Black Jasmine

A Lei Crime Novel

Black Jasmine

A Lei Crime Novel

Toby Neal

Black Jasmine

Copyright © 2012 by Toby Neal

ISBN 978-0-9839524-7-3

Photo credit: Mike Neal © Nealstudios.net
Cover Design: © JULIE METZ LTD.

Book design by Mythic Island Press LLC

Rom. 12:19:

Beloved, do not avenge yourselves,

but leave room for the wrath of God; for it is written,

"Vengeance is mine, I will repay, says the Lord."

Chapter 1

*D*etective Lei Texeira tested the rope running through the cleat, giving it a yank before nodding to the fireman controlling the winch. He switched the engine on, and she rappelled down the cliff, keeping her knees bent as she began a slow descent. Blasts of wind off the ocean whirled her curly brown hair. The rocky bluff was marbled with pockets of underbrush, and minutes later she became tangled in a thick clump of strawberry guava.

"Stop the winch!"

The grind of the machine and the crash of waves masked Lei's voice, and the rope kept paying out until her full weight rested on the bush. She spread her arms across the springy branches, resting horizontal and horrified thirty feet above the rocks for a few long seconds—and just as suddenly the bush dumped her. Lei yelped and flailed as she hit the end of the rope like a plumb bob, torquing her neck, the harness digging into her crotch and hips.

"Dammit!" She dropped as gracelessly as a load of laundry the last ten feet onto the lava ledge beside the upside-down sedan.

Her burly partner, Pono Kaihale, hurried forward to help her unfasten the harness. He'd been her first partner on the Big Island, and had preceded her to this new assignment on Maui.

"Shit. You okay?" He pushed mirrored Oakleys up onto his buzz-cut head, a worried crease on his wide brow as he unclipped the cable. She groaned, fumbling at the buckle in the front and prying the straps out of her ass.

"Gonna have whiplash tomorrow. You sure there's a body in there?"

The fireman who'd made the discovery came forward, hand extended. "Ouch. Sorry about that descent. I couldn't call Ben fast enough on the walkie. Ron Vierra." Lei shook his hand: strong, calloused grip, big local guy who wore his fire gear like a proud second skin.

"Eh, Ron. What we get?" She slid into pidgin, liquid dialect of the islands, to establish rapport. In Hawaii, a magnet for transients, it was important to be *from here*, a "local," and that identity was established within minutes.

"We get one call from the public phone in Haiku early this morning. Wouldn't leave a name. Said one car wen' crash, no one inside. Probably stay from the tent village on top da cliff. Soon as it got light, we came out wit' responding officers. Me and Ben, we rappelled down. That's when we seen her."

He gestured to the wrecked car.

Lei and Pono followed him over to the vehicle, snapping on latex gloves. Cubes of glass glittered on the rocks, adding sparkle to the turquoise sea, which had retreated with low tide, leaving the wreck shiny with moisture. Lei squatted down beside the blown-out driver's window and peered in.

The body was upside down, belt still in place, long red hair trailing in pinkish water collected on the roof of the aged sedan. The girl's neck was broken at such an extreme angle that her face, intact and wide-eyed, looked up in surprise at her crushed body folded around the steering wheel.

The hood of the car had hit the rocks first. As it compressed backward, it had jammed the steering wheel into the girl's torso, almost bisecting it, before tipping upside down. A regular rinse of seawater through the blown-out windows had washed most of the blood away, leaving the body soggy and bleached-looking.

Lei hated it when the eyes were open. These were blue, glassy as marbles. She resisted the urge to close them, tucking her hand in her pocket, where she rubbed a small, round black stone. She looked at Pono. "Medical examiner on the way?"

"Yeah." He folded Cupid's bow lips, hidden by a bristling mustache, into a thin line and rubbed them with a forefinger as he looked at the girl. "Looks like a teenager. Suicide?"

"Could be." Lei steeled herself and reached in to rifle the pockets of the voluminous jean jacket the girl wore. Empty. No purse on the seat or anywhere in the vehicle. She went around and reached in from the other window to push the button on the glove box. Nothing inside but a dripping map of Maui.

Lei straightened up, slipping the map into a plastic evidence bag. "If there was any trace here, the ocean doing the washing machine all night isn't going to leave much."

They continued to check over the vehicle. Nothing in the back-seat and nothing on the roof of the car. Lei radioed in the plate number, and it came back as stolen last week out of Lahaina—nothing there to help with the identity of the red-haired Jane Doe.

She turned back to Vierra, who was guiding the Jaws of Life down the cliff on the cable. He unclipped the heavy hydraulic spreaders and cutters and set them on the rocks out of reach of the surf.

"Wish I'd known she was in there last night," Vierra said. He looked pale under his brown complexion. "I've got a teenage daughter."

"She was gone at the impact—way too late for the Jaws of

Life to do her any good, and you guys couldn't have done anything much at a site like this in the dark."

Lei looked back up at the cliff. The uniforms who'd first responded were peering over; then the winch rumbled into action again. This time it was the ME on the line, a pudgy doughball of a man in an aloha shirt and jeans. He made no effort to manage the descent, just clung to the line, and still somehow avoided the protruding guava clump.

He landed on his feet but tipped back onto his rump. Pono helped him unclip the cable and hoisted the man back onto his feet. He clutched his crime scene kit to his chest and reached up to wipe his pallid face with a trembling hand. Apparently he was not a fan of heights.

"Hey. I'm Detective Texeira." Lei hadn't been on Maui long enough to have met all the essential personnel. She extended a hand.

"Dr. Gregory." He shook her hand with a soft and clammy one.

She resisted the urge to wipe it immediately on her black jeans and pointed to the body instead. "Teenager. We're thinking suicide."

"Never jump to conclusions." Dr. Gregory awkwardly hopped on one leg as he wriggled the harness off his wide rear end. The metal fittings clanged as they hit the lava, and Pono stabilized his shoulder with a tiny eye roll. The harness jolted its way back up the cliff.

"My assistant is coming down next, but tell me what you know." Dr. Gregory approached the vehicle, donning his gloves, as Lei recapped the story.

The ME took out his camera and a handful of plastic markers and went to work. Lei could tell that, Humpty Dumpty appearance aside, he knew what he was doing—so she turned to Pono.

"Let's do a search along the rocks here, see if anything might have fallen out of the car on its way down."

They picked their way to the edge of the lava that jutted out from the base of the cliff. Like many ocean-facing areas on Maui, the black volcanic bones of the earth were exposed by the relentless wear of wind and sea, forming a promontory that belled out from the edge of the bluff. She and Pono began a slow survey at a considerable distance from the impact site, walking a few feet apart, eyes traveling in what she liked to call "see mode"— a relaxed systematic pass back and forth, focusing only when something odd blipped in her vision.

Nothing but tide pools filled with blennies and tiny hermit crabs, a few of the local single-shelled delicacies known as *opihi*, brown *limu* seaweed, and darting silver *aholehole*. Then something else silver caught her eye, about fifty feet from the wreck. She bent and spotted a shiny key in a tide pool.

"What do you think?"

"I think that has to be from the wreck, because even a week in the ocean and that key wouldn't be shiny anymore." The sun was getting hotter, and sweat gleamed in Pono's black hair. He pushed his ever-present Oakleys up to investigate the item in question. The key was a nondescript Schlage, no markings but the name brand. "Looks like a door key, I've got one to my house that looks like this."

"Better shoot the site." She stood over the pool, and Pono went to the crime kit they'd brought and fetched the camera.

Dr. Gregory's assistant had arrived, dressed in scrubs as if she'd just come from the morgue. Glossy black hair in a ponytail emphasized an angular Japanese face. She squatted beside Gregory, who was semi-inserted into the broken window beside the body.

Pono came back, photographing the tide pool with the digital Canon and then turning to take a few shots of the soaring cliff. Pono, with his sociable personality, usually had the inside scoop on departmental business. They'd been partners when they were both patrol officers on the Big Island, and when Pono made detective he'd moved his family to Maui. He'd contacted Lei and her boyfriend, Stevens, on Kaua'i about job openings, and the two had moved to the Valley Isle six months ago.

Lei and Pono continued their sweep and found a few other items: some coins and bottle caps, a rusty beer opener that was probably detritus from the tent village on the bluff. The light-house area was a well-known party and drug zone in addition to being a homeless encampment.

The sun felt like a hot lance in Lei's eyes, and she wished she'd remembered sunglasses, sunscreen, or a hat—preferably all three. Even with her Hawaiian and Japanese blood, her greater Portuguese heritage caused her face to freckle and burn. By then they'd worked their way back to the wreck, and Lei watched the firemen cut the body out of the car.

Ron Vierra handled the bulky hydraulic cutters with the ease of experience. They clipped through steel, foam, and plastic with a guttural roar, like a T. rex dining.

The girl in scrubs approached Lei, hand out. "Hi, I'm Angie Tanaka, ME intern."

More introductions. Dr. Gregory joined them, glancing nervously up the cliff as he packed his kit.

"So what do you think, Doctor?" Lei asked.

"Seems apparent she died on impact." Gregory swiped sweat off his brow again. "And she's a teenager. But I have to do a full workup back at the morgue to make sure. Liver temp appears consistent with death last night sometime. The ocean activity inhibited onset of rigor, but she's begun now."

The two firemen, grunting with effort, lifted a section of the steel car frame away from the upside-down corpse. They'd cut the steering wheel loose from the dash, and Vierra pulled it out of the girl's jacketed midsection.

Lei found herself massaging the stone in her pocket, seeing lost faces as she gazed at the girl's mutilated body. She'd learned to use a worry stone in therapy some years ago, but this black one was special—she'd picked it up at the funeral of a friend. The stone worked to help her manage her feelings—but it had a price, and that price was remembering.

The body remained upside down and folded into a C shape with the onset of rigor. Gregory and Tanaka moved in, tipping the corpse onto its side into an opened body bag. With some effort, they stuffed and straightened the body enough to fit, and the sound of the zipper closing, one long screech, set Lei's teeth on edge.

She and Pono helped the MEs lift the bag onto the wire mesh body-retrieval basket that had trundled down the cliff on the winch. They clipped the mesh shut; then Vierra checked the cable attachment and gave the go on his walkie.

Lei took a second to look out to sea, away from the wrecked car, black cliffs and yellow fire truck perched atop them. The ocean was a wind-whipped cobalt, lightening to foamy cerulean near the rocks, and her eyes scanned the horizon automatically for humpback whales.

The winch began with a grinding rumble, and the wire casket lifted. The body bounced and banged its way up the cliff. It caught on the same clump of guava that had impeded Lei's descent, tipping vertically. They'd closed the cagelike mesh door, but they all gasped as the body tilted upright and slammed against it, swaying and stuck like a bundled black fly dangling out of a spider's web.

Vierra screamed to stop the winch. After much raising, lowering, and debating, the body remained stuck. Finally, one of the other firefighters on the bluff rappelled down off the truck and untangled it, and the metal cage resumed its undignified ascent.

Lei was the last to go up. By the time she did, she could feel how matted her curly hair had become, how sunburned her normally olive complexion was. She imagined the hated handful of cinnamon freckles on her nose multiplying as the winch hauled her up the precipitous cliff—this time avoiding the guava bushes. She glanced down at the wreck below her as she rose. The Volare was going to be hauled up with a crane eventually, and it was a good thing, because an oily rainbow already polluted the pristine tide pool around the vehicle.

Unhitched from the winch at last, Lei got into her silver Tacoma truck and cranked on the AC. She chugged a tepid bottle of water. Pono hopped in beside her, sweat rings marking his arms. He flopped the seat back.

"Get me to something cold and wet, please, stat." Tiare, his wife, was attending nursing school at University of Hawaii Maui and his speech was peppered with medical terms.

"Ha." She handed him another warm bottle of water and broke open a packet of pretzels. "Let's take ten and then go canvass those campers in the tent village."

"So—you thinking suicide?" This was the second time Pono had mentioned it. Something was bugging him, too. She glanced over and, sure enough, he was rubbing his lip with a meaty forefinger, an old habit from when he'd given up smoking.

"Too soon to tell. Usually the obvious is the obvious, but there's something about this that's just…weird." She tapped her fingers on the steering wheel. "It was a stolen car, so that bugs me. If she committed suicide, why here, in the armpit of nowhere? Why in some anonymous car we can't trace, without any ID or note? It's just seeming like too much work, like she was trying to disappear."

"What I was thinking." They continued to hash over the possibilities, finishing the pretzels and a browning banana Lei found in the cup holder.

Lei didn't want to lose any time; she'd spotted the camp dwellers watching the retrieval of the body and wanted to get to the canvassing while the scene was fresh. Slightly restored, they got out of the truck, which Lei had parked near the huge lighted steel pole that constituted Pauwela Lighthouse.

It was a poor excuse for a lighthouse, dreary on a good day and downright creepy in the dark. The spectacular setting of cliffs and restless sea somehow failed to counteract a sense of misery left by a collection of abandoned, rusting cars and the graffiti-scarred broken cement structures that had been bunkers in WWII. The bluff was bare and empty without the emergency vehicles, breeze humming in the twisted brush that hid the tent village, the site of several unsolved murders.

Lei patted the Glock 40 holstered against her side. She made sure her baton and pepper spray were handily stowed in their holsters on her belt and her badge was clipped in plain view. As a detective, she'd come up with her own "uniform"—black jeans with dark running shoes, plain tank tops, and a light blazer to hide her gun, if needed. Today the blazer wasn't needed. And better late than never, she put on a ball cap her friend Marcella had given her.

"Ready?" Pono slammed the door of the truck.

"As I'll ever be." She followed him into the hollowed cave of underbrush, the wind keening in the interlaced branches overhead.

Chapter 2

*T*he first tent was camouflage patterned, a still, hunkered shape in the green gloom.

"Maui Police Department. Anybody home? Come out and talk to us, please," Lei said.

A zipper opened in a slow parabola, and a thin young woman wearing stained jeans, her hair in dreadlocks, crawled out, accompanied by a draft of garlic and urine. She sat in a camp chair beside the tent opening, eyes flashing defiance.

"Yeah?"

"Did you hear the crash last night?" Pono asked.

"No."

"You sure about that? It must have been pretty loud. Shoots, you're lucky the car didn't run through your tent here on the way off the cliff." Lei played bad cop, her favorite role.

"I'm a heavy sleeper."

"Could be you had some help with that." Lei nudged an empty Jim Beam bottle near her foot.

"I said no. I never heard nothing." The woman folded scrawny arms across her chest.

"C'mon. We're not saying you had anything to do with it. Someone died, though, and we're trying to at least establish when it might have happened," Pono said, conciliatory, warm as honey in summer.

"I told you, I was sleeping."

Lei'd had it. She pulled a pair of rubber gloves out of her back pocket, snapped them on, and reached for the zipper of the tent. "Did you hear my partner tell you someone died? I'm guessing there were some illegal substances in here, helping you sleep that heavy."

"Hey, stay out of my tent!" The woman scrambled up. "Yeah. I heard it, around two a.m. I know because the kid woke up, was crying."

Kid? They both leaned forward, and in the gloom of the tent they could see the faint gleam of a toddler's face through the screen insert of the door, wide dewdrop eyes tracking them like a tiny wild thing in its den. The urine smell must have been diapers.

"Tell us more, or I'll take that kid straight to Child Welfare," Lei said. A familiar rage swept over her with white-hot power. There was nothing she hated more than child abuse and neglect. She wanted to grab the baby and run away with it—to somewhere light and clean, where there was no drinking, drugs, or danger.

"You're right, Lei. We could do that." Pono redirected his gaze to the homeless woman. "Or we could get you into the shelter."

Lei shrugged. "Guess it's up to her, what we do with the kid."

"Fuck you, cop. It's not against the law to be homeless, and I never did nothing wrong. I take good care of my baby." The young mother snarled. On second glance, she probably wasn't out of her teens, and her eyes welled with furious, terrified tears.

"Watch your mouth. I'm taking that baby." Lei reached for her handcuffs.

Pono stepped in.

"I'm sure you take good care of your baby. Just tell us what you heard." His big, warm hand landed on Lei's arm, both restraining and anchoring her.

"Just heard the crash. And you're right; it was loud."

Lei sucked in some relaxation breaths, realizing she'd been too aggressive. But she was still going to call Child Welfare. This tent in the bushes was no place for a baby. Maybe the call would help get the girl some services, a real place to live.

The young mom didn't have anything else for them. No, she hadn't come out of the tent. She didn't go out late at night with the baby. She hadn't seen anything until that morning when she'd gone out to look at fire trucks and the commotion on the bluff. What did she think? Someone drove their car off the edge—it wasn't the first time there was a suicide out here. Which was true, Lei remembered. There had also been some suspicious overdoses, and prior to this, a missing woman and a teenager beaten to death, both cases unsolved.

Pauwela Lighthouse was not a homeless camp for the faint of heart or those with any other options.

They worked their way from tent to tent, hearing much the same story, a big crash at around two a.m. Lei wondered aloud where the campers got their water, and one obliging toothless denizen showed them the former pineapple field irrigation system that had been breached. Water was brought into the central camp area under the biggest ironwood tree via a series of screwed-together garden hoses.

They went to one last tent, a little bigger and set apart from the others, where an imposing Hawaiian woman sat at a table made from an upright cable spool. She was sorting long, sword-shaped hala leaves, which hung, drying, from a line under the tarp outside her tent. Lei wondered what a dignified woman like this was doing at the seedy camp. Usually Hawaiians took each one another in; it was shame to the family for a relative to be in need.

The woman looked up at their approach. Long iron-gray hair was wound into a bun and pierced by a bamboo chopstick, and she wore a drab muumuu and had rubber slippers on her swollen feet. Her eyes were dark, inscrutable wells.

"What you cops stay looking for?"

Lei held up her badge. "Eh, Aunty. Know anything about the crash last night?" She called the woman by the title of respect used in Hawaii by younger people to elders.

The woman picked up a long piece of hala, pandanus used to make basketry, hats, and floor coverings. She worked the long leaf with her fingers, expertly shredding off a row of spines that edged the length of the leaf with a thickened thumbnail.

"I saw someone leaving after the car went off."

"What? I mean, you sure, Aunty?" Lei's attention sharpened.

Dark eyes glanced up, a tightening of contempt at the corners. "I know what I saw."

"What's your name, Aunty?" Pono had his notepad out.

"Ramona Haulani."

"Well, Ms. Haulani, tell us more."

"I don't sleep so good." The woman shredded the stripped hala leaf into half-inch sections, each about eighteen inches long. The thumbnail appeared to work as well as any paring knife. "I was awake, and I heard the car drive up to the edge. I came out of my tent." Ramona gestured. From the door of her tent, she had a clear view of the bluff where the car had gone over.

"I wanted to see what was going on. I knew it was late, the hour of no-good."

Lei considered asking about that but decided it was more important to keep the woman talking.

"Then, after the engine was off and it had been sitting awhile, it rolled forward and went off the edge." Lei and Pono darted a glance at each other. This scenario didn't sound like a teenager driving off the cliff in a suicide.

"It was loud." It must have been; everyone had mentioned that. "Then I saw a little light, just a flash, like one of those mainland lightning bugs. It would go on and off, moving away from where the car went over."

"Did you see anything else? Who was holding the light?" Lei tried not to rush her.

"No. It was dark, hardly a moon even. I saw the light—flash, flash—moving down the road." She gestured back toward the main road. "I thought it must be someone walking, using a small-kine flashlight."

They pumped her for more information, but that was basically all she had. She hadn't talked about what she has seen to anyone, and Pono encouraged her to keep quiet.

"I can keep a secret."

Ramona picked up another hala leaf, slit the edge. The older woman's nail must have been sharpened, the way it cut through the plant material with a zipping sound that reminded Lei of the body bag closing. Lei found her hand in her pocket again, rubbing the black stone.

"Why you stay out here, Aunty?" Pono asked.

"I nevah like the family tell me my business. I do what I like," Ramona Haulani said, and the darkness behind her brown eyes hinted at secrets. They thanked her and hiked back to the truck.

Lei drove them to the station while Pono wrote up notes on his laptop. She was still entertained by the sight of his big sausage fingers flying nimbly over the keys. Sunset slanted across the dash, and her stomach rumbled again. Those pretzels hadn't lasted long.

"We'll have to meet with the lieutenant in the morning," Pono said, still typing. "She's going to want to get up to speed, stat."

"I know—but I don't have to like it." Lei and the lieutenant weren't fans of each other. "I'm not thinking suicide anymore."

"It'll be interesting to meet with the ME and go over the autopsy report. Somebody walking away from the wreck looks bad. More paperwork." Pono liked to grumble about that, but they both knew he was better at it.

Her phone vibrated in her pocket and she flipped it open. "Hey, Stevens."

"When you getting home? Dinner's almost ready."

"Half hour."

"'K, then. Love you."

"Likewise." Lei closed the phone.

Pono looked up. "How's loverboy?"

"Hungry. He's almost got dinner ready."

"When you guys going to get married?" Pono never tired of trying to get others into his own debatable domestic bliss. He and Tiare had stopped at two kids, something Lei considered a good thing, but the struggle to make ends meet with a family wasn't something she was in a hurry to duplicate.

"Mind your business." Lei dropped Pono at the station lot, where his lifted purple truck was parked.

"See you tomorrow, Sweets." The ironic nickname her Kaua`i partner, Jenkins, had dubbed her with had been bequeathed to Pono. She'd finally given up fighting it.

"Too soon, bruddah."

* * *

I stretch out on my four-hundred-thread-count Egyptian cotton sheets and flick on the flat-screen TV to the news, looking for something about the crash. I sip my evening cosmopolitan, waiting through school budget crises and a whale watch gone awry. It's been another long, productive day managing the company, doing what I love. I'm lucky—or no, that isn't right. I've made my own luck, starting a long time ago when I stole that name that felt so much more a fit than the one I'd been born with.

Finally, a grainy video, obviously someone's cell phone—a fire truck hoisting up a yellow metal mesh body stabilizer on a windblown bluff. A cluster of uniforms wrestle the basket to the ground beside the fire truck as a voice-over begins.

"Tragedy struck on Maui when an unidentified young girl in a car went off the cliff at Pauwela Lighthouse. Authorities are still determining if the crash was an accident. Neither of the seasoned detectives assigned to the case were available for comment."

Just a quick blip. The "seasoned detectives" will have the devil of a time finding out who the mysterious dead girl is. I've made sure of that. I close my eyes to savor the high from the night before. I felt like I could fly, soaring like an owl over the moonless nightscape. That high. God, it was something. Maybe that was it—I felt like God, granting life, taking it away.

I need to do a little research. I take out one of the prepackaged burner phones that I keep around for such moments and dial a number I've memorized—my contact at MPD. He doesn't know who I am, but he likes the deposits I make every time I need him. That, and I have a few choice photos that ensure cooperation.

I get info on Texeira and Kaihale, detectives on the case, and tell him to keep me informed. I boot up my Apple Air, thin as a wallet. In moments, I'm online, pulling up everything I can find on Pono Kaihale.

There isn't much. Until recently, he'd been a regular patrol officer on the Big Island. After he was promoted to detective, he moved to Maui. He looks like a tiki god come to life in his departmental photo. Buzz-cut hair, wide brown face with a bristling mustache, even wider neck. Typical moke cop.

Leilani Texeira is another story. A slender, athletic-looking woman with a lot of curly hair, she has tilted almond eyes, a smatter of freckles, and a full mouth. That mouth, cut wide and set hard, shows attitude.

Texeira's got a face that's more than pretty; it's hard to forget. I feel a little frisson of unease as I read about the Cult Killer case on Kaua`i—biggest case the sleepy island had ever seen, and Texeira was in the middle of it all the way to the end. I look at her photo again. Attitude is right. I'd better monitor things closely, and that means more payments to the mole, more hassles.

That stupid little redhead is still costing me money and I hate that. I never let anyone beat me at anything. I can't stand losing. But she's already dead, so I can't take anything more out of her, goddamn it. I need something to take my mind off things. I punch in a number on the bedside phone.

"Kimo. Send up some merchandise. I'm in the mood for dark meat."

I mix up the drink in a highball glass—a potent cocktail of Rohypnol and Viagra that guarantees me a good time. For this one, I go light on the roofies and heavy on the Viagra—might as well teach him something he'll remember. When Kimo pushes the merchandise in the door, I hand him the drink with a smile.

He's not sure what to think, doesn't know what's coming, so he drinks it after I clink his glass with mine...and pretty soon he's just what I need to get the kinks out. I like the way my beautiful white skin, so silky, looks against his mocha hide. I like the taste of a little blood, spread around like finger paint. It's a good session.

When Kimo picks him up, my sheets are messy so I have the maid come change them while I take the SIM card out of the phone, stick it in a chunk of apple, and grind it up in the disposal. I toss the plastic phone body into the recycle bin.

I go back into the bedroom. It's white and pristine once again, creamy drapes hiding the door to my bondage room, toys cleaned off and put away. I pay that maid well to not be seen and not be heard.

I take a shower, but now my shoulders are sore from the work-out. I use my regular cell to call the masseuse to come work the knots out, which he does rather nicely. Finally, oiled, perfumed, and pleasantly tired, I turn off the crystal bedside lamp and gaze out the sliders to the night sky reflecting off the black sea.

It's taken all that to get me to the state of relaxation I was in before I heard the name Lei Texeira.

She owes me for that.

Chapter 3

Lei pulled up into the wide driveway of her and Stevens's rental cottage in ʻIao Valley. A six-foot chain-link fence held back her Rottweiler, Keiki, who'd heard the truck drive up and had her paws up on the fence in ecstatic greeting, muscular hindquarters waggling with joy.

"Hey, baby." Lei gave the dog a head rub, then snapped her fingers as she unlatched the gate. Keiki sat obediently. She gave the Rottweiler another pat in reward and went up the slightly sagging wooden steps onto the porch, the dog glued to her side.

Lei loved the house's location, only ten minutes from the Maui Police Department station in Kahului. Set slightly off the two-lane, winding road that dead-ended at a state park at the back of the valley, the cottage was isolated enough to feel a world away from work. They could afford something newer, but she and Stevens enjoyed the feeling of vintage Hawaii embodied in its older plantation-style cottages. This one had a wide, extended tin roof painted a red that was fading to terra-cotta. The roof contrasted with traditional dark green paint trimmed in white around windows and doors.

They'd replaced the elderly screen door with a new iron security door that still allowed airflow, and he'd left it unlocked for her. The door opened straight into the wooden-floored living room, and the modest kitchen at the back looked out onto a hillside covered in green jungle.

A delicious smell of teriyaki chicken filled the air. She looked at Stevens as he stirred something on the stove, dark head bent. The height and breadth of him set loose a flight of bubbles under her sternum, an unfamiliar feeling she'd finally figured out was happiness. She went across the room on quick, light steps and encircled his whipcord back from behind, laying her cheek against his shoulder blades.

"Honey, I'm home."

"So you are." He set a hand on the crossed wrists around his waist, gave them a pat and a squeeze as he sniffed audibly. "You stink."

"Thanks. Nothing like a little rappelling and body retrieval followed by a long day canvassing homeless to get the heart rate up. Do I have time for a shower?"

"I think that would be best," he said, and handed her a Corona he'd opened and placed beside the stove. "When you get out, it'll all be ready."

"I think I could get used to this."

Lei showered the grime of the day off her lean frame, using a loofah sponge to scrub her arms and legs. She had an athletic build, slender-hipped and round-breasted, and she particularly liked the smooth dip of her waist and the fact that nothing jiggled that shouldn't.

Lei looked at her scarred arms, letting herself really see them. She rubbed the thin silver lines of past self-injury gently with body soap. She no longer needed to resort to that hollow form of coping—she'd come a long way in therapy on the Big Island. Lei rubbed the bite mark on her collarbone, feeling the throb her wrist sometimes still gave from being broken two years ago in a battle for her life. Scars marked you, but they didn't have to hurt anymore.

There was just one human scar she still needed to take care of.

Charlie Kwon, her childhood molester, was in Lompoc doing time for sexual abuse of a minor, and knowing she'd been only one in a string of victims didn't make her feel better. She had an acquaintance who worked at Lompoc keeping an eye on him. Charlie aside, she was grateful for all the people who'd come into her life, one after the other, to heal her.

Chief among them was Michael Stevens. They'd met working a case on the Big Island, fallen in love. She'd accepted his marriage proposal only to panic, dump him, and run away to Kaua'i. Stevens had followed her over to help with the big serial case she'd uncovered, and they'd eventually reconnected. It hadn't been easy. It had never been simple. But the poor guy couldn't seem to stay away. He even had a purple heart tattoo on his forearm with her name in it.

Lei looked up at a note card reminder from her therapy, tacked to the drywall above the shower surround. *Trust your heart.* She was getting better at that, now that her heart wasn't so fucked up.

She got out, drying off and squishing a handful of Curl Tamer into her hair. It was still short from when she'd shaved her head to go undercover for the Cult Killer case. That case on Kaua'i had garnered so much media attention that she and Stevens had been marked at the station for nonstop harassment in the form of jealousy and practical jokes. It had gotten old being recognized everywhere they went on the small island, especially after a TV movie was made of the whole thing. Six months later, when Pono called, she and Stevens had been ready to put in for transfers.

Every month or two she got little prodding e-mails from Marcella Scott, the FBI agent she'd worked the case with on Kaua'i.

Marcella was still trying to recruit her to the Bureau—and Lei was still thinking about the opportunity.

Lei pulled on old sweats and rubbed face lotion into her sunburn, squirted her eyes with Visine for the windburn, and went back into the kitchen.

The dining room consisted of a small bump-out area with a circular Formica table, and Stevens had set it with a pot of rice, a green salad, and a lasagna pan of chicken swimming in teriyaki sauce. Lei set the beer down by her plate and put her napkin in her lap, mouth watering.

"Damn, Michael. This is really awesome."

"Glad I can get something right."

There was an edge to his voice, and she realized that he hadn't really looked at her. She decided to ignore that and dug into the meal, which was as good as it smelled. When she'd finished the first ravenous plateful, she sat back, sipping the Corona, studying him.

Big, sensitive, long-fingered hands worked the chopsticks as easily as a local. When she'd first met him, he hadn't known how to use them and she'd teased him for it. Dark, rumpled hair fell over a high forehead, casting a shadow over his face. Blue eyes hid under thick lashes as he looked at his plate.

Something was wrong. She wondered if she had what it took to ask about it. Decided she didn't. She'd never been good at the talking part of being a couple—Pono said she was more like a dude that way.

Lei helped herself to seconds. He'd bring up the problem when he got tired of waiting for her to ask, and the truth was that she wanted to talk to him about the case. He'd been promoted during the transfer and was now detective sergeant for Kahului Station, while she was still only a detective grade II at the small Haiku station. She missed working with him, but now that they were living together, a little distance had been a good thing.

"So we got a weird one. Teenage-looking Jane Doe went off a cliff in an old Plymouth at Pauwela Lighthouse. Plates come back to a stolen Lahaina car."

"Suicide?" He perked up. They could always talk about work. She got to see his eyes finally, and there was sadness behind them that interest in a murder couldn't dispel.

Shit. She hoped it wasn't the marriage thing again.

"We'll know more at the autopsy, but when we canvassed we found a wit who saw the whole thing, says the car drove to the edge, shut down, and then a few minutes later, rolled off. Says she saw a penlight turning on and off as someone walked away from the scene."

Stevens straightened up, that spark of intensity back in his eyes. She loved that about him.

"Does sound weird. The scene tell you anything?"

"Nothing but a shiny door key I found in the rocks. Interior of the car was empty, no purse or anything left inside. Body spent the night in the ocean rinse cycle, so I wonder how much it's going to tell us."

"Interesting. What are you going to do about those other cases? They've been taking a lot of time."

"Oh, that." Lei plunked down her beer and sighed. "You know, I don't know why we try. Damn chicken fighting is a whole layer of economy around here. A part of me hates even busting these people. It's their main source of income."

"That's why the Maui Police Department's kind of been turning a blind eye for years. But with Mayor Costales in office on his reform platform, we gotta bring in some numbers."

Now that Stevens was doing administration, he'd developed a sensitivity to what he liked to call "The Big Picture" and Lei called the "Company Store Line of Crap."

"Yeah, I know. We've got some good confidential informants on it; Pono's amazing at working that end. Good thing, too, because I suck at getting people to talk without giving 'em a smack upside the head."

"Yeah, you have a way about you." The tension around his jaw had eased; he patted his knee. "C'mon over here, shrew."

"What?" Lei felt a grin moving across her sunburned face. He wasn't going to bring up whatever-it-was—she'd dodged a bullet again. "What's a shrew? This isn't a Hawaii thing, is it?"

"It's a Shakespeare thing." He'd minored in English lit and liked to show off now and then.

"I know to come when I'm called."

She sat on his lap, put her arms around his neck, and stroked the hair out of his eyes. He felt so good in her arms, like everything about him fit everything about her.

"I'm gonna be sore tomorrow. Fell out of a bush on the way down the cliff and tweaked my back. Not to mention my ass. Think you can help me with that?"

"I can do something with my hands, yeah."

He demonstrated, and she forgot to ask more about what it meant to be a shrew.

Chapter 4

*T*he next morning, Lei and Pono sat with the commanding officer of Haiku station. Pono had downloaded their pictures from the crime scene and printed color copies for the lieutenant to review.

Lieutenant Omura was a petite Japanese woman with a poker face and the imposing presence of a much larger person. Lei had heard a rumor that Omura had an IQ of 155, a black belt in judo, and a master's in criminology. Her flinty dark eyes scanned the hastily written paperwork and photos.

"Homicide or suicide?"

"ME hasn't said yet. Initial impression is suicide. Our meeting's at ten a.m. He said he was still working on it." Pono got along better with the "Steel Butterfly," so he did the talking.

Lei was still smarting from the dressing-down she'd received for being late. She'd awakened stiff and sore and had tried to fit a run in before the briefing. The run hadn't helped with the stiffness and it had made her late—something the lieutenant looked upon as a sign of bad character.

The commanding officer was immaculate in a trim navy uniform she must have had altered to hug her perfect figure. She wore a pair of decidedly nonregulation heels on her tiny Asian feet—Imelda Marcos shoe habits had contributed to the nickname she didn't know she had. Lei felt lumpy and unkempt beside her, and nocturnal activities with Stevens hadn't done good things for her hair. She wriggled in her plastic seat, feeling like she had to pee. The lieutenant did that to her every time.

"Hear you made a Child Welfare call, Texeira." Those sharp eyes were on Lei now. Her bladder cramped.

"Yeah, there was a baby out there. Not a good situation. Wanted to have it looked into, just in case."

Omura clicked her tongue, looked back at the paperwork. "Your complaint isn't going to go anywhere and you might need the parent as witness, so I wonder at your judgment." She assembled the materials into the folder and handed it to Pono, giving a tiny flick of dismissal with glossy red nails. "Keep me informed."

They got up and filed out.

Lei contained herself until they got to their cubicle.

"I hate her. I mean, I really hate that bitch."

"I get the feeling it's mutual, and we know who's on top." Pono gave her a worried glance, stabbed a thick finger at her. "You don't want to piss her off, Sweets. She's made tougher men than you cry. How do you think she edged out the competition in a department that's never ranked a woman higher than sergeant?"

"Okay, I know. I'll keep kissing the toes of her shoes. How much do they cost, do you think?"

"More than you make in a week."

Lei sighed. "So let's work on the cockfighting thing until the meet at the morgue." She fumbled in her drawer for a rubber band, but her hair was too short to pull back. She took an MPD ball cap and stuffed it on her head, booting up her computer to review their contacts on the underground gambling and cockfighting case.

Lei and Pono took the stairs to the basement floor of Maui General Hospital, where the only morgue on the island was located. Lei practiced some relaxation breathing—in through the nose, out through the mouth—as she approached beige double doors bisected by a steel push handle. Pono glanced at her, patted her elbow.

He knew how she felt about morgues.

Dr. Gregory was hosing something nasty off one of the long steel tables as they breached the inner sanctum. He looked up, pushing multilensed glasses up onto his egg-shaped head.

"The report's not done."

"That's all right," Lei said. "We're just hoping for some preliminary results. The lieutenant's on us for a homicide ruling—or whatever you think."

"Okay." He gestured for Tanaka, who was tying a toe tag onto a body, to come take over his cleanup.

He led them over to the bank of refrigerator boxes, flipped the compression handle on one. It made a sound like popping the lid of an old-fashioned Coke bottle that had been shaken up. He picked up a clipboard and rolled the shelf out.

The body wasn't draped and the girl's eyes were still open, the Y incision on her chest cartoonishly stitched into rubberlike skin. Lividity had set in, mottling her face, neck, and shoulders to a dusky shade. She looked like she'd been dipped headfirst into something purple. The girl's midsection was pulverized, organs barely contained by perforated skin blackened by bruising, the rib cage crushed.

Lei breathed through her mouth, slipping her hand in her pocket for the stone, but she'd forgotten to pick it up in her hurry that morning.

"I should be able to get the report done by tomorrow, but I can give you an oral recap." Gregory read from the clipboard. "Female, approximately seventeen years old. She has a butterfly tattoo on her ankle. Maybe that will help identify her." He indicated a tiny, optimistic yellow butterfly on the girl's anklebone, tapping it with his pen. "Cause of death is massive blunt force trauma."

"What about her broken neck?" Lei was glad the girl's head was held upright in a small metal stanchion on the shelf, but her imagination supplied a picture of the head flopping off the table, held on with nothing more than skin.

"Broken neck also a result of blunt force trauma, simultaneous with impact of the steering wheel. Premortem injuries indicate the victim was alive when the car crashed. She has some interesting bruises. Look here." He held up a hand. A sharp, dark line encircled each wrist. "She was bound at some point. There are no other injuries, except the obvious." He made a dismissive gesture that encompassed the girl's mangled torso.

"Any signs of sexual activity?" Lei asked.

"No, but we did all the usual swabs. The toxicology report will tell us more, but it's going to be at least a week." He handed her a card with the girl's fingerprints on it, then pressed a couple of buttons on his computer keyboard and the printer spit out an image on photo paper. "Jane Doe's picture, for your canvassing. I scanned the prints into the computer as well. I'll send 'em to you with the picture."

"Thanks." Lei was impressed with his efficiency. "So, you said blunt force trauma. Suicide or homicide?" She knew the answer but wanted to hear him say it.

"Given the ligature marks, homicide. Vehicular homicide."

Chapter 5

Lei ate a cold piece of leftover teriyaki chicken at her workstation as she ran the girl's scanned-in fingerprints through the AFIS database. It didn't take long for the dialogue box to pop up. NO MATCH.

"Shit." The case had just gotten a whole lot harder. She wiped her hands on a paper towel and hit Print on the page for the file. She and Pono had already sent the photo of Jane Doe out over e-mail to all the stations. They'd need to send it to the newspaper, blanket the town with flyers. Surely someone knew this girl.

Lei glanced down at the newly doctored photo of Jane Doe. Pono'd taken the e-mailed shot from the doctor and run it through NCMEC. The National Center for Missing and Exploited Children's database had sent it back with a disappointing NO MATCH and a digitized version that washed out the ugly mottling of lividity that would distract from identification.

Lei was finally able to really look at the girl's face, now that the eyes were closed and the dusky purple was bleached out of her skin. Jane Doe had full lips and winged brows, and with that long red hair and knockout body, she'd have been a traffic stopper.

Sometimes Lei's brain made unfortunate puns.

What was a seventeen-year-old girl doing in an old, stolen Plymouth Volare in the ass-end of nowhere, plummeting off a cliff?

Lei studied the photos of the girl's clothes that Gregory had e-mailed. She hadn't really noticed them at the crash scene. The clinical layout of the short, black pleather skirt, thong, lacy black bra, and hot-pink tank top added up to one kind of job that would put a beautiful teenage girl in danger.

The oldest profession in the world.

There were no shoes on the girl's feet—another oddity. Included in shots of the clothes was the girl's oversized jean jacket, the reason Lei hadn't jumped to the obvious conclusion at the scene. Because, as she'd told Pono, a lot of the time the obvious was just the obvious. Lei was so deep in thought that the ringing phone made her jump.

"Texeira here."

"Hey. It's Pono. Looks like there's going to be a big cockfight this afternoon out by Giggle Hill." Giggle Hill was a nickname for the WWII memorial park out in the lush East Maui area of Haiku, surrounded by jungle and abandoned pineapple fields. "Can you round up some uniforms? Let's see who we can rope in and shake down. Get those numbers the lieutenant's after." Pono's voice was tight with preraid adrenaline.

"What time?"

"Three o'clock." It was now two p.m.

"Yeah, I'll speak to the shift commander. Call me when you have the exact location."

"Copy that."

Lei printed several more copies of Jane Doe's face. Might as well show them around to whoever they rounded up at the cockfight. She closed the file, grabbed her jacket off the office chair, and headed for the shift commander's office.

Lei's Tacoma bounced down a rutted dirt road, Pono clutching the dashboard and sissy handle. The fight was going to be in an empty field behind a grove of banana trees, someone's abandoned foray into farming. Lei's bulletproof vest, procedurally required on any kind of raid, restricted her breathing as she wrestled the steering wheel.

"Hadn't noticed before with that big jacket on her, but Jane Doe's clothes are hookerwear." Lei spoke in little pants.

"Doesn't every teen girl dress like a hooker?"

"Maybe. That would put her on the wrong side of bad news, though. Might be a reason someone offed her."

They passed the banana trees and reached an open area marked by a ring of trucks. Behind them rolled several unmarked squad cars and the station's Bronco. Lei pulled her Tacoma in behind another truck, and the others did the same, physically blocking in the rest of the vehicles. Adrenaline brought Lei's heart rate up, but the tight vest restricted her breathing. Lei wished for the hundredth time that day that she'd remembered to pick up her little black stone, even though both hands were occupied.

Her eyes flicked here, there, everywhere, scanning for threats as she put the truck in park. A raid like this was one of those situations where anyone anywhere could be carrying a weapon, and a seemingly low-risk operation could turn deadly.

Pono gave the signal in the radio, and they all hit their sirens and lights at the same time, jumping out of their vehicles and running to the collapsible fight ring, a structure made of three-foot-high sections of heavy wire fencing.

Lei had her zip ties out, and Pono worked the bullhorn as they ran toward the fight area, the other officers right on their heels.

"Maui Police Department! Get on your knees and put your hands on your heads!"

Of course, that wasn't what they did. Lei was reminded of hitting the floodlight on the side of the house and surprising cockroaches covering one of Keiki's beef bones—the way they'd scattered in all directions. At least fifty men and boys bolted for their vehicles, headed into the deep grass, or hoofed it for the bananas. Many of them stayed, though, holding cages, unwilling to leave their prize birds.

The two cocks in the ring, oblivious of the human chaos, continued to fight. Lei was struck by their savage commitment, the height of their jumps, the whirl of red and black color like flamenco dancers in full swing.

The owners of the two birds hadn't moved, eyes intent, screaming at the birds. Lei grabbed one of them, a burly, bald Hawaiian in a Kirin beer shirt, and kicked the back of his knee so that he folded as expertly as a collapsible chair. He never took his eyes off the fight as she whipped his arms behind his back and bound his hands with a zip tie.

She ran and did the same to the other man. Several other spectators, committed to the match, merely dropped to their knees and put their hands on their heads while continuing to cheer on the birds. She was putting a tie on the last one when the black cock got the upper hand.

Lei looked up as Kirin Beer Shirt emitted a groan. The black cock stood on the red's back, the blade tied to his leg embedded and tangled in the other bird's neck plumage, and as the red collapsed, he continued to peck at the bird's head and eyes with an intensity that was unnerving.

"Son of a bitch," the man she was holding said. "Could this day get any worse? I just lost a hundred bucks."

"That's not all you're going to lose," Lei said, giving his arms a little yank. The owner of the red cock—the bald guy she'd first restrained—emitted a cry as the black continued to mangle the bloody head of the downed red.

"Get that fucking black off my bird! He'd have won if the cops hadn't distracted him!"

"He got the eyes fair and square!" yelled the black's owner. The big, bald guy uttered a roar, lumbered up from his knees with his hands still tied behind his back, and hurtled across the ring to ram the other owner.

The two huge Hawaiians went down in front of Lei in a cloud of dust and curses.

Lei blew her whistle for help as the men she'd zip tied, realizing there was a distraction, jumped up and took off, since she hadn't had time to do their legs. More chaos ensued as the other officers tackled them. It took Lei, Pono, and another officer to pull the two rooster owners off each other.

They eventually got the scene under control and secured eighteen cockfighters for the station's arrest count. Lei glanced back at the ring. The triumphant black cock stood square on the red's body, stamped his long, elegant bladed legs, flapped his wings, and crowed.

Pono called Animal Control to come take charge of the stacked, portable cages of birds that had all begun to crow once the black got them started. Pono approached the black cock, crouching low and speaking in a soothing voice. The bloodied bird was reluctant to leave his trophy, bobbing a sleek head that had been razored of the comb and wattles, prancing back and forth over the corpse of his enemy.

Pono took a handful of grain from one of the fallen cages and, clucking his tongue softly, extended it to the bird. Mincing like an eighteenth-century dandy, the cock approached and deigned to eat from his hand. Pono encircled the bird's body, and the rooster seemed to go limp as he untied the wicked, bloodied spurs from the cock's legs.

"You look like you know what you're doing," Lei said as Pono put the bird into one of the cages, still talking to it, and gave it some more grain. Her partner's teeth flashed in a grin.

"I wasn't always a police officer."

Lei laughed. The aftermath of adrenaline was making her a little punchy. She took the picture of the dead girl to the three captives they'd stowed in the back of her Tacoma.

"Anyone recognize this girl?"

The guys all looked at it and shook their heads. "She looks dead," one of them said. He was just a kid, no more than sixteen, and Lei knew they'd be letting him go later.

"She is. Went off the cliff at Pauwela Lighthouse. We're just trying to figure out who she is."

"She a hooker?" one of the men asked.

Lei looked up sharply. The man was in his fifties, a belly straining the oversized board shorts he wore under a fraying UH football jersey. His eyes, sunk in dark folds, got shifty.

"What makes you think so?"

"That red hair. Can't be real."

"We're just trying to identify her at this point," Lei said. "What do you know?"

The man pinched his lips shut and sat back. "I don't know nothing. Never seen her."

Lei moved on, making a note that James Silva, age fifty-two, bore more questioning down at the station. Lei showed the photo around to everyone they'd caught. They all denied having ever seen Jane Doe.

The officers and Pono worked the group, getting names and addresses and writing up charges so they could be put in the group lockup at Kahului Station. Pono was working on trying to identify who'd organized the fight. The "paddy wagon" finally arrived, an old pineapple ag worker transport bus that had been modified for the MPD.

The transport rumbled off with its load of downcast defendants, most of whom would be out that afternoon. Several teens and young boys had been caught up in the raid; they were often used to prep and care for the birds because they wouldn't be arrested. Lei had seen the rolls of cash those kids were carrying. What was the incentive to stay in school with so much easy money to be had and Uncle or Dad raising birds worth thousands in the backyard?

She and Pono leaned against the hood of her truck as Animal Control loaded up the rooster cages, still emitting agitated crowing. They'd take them down to the Humane Society, where they'd be adopted right away by their former owners or someone else using them for breeding stock.

"I wouldn't mind taking home that black bird," Pono said thoughtfully. "It's not illegal to raise chickens, and he'd be a valuable breeder."

The black pranced in his cage, sun reflecting off iridescent feathers.

"Bet Tiare would have a few words to say about the crowing," Lei observed. "Not to mention, his owner seemed ready to defend him to the death."

"These birds're confiscated. He can't have him back."

"Yeah, but the only way to make sure the birds don't get back into the game is to destroy them. You ready to do that?"

They both looked at the colorful birds filling the back of the Animal Control van. Pono looked at Lei. "Be a shame."

"Lotta things are a shame."

The dust was settling on the whole operation and they got in the truck. Many abandoned vehicles still cluttered the area. As she turned on the Tacoma, Lei had an evil thought.

"Let's impound these cars. Raise a little money for our department with some fines." Lei stuffed down the conflicted feeling she had about straining the finances of subsistence-level families. These men had chosen the illegal blood sport with its risks—and they'd probably make up the fines next weekend.

"Damn, girl, you're good. Lieutenant's gonna love that idea."

They called the tow company that subcontracted for the

county. In short order, several trucks arrived, winching up a host of vehicles to be locked into the MPD Station impound yard, a big fenced lot behind the central Kahului station.

"This is double genius. To claim the vehicle, they're going to have to admit they were at the fight, or at least their vehicle was somehow there, and we can flag them in the system." Pono grinned, thick fingers flying over his laptop as he updated the incident report.

They headed back to Haiku Station in the village. The police station building was a renovated gray warehouse squatted behind the Haiku Cannery Mall, a giant Quonset hut pineapple packing plant in another era.

The lieutenant was in her office. Somehow she kept the surface of her metal desk immaculate except for her computer and a stack of in-and-out trays. Her eyes were on her monitor when Pono knocked on her doorway; she beckoned without looking up, and they took the two hard plastic chairs facing the desk. When she was good and ready, she pushed a button on whatever she was doing and turned her attention to them.

"We brought in eighteen arrests at the cockfight bust." Pono had taken a few moments to print his report and he pushed it over. He'd told Lei never to approach the throne without an offering. Omura shuffled through the write-up. Lei hoped Pono had taken the time to run spell-check.

"Nice work. How many of the detainees were juveniles? That will affect the final arrest count."

"Six."

"Well. You can't include them in the arrest report. They can be included in the total count, though. So did you get any of the organizers of the fight in the roundup?"

"Hard to tell. They all said they just got a text message about the date and time, that none of them had anything to do with putting it together. That's all my CI knew as well. We'll do follow-up interviews with them alone." Pono gestured to Lei. "Impounding the cars was Lei's idea. We think that will bring our station some fine revenue, and we can also flag those vehicle owners for monitoring in the future."

Brown eyes so dark the pupils were invisible traveled slowly over Lei's grubby clothes and disordered hair. Lei shifted on the plastic seat. She tucked dusty athletic shoes under the chair.

"Impounding vehicles is standard procedure in a raid like this. I think I'd have had something to say if you'd forgotten to do that."

Lei glanced over at Pono. He looked blank. This was their first raid of this type; obviously they'd gotten lucky by covering it. Lei's stomach clenched in a familiar cramp.

Omura seemed to relent. "Next time, I'd like a quick briefing before the raid; then we can make sure everything's covered. What's nice about the impound is that those fines will be directly credited to our station in terms of district funds, so you're right, we can use the money."

She looked back down at the paperwork. "Says you had Animal Control take in the birds. What's happening to them?"

"Animal Control takes them to the Humane Society. They're adopted out."

"More likely picked up by their former owners." She picked up the phone, dialed a number she appeared to have memorized. "This is Lieutenant Omura at MPD. May I speak to your director?"

Lei had an intuition of what was coming. She glanced over at Pono and saw color drain out of his face, leaving it ashy. He rubbed his lip beneath his mustache.

"Hello. This is Lieutenant Omura, commanding officer of Haiku Station. Our officers performed the raid that resulted in the fighting cocks you're currently holding. I'm requesting the euthanization of the birds that were brought in this afternoon." A pause, obviously objections on the other end.

"Yes, I know that's not your policy. However, if you won't do it, I'll send some officers down there and we'll destroy them ourselves. These birds are going to end up back in the ring or breeding more birds for fighting, so we have to make sure we are taking permanent steps to eradicate the problem."

More arguing. The lieutenant's threat was empty, Lei hoped.

"Well, if it's humane you're concerned about, you should consider what means my officers will use to dispatch the birds."

A shorter pause this time. Lei rubbed her hands on her jeans, missing the black stone.

"Great. Thank you for your cooperation in reducing the gambling, violence, and negative community impact that go along with cockfighting. Oh, and if this gets to the papers, I'm going to know it was you who leaked it, and I don't like leaks…No, I'm not threatening, just communicating clearly."

Omura hung up the phone.

Lei's hands were fisted on her thighs as she restrained herself from patting Pono's rigid arm.

Omura looked up. "I know it must seem harsh, but those birds have no other purpose or function than fighting. If this were a drug raid, we wouldn't let the merchandise back out on the street. In the future, I don't want the Humane Society involved. It's going to be a mess if the media gets this, and with the way they sounded, they may try to leak it. In the future, we'll just eliminate the birds ourselves after we confiscate them." Omura must have seen something in Pono's expression because she addressed him directly. "I know it goes against local culture, Kaihale, but they're just chickens. Dismissed."

They got up and went out. Pono turned and went into the men's room, probably punching a wall. He wouldn't be the first to leave the Steel Butterfly's office and do that.

Lei went to the cubicle. Two new files were on her workstation; she booted up her computer as she leafed through them. One was a report of a possible meth lab near the junior high, the other a questionable disappearance of a passenger off the cruise ship in Kahului Harbor. The responding officer had almost immediately bumped it to the detectives since the passenger's home address was Haiku.

Lei was on the phone with the guest coordinator of the *Rainbow Duchess* when Pono returned, stone-faced. He didn't boot up his computer, just picked up his lunch box and jacket and headed for the door. She let him go without comment.

The passenger, one Robert Simmons, had been taking a honeymoon cruise with his new wife. They'd just returned to Kahului after a "great week at sea," where they'd apparently been physically affectionate enough to have drawn the attention of other passengers—but when they went to leave the ship, the bride had been unable to locate the groom.

Lei corroborated the details and made an appointment to see the ship's staff and the wife first thing in the morning, then closed up the workstation. It was four p.m. by then; she had just enough time to swing by Kahului Station on her way home and question Silva about his hooker comment.

She called Pono's phone as she drove into town, but it went to voice mail.

"Sorry about the black rooster, Pono. She's a bitch, but the lieutenant had a point about where the birds will end up. Listen, meet me at the *Rainbow Duchess* dock tomorrow morning at eight; we have a missing passenger to follow up on. I'm interviewing one of the dudes we busted who said something about Jane Doe."

She folded the phone shut and slid it into her pocket.

Lei had Silva brought out of the general holding cell and escorted to an interview room by Gerry Bunuelos, one of the detectives at Kahului Station. Bunuelos had agreed to sit in and assist. He escorted Silva in, clipping the man's handcuffs to a ring on the bolted-down steel table.

"Don't know why I need all this." Silva spread his hands wide. "I went to a cockfight. So what? I'm not a criminal."

Lei sat in the aluminum chair across from him and tried for good cop.

"Standard procedure. Sorry, buddy."

"Well, my wife is on her way, so hurry up with this—whatever it is."

Good cop wasn't a fit, Lei decided.

"You said this girl was a hooker. Why?" She pushed the eight-by-ten glossy print of the girl's face over.

"I just said she looked like the type, with that fake red hair. Girl like that. . ." He shook his head.

"Girl like that, what? Deserves what she got?" Lei felt heat roar up the back of her neck. "This girl was just that—a girl. She was a teenager. Whatever she was, she didn't deserve to die like this." She pushed a full-length, unretouched shot of Jane Doe's mangled body over to Silva, who recoiled. "Take a good long look—buddy."

"Hey, man, I'm sure you didn't mean any disrespect by that," Bunuelos chimed in, picking up the good cop thread.

"I didn't. I didn't!" Silva cried, looking ill as his eyes refused to look away from Jane Doe's hamburgered midsection.

"Guy like you has needs, right?"

Silva's head bobbed. "Uh-huh. Uh-huh." Then he seemed to realize what he was saying and shook his head. "No, no, I'm married. Happy married man."

"So you go to hookers now and again. You ever see her? Lahaina, maybe? She with a massage company or something?" Gerry sounded so sympathetic that Lei narrowed her eyes at him.

"No. No needs. No hookers." Silva seemed to be withdrawing into himself, still shaking his head.

Lei smacked the photo with her open hand. The loud crack made him jump and look her in the eye. She kept his gaze with sheer willpower and meanness. "Tell me. I just want to find out who she is. You won't be in trouble, I promise." The velvet of her voice contrasted with an implicit threat.

Silva rested his head on his cuffed hands, closed his eyes in surrender. "I saw her once. She was in a lineup."

"What do you mean, lineup?"

"Like, when you pick a girl. For the night." His voice was just a whisper. Lei pushed the tape recorder closer to pick it up.

"Where was this?"

"Miramar Hotel." A classy place, the Miramar had been open since the 1970s. It was an elaborate Moorish-style Lahaina landmark.

"What's a guy like you doing in a place like the Miramar?" Lei's voice dripped contempt.

"Construction wrap party. We finished a job, and the owner had us all there to celebrate. He ordered up what he called 'room service.' She was in a lineup, like I said."

"So you recognize her. Sure you didn't do more than that? Does she have any special features, distinguishing marks?" Lei wanted to know if he knew about the butterfly tattoo. Silva shook his head, sweat pearling across the top of his lip.

"No. I never saw nothing. She had on a little white robe. They all did."

"White? That's odd for a hooker."

"It was shiny white stuff, you know, like satin. They're a classy outfit. I mean, according to the owner. He said he was ordering the best. Since we'd made his dream house come true, he was going to make some of ours come true, too."

"So what did you have?"

"A blonde. She was older."

"Right. Older. Okay." Lei tried to keep the sarcasm out of her voice but failed. "Anything interesting about these whores beside the white robes? Anything you remember?"

"The girl I was with. She had an accent."

"What kind?"

"How should I know what kind?" He finally showed a little spirit, clashing the cuffs against the table. "I wasn't there to talk to her."

Lei paced as Bunuelos took over.

"Anything else stand out to you about that evening?"

"No. Is my wife going to find out about this?" He glanced nervously at the closed door.

Lei let an evil grin move across her face. She had a wide mouth with a lot of teeth, and Stevens had said her evil grin gave him bad dreams. "I don't know. Anything your wife should know?"

"I told you everything. I can't stay in here. I have a health condition. . ." Silva degenerated into a whine.

"So we need your boss's name. The guy who threw the party."

"He can't know I ratted about the whores!"

Lei smacked the table again. "Shut up and focus. You get no promises. You don't deserve any until you give us something we can use."

Bunuelos put his hand on her arm. "Settle down, Detective. The man only did what anyone would do when presented with that kind of opportunity."

He winked where Silva couldn't see it. Lei whirled up and paced again. Bunuelos turned back to Silva.

"We'll do what we can. No reason your wife needs to know anything but that you got picked up with a lot of other guys at the cockfight, and the contractor won't know who told on him about the hookers. We aren't trying to bust anybody for that—we just want to find out who this girl was."

"John Wylie. He's a pretty big developer, does a lot on the west side of Maui." Silva hung his head. Sweat rings marked his armpits in the dusty shirt. Lei wrote down the first note she'd taken for the interview on a pristine yellow pad she'd set beside the tiny recorder.

"So what do you know about who organized the cockfight?" A stab in the dark but worth a try now that she had him talking.

"Nothing. I don't know nothing! I got a text with the date and time like everyone else!"

"Someone sends the texts, keeps track of who's fighting their birds, who's attending. Someone organizes these things."

"I don't know anything real. I swear. But I hear it's a guy on Oahu who gets a cut. All the owners who put birds in the ring pay a fee to him; he's the 'house' you can bet against, and somehow the 'house' does better than most."

"That's gambling for you. So what do they call this guy?"

Silva looked up. "My wife could leave me over this. You think it's a good idea for me to get two in the head, too?"

"C'mon, quit being such a drama queen. This is Maui. No one rolls like that around here."

"You just never find the bodies." He looked down, shook his head, his voice a whisper of defeat. "I don't know anything worth anything. He's called the House. That's all I know."

"Oh. Didn't realize that was his handle." She gave a nod to Bunuelos, who unclipped the handcuffs from the ring. "Thanks, Mr. Silva. We appreciate your cooperation. Now, was that so hard?"

"You sure my wife won't find out? She'll just leave me in here if she knows. . ."

"You gave us a name, so we're square. Couple of names, in fact. But we know where you live." Lei did the grin again.

He nearly ran out of the room, followed by Bunuelos. Lei collected the recorder and notepad and followed him out. Stevens was waiting in the hall. Her heart gave a familiar thump at the sight of him.

"Michael!"

Lei knew Stevens was ever aware of setting a good example in front of the men, so while not keeping their relationship a secret, they weren't advertising it either. The echoing linoleum hall was empty, so he leaned over and gave her a kiss, a hard stamp on her mouth that left her wanting more.

"Why didn't you tell me you were here? I caught about half your performance from the gallery." The back wall of the interview room was two-way glass.

"Sorry. I was in a hurry, wanted to get to the interview before Silva got released." They walked side by side toward the main work area. Lei slid her hands into her pockets, familiar guilt irritating her. She seldom remembered to do the right girlfriend shit, like calling him. She turned to him with a bright smile. "Well, it's time to head home. Want to go get something to eat on our way?"

"We can hit Ichiban. I have to shut down the workstation first."

"I'll meet you there; just want to wrap things up with Bunuelos. He was a big help."

Stevens peeled off to the left, and Lei went onto the main floor, a typical government maze of soundproofed cubicles in industrial gray with the occasional "inspirational" print to liven things up. Bunuelos met her at his cubicle after releasing Silva. He gave her a high-five.

"You have a gift. Silva is totally paranoid now. He was practically peeing himself."

"Good. Maybe he'll keep it in his pants now. What a scumbag, so worried about his wife finding out."

Bunuelos's partner, Abe Torufu, came in. Lei had noticed the contrast between the two of them from day one—Bunuelos was a wiry Filipino with the build and energy of a rat terrier, while his partner loomed, a slow-moving Tongan mountain. Torufu sat down on his chair. The overwhelmed equipage squealed and moaned, but held.

"Well, I'm off for the night, but I just wanted to thank you for helping me out. We got some names to follow up on, and that's huge. I'm crazy to know this girl's name." Lei tapped the folder with the photos.

"A pleasure. Interesting case. Keep me posted on it, and if you need any help, let me know."

"You and Stevens a thing?" Torufu asked, spinning his chair in her direction, a toothpick protruding from between Chiclets-sized teeth.

"Uh. Yeah." Lei felt a blush prickle her hairline. "Is there a problem?"

"No. Just explains it; that's all."

"Explains what?" Lei put her hands on her hips.

"Nothing." Both of them turned to their computers.

"C'mon, guys. Really. He a bad boss or something?"

"No, fine; it's all good." They'd become very intent all of a sudden, eyes on their monitors.

"Okay, then. Bye." Lei shook her head as she left.

"Lemme know if you need me," Bunuelos called after her again.

"Will do." Lei hurried down the hall. She didn't have time for male mind games. Japanese food sounded delicious, and the sooner the better.

Stevens was already seated at the little hole-in-the-wall restaurant minutes away from the station. He'd ordered a Kirin for her, which she sipped while perusing the menu. They chose tempura and teriyaki beef, and when the waitress left, Lei bounced and wiggled a bit in her seat.

"Got a good lead. The name of a guy who hired a company that provided the girls. Our Jane Doe was one of them."

"I know. I was there for that part," Stevens said dryly. "I like your bad cop. Nicely done. The smacks on the photo were a tad theatrical, but they worked."

"I shouldn't enjoy it so much, but damn, that guy was so gross. I mean, can you see him with some poor little teenage girl?" She shuddered. "I wanted to put the fear in him so bad he can't get it up for a hooker ever again."

"That's the world we live in. Nasty people doing nasty shit." Stevens rubbed his eyes with his hand. She noticed for the first time they were even more deep-set than usual, ringed in shadows. She put her hand on his on the table; he turned it up and warm energy flowed between them. They laced their fingers together. Lei felt a rush of compassion for him.

"What's the matter?" She finally had the nerve to ask.

"Nothing really. Just getting tired, I guess. Office politics." He still wasn't telling her.

"Okay." Lei couldn't tell if the feeling she had was relief or disappointment.

The food arrived, and Lei ate with her usual focus and enthusiasm, hungry from all the exercise. Between bites, she told him about the raid, making Stevens laugh with her rendering of the irate rooster owners tackling each other with their hands tied. It felt good to hear him laugh, see him relax, the darkness around his eyes pull back a bit.

"Pono took it hard about the birds, though." She finished the story. "He left work early—meaning on time for once. I've never seen him so upset. The Steel Butterfly finally got to him."

"Watch out for her," Stevens said. "I hear she can be a bad enemy."

"I'm doing my best. I never speak unless spoken to. I can't help that she thinks I'm a train wreck, though." Lei took a sip of her beer, swallowing past the lump in her throat.

"Hey." She looked up. His penetrating blue eyes were on her, stripping her bare. He saw past her defenses—he'd always been able to. Then Stevens smiled, the crooked flash she loved so well.

"You could take her. That's a chick fight I wouldn't mind seeing."

"I don't know. I hear she has a black belt."

"Well, what are you up to in Tae Kwon Do? Red?"

She ducked her head. "It's going okay, yeah." She'd joined a nearby dojo in Wailuku and took a class twice a week. "So what's got you so bothered? I've been telling you a lot about my cases. I'm not hearing anything about yours."

"Not much to tell. They got me doing a lot of training with the new detectives. That's not what's on my mind, though." He sighed. *Uh-oh.* Here it came—the problem he'd been holding on to.

"I'm just...wondering where this is going." He gestured back and forth between them. "This. Us."

"I don't know. We're living together and having some excellent sex? What more is there?" She tried a smile.

He shook his head. "I just feel like we're...not going in the same direction. Maybe it's that I'm older, got this promotion, starting to build something here that I know I won't want to leave. I don't get that feeling from you. You're still thinking about the FBI, aren't you?"

"Marcella keeps in touch, yeah. You know she thinks I'd be a good agent out here because of the multicultural thing."

"So I'm wondering, where does that leave me if you take off for the Academy?"

"Well, it's not forever, the Academy. I'd be back. Eventually. Marcella says they'll want to post me some places after training, so I can get some seasoning."

"I'm not getting any younger. I can't go with you."

"Thirty-four isn't old." She took his big, warm hand, bit his finger, and laid it against her cheek. "My biological clock's not even wound yet. We've got plenty of time."

He pulled his hand away. "You're not the only one with a biological clock."

He reached into his pocket, set the little black velvet box on the table between them.

"Dammit, Michael, you promised you wouldn't do this to me again." Tears prickled the backs of Lei's eyes, and she blinked rapidly. "You know this freaks me out."

"I need something, too. I need to know we're going to be together. If I know that, I can wait. I can tell myself, someday she might be ready to settle down—have a family."

"I can't make those kinds of promises." Her heart had begun thundering, blood roaring, claustrophobia bringing blackness around the edges of her vision. She pinched her leg through her jeans to anchor herself.

"Then I'm thinking I need to get this over with. I can't put my life on hold forever, hoping you'll be…ready for more."

"Isn't what we have enough?" Her throat seemed to close, strangling words to explain. Their relationship was perfect to her; it was all she wanted. She loved what they had—the little house, runs with Keiki, leisurely weekends having adventures or making love all afternoon. Why couldn't that be enough for him?

"I love you. I love what we have." He must have seen the panic in her eyes, because he took both her hands, rubbed the palms and then the backs with his thumbs, touch keeping her in her body. "I just want that and to know we'll always be together—and throw in a couple kids someday, too."

She closed her eyes, did some relaxation breathing, feeling the calm his touch brought. His thumbs caressing the thin skin of her wrist, the pulse point of her blood, seemed to be the only thing that meant anything. Panic brought on by her inadequacies, his possible abandonment, and the use of the word "kids"—all gradually receded. After a long moment, she opened her eyes and found herself looking into his—eyes so blue they held bits of white like stars. Those eyes reflected everything he felt, always had.

"I can't promise," she finally said, her voice a whisper. "But I can think about it. I can try."

She took her hands out of his, opened the box. In it was the old-fashioned ring his grandmother had left him, a cushion-cut diamond surrounded by baguettes set like petals on a daisy. She knew that ring and had missed it. She'd worn it for several months before the actual wedding plans had sent her running away in terror to Kaua'i.

"I love this ring." She picked it up. "You don't even know how much I wish I could be what you want, say yes, do the whole white picket fence thing. But I tried already and broke your heart. I don't want to do that to you any more than you want me to. But I can wear this on a chain, and when I know one way or another, I'll either give it back to you and we'll be *pau*, finished, or I'll put it on my finger, and we'll get married. That's the best I can do."

"That's fair." She could tell it wasn't what he wanted to hear by the way he sat back against the orange plastic of the booth, dark brows lowering—but it was all she could give.

"It's Charlie Kwon's fault. If I do something about what he did to me—I might be able to move on."

"Fuck Charlie Kwon and that old pedophile shit. This is you; this is me." He leaned forward, intense, and lifted the hand she'd slipped the ring on. He nibbled her fingertip, drew it into his mouth. Tingles of feeling shot down her arm and headed south. She'd forget about Charlie, forget anything, if he kept that up. The waitress appeared, and Stevens let go of her hand and picked up the check.

"Let's get home so you can start convincing me to get married," Lei said, leaning forward to put her hand on his leg, working upward.

"On it," he said, fumbling for his wallet.

They hurried home. Lei's hair was sure to be a wreck again in the morning.

Chapter 6

*T*he dark was blooming with dawn when Lei got up. She padded into the bathroom, washed up, brushed her teeth, and got into running clothes. Back in the bedroom, she looked over at Stevens, his body a dark outline against the white sheets. Her mind filled in the long, solid contours of his body, the warm hollows and ridges she'd come to know so well, fitting under his collarbone, tucked against his side like she'd been measured for the space.

She wanted to climb back into bed, spoon up against the long, elegant curve of his body into that spot that was hers. But inside her, an inner restlessness wound tight in her sternum, pounded along her veins, demanding freedom and movement.

It hurt to leave, even while that tension drove her.

Lei opened the simple koa box Stevens had given her to hold her few jewelry items. Coiled in the bottom like a handful of rose petals was the Ni`ihau shell necklace she'd been given on Kaua`i, her Tahitian pearl earrings, and an eighteen-inch gold snake chain with a cross that Aunty Rosario had given her for Christmas. She slipped the cross off of it and fumbled the diamond ring out of its box. She threaded it onto the chain, tucking it under her shirt as she headed for the door.

Keiki danced happily by the gate as Lei put on her running shoes. She slipped the choke chain over the big dog's head, snapping the leash to get her back on task.

They set off down the deserted two-lane road, a few wild roosters crowing greetings from the tops of mango trees as mynahs began their morning gossip against the lightening sky. The steep, jungled green slopes of `Iao Valley rose around her, cradling her with the ancient intensity they'd always held, making the Valley one of Maui's most sacred places. Keiki lunged and snorted.

"Okay, girl."

They picked up their speed to full blast, running down the deserted two-lane road toward the back of the valley, and the relaxation she'd been looking for came to Lei at last. At the park at the end of the paved road, they turned back, jogging beside the stream.

The liquid song of the stream was pierced by the chirping of her phone from her pocket, a jarring mechanical note. Lei checked the number—someone on the Mainland. They must not know it was only six thirty a.m. here.

"Texeira."

"Lei Texeira? This is Diane Buchanan at Lompoc Federal Correctional Facility."

"Oh hi, Diane. Something up?"

"You asked me to keep an eye on what's happening with Charlie Kwon. Well, he was granted parole."

"No. Seriously?" Lei stopped, bent over to suck in some air. She wasn't just out of breath from running. Scumbag was supposed to be in for fifteen years and had served only five.

"Well, we've got a crowding problem, and he successfully completed the sex offender rehabilitation program. The psychologist signed off. I did what I could at the hearing, but in the end I think it was the space issue that did it. His parole is being handled by Corrections Aftercare Solutions, and he's being returned to Oahu next week."

Lei tried to get air, but it didn't seem to want to go into her lungs.

"You okay?" the social worker asked. She'd been very sympathetic when Lei visited the year before and talked to her about being abused by Kwon; she'd agreed to keep Lei informed of his progress and whereabouts.

"I'm fine, thanks. I'm just out running." Lei's mind raced. Aftercare Solutions. She was familiar with them because of her father's process last year upon his release after a long-term stretch for dealing. The private nonprofit handled parole monitoring and reintegration of ex-cons into the community with the end goal of lowering the recidivism rate. As far as Lei could tell, they were accomplishing that while saving the state some money.

The reintegration program was probably beefed up for sex offenders. She should be able to get Charlie Kwon's location out of them with just her badge.

"Diane, I know you must have done what you could. Thanks so much for letting me know."

"I just want victims to get help and closure."

"I so appreciate your advocacy." Social workers loved words like "advocacy," and Lei definitely planned on getting closure on Kwon.

Lei closed the phone and slid it into her pocket, then cranked up the speed again to get home quickly. She'd waited a long time to deal with the man who'd stolen her childhood, and now he was almost within reach.

Chapter 7

L ei pulled the Tacoma into a parking spot at Kahului Harbor. The *Rainbow Duchess* loomed above her, a vast floating wedding cake of cruise ship fantasy, glowing in the morning sun. Pono jumped out of his purple truck beside her, slamming the door. He looked fresh and sassy in a big man's hibiscus-flowered aloha shirt and chinos.

"Hey, partner. Glad you got my message." They fell in step toward the ship.

"Yeah, no problem."

"You seem in a better mood. You okay about the chicken thing?"

"Sure." He paused midstride, glanced at her. A dimple appeared in the brown wall of his cheek. "We have a new pet at the Kaihale house."

"You're kidding!" Lei stopped, put her hands on her hips. "Tell me you're kidding!"

He walked on. "Nope. His name's Jet. I know a guy who can do something to his vocal cords to chill out his crowing; once I promised Tiare we'd do that, she said it was okay. He's bedded down in the laundry room."

Lei laughed aloud. They did a fist bump.

"That's my boy! What'd the Humane Society say?"

"Nothing. I said I needed the bird for evidence collection. I'm sure they thought I was going to take him out back and chop his head off."

"Gotta catch you up on the follow-up from the raid, but here's what we know so far about the missing guy off the ship." Lei sketched in the details she'd picked up about the Simmons disappearance.

They boarded the ship and were met by the coordinator, a dapper young man with a wannabe mustache who led them up to the captain's office. It was a handsome wood-paneled room with a magnificent view, fifteen floors above the harbor. Lei tried not to let on how impressed she was as the captain shook their hands and sat them at the conference table.

He was an imposing silver-haired man dressed in crisp whites, radiating authority.

"I hope we can get some traction on this soon. We're set to sail out of here at nine a.m.," the captain boomed.

"I'm sorry. That's definitely out of the question," Lei said. "You're missing a passenger who may have met foul play or an accident on board. We have to at least have time to search the ship."

"We've already done that. I had my crew do a top-to-bottom. We didn't find him."

"I'm afraid I can't just take your word for it," Lei said. Pono was already dialing Lieutenant Omura.

"You can speak to our commanding officer," Pono said a moment later, and handed the cell phone over.

The captain had met his match in the lieutenant, and in the end he threw his hands up in disgust after handing back the phone. "Take the time you need to interview people and do your search, but I warn you, the natives are going to be restless. I'm going to make the announcement that we can't leave port on schedule."

The detectives ensconced themselves at the conference table. The purser brought in the red-eyed bride, a large woman in her fifties with orange hair and a flowing purple caftan. A gigantic square-cut diamond glittered on her finger.

"I can't believe the police have had to be called. This is a nightmare." The newly wedded Mrs. Simmons waved the hankie wadded in her hand. "Where could Robert be?"

"Ma'am, we'll do all we can to find your husband." A suspicion niggled at Lei's mind as she looked down at the photo taken of the happy couple when they'd come on board, handed to her by the purser. Clara Simmons, looking almost pretty, embraced a muscle-bound spray-tanned man with a head of Fabio-like wavy locks.

After a few warm-up questions, Lei followed her hunch. "After your wedding, did any money change hands between the two of you?"

"What do you mean? What are you saying?"

"Nothing. I'm just asking, did you pool or exchange any money?"

"He signed a prenup, if that's what you're asking." Clara sniffed, gathering her dignity. "That's what all my friends insisted on. I mean, why else would a man like Robert be with a woman like me—at least according to my friends." She shook her head. "I did transfer a hundred thousand for the down payment on our house in Napili into our joint account. We shopped for it for weeks before the wedding, and it's going to close now that we've returned."

"What bank?"

"Bank of Hawaii. But I'm sure—that can't be it." Tears threatened again. Lei turned to Pono, who was already standing up and dialing his phone.

A few minutes later, he had the bank manager on the phone, wanting confirmation from Clara, who gave it. The bank manager must have told her what was left in the account, because she gave a ululating cry of mortal pain and sat down abruptly on one of the cushy chairs.

The coordinator hurried forward, soothing, patting, and waving tissues.

"I think it would be best if we get Mrs. Simmons installed in a hotel, and we continue our investigation in Kahului after a quick check belowdecks, in case he's still hiding on board." Lei gestured toward the door, and the coordinator escorted the weeping woman out.

Pono was already calling the airport and Dispatch to put out an alert on one Robert Simmons, age thirty-two, six foot two, muscular build, wavy blond hair, probably traveling under an alias—if his name was Robert Simmons at all.

Lei went down to the cabin the honeymoon couple had stayed in. Empty, but for a set of matched Louis Vuitton luggage. Clara Simmons would have been good for more if he'd waited awhile, but apparently the honeymoon had been all that he could handle.

A staffer took them below and unlocked doors for them. After they'd done a sweep of the most likely hiding places, Lei glanced at her phone. It was eleven a.m., and the ship had already been delayed two hours. It was unlikely Robert Simmons was still on board; he'd probably hopped a plane yesterday. She signaled Pono.

"Check with the lieutenant, but I think we should let the ship go and focus on trying to catch Simmons at the airport."

Pono nodded and made the call, then motioned toward the metal ladder back up to the next level, far from the luxurious upper decks.

They said respectful goodbyes to the captain. Clara Simmons had been taken in a cab to the nearby Maui Beach Hotel. Lei followed Pono off the ship with an echoing clang of footsteps on the metal gangplank, holding on to the rope baluster as the giant engines fired up for departure.

"Want to get lunch?" she asked Pono. "I need to tell you about the interview with Silva and what Bunuelos and I found out about Jane Doe."

They pulled into Pinatas on Dairy Road in downtown Kahului and took a corner table with their burritos. Lei told Pono about the "House," mysterious organizer of the cockfighting ring, and the white-robed hookers, including the name of the developer who'd bought hookers for his construction wrap party.

"I gotta follow up on that next," Lei said, taking a bite of her kitchen sink burrito, the size of a small coconut. Pinatas didn't stint on portions.

"I don't think he's going to just tell you who he ordered hookers from over the phone," Pono said. "We should drive out there. Get eyes on him. What if he has a hand in it somehow?"

They flipped a coin, and it was the purple truck this time for the ride to Lahaina, where Wylie's construction offices were located. Lei called back to the station and checked in with Dispatch as they drove along the Pali, asking if the lieutenant could send someone to work the meth house case that had shown up on her desk that morning.

She put her head back against Pono's sheepskin-covered seat, surprisingly comfortable even in hot Hawaii. A tiny imitation Hawaiian war helmet decked with red and yellow feathers dangled from the mirror, and Pono's gearshift was a chrome skull. Riding in Pono's truck was always interesting.

"How are we going to do good work with so many cases? That's not to mention the ones we had before these new ones started piling on." Lei unscrewed a water bottle and sipped.

"Well, at least the cruise ship one isn't a homicide."

"We don't know that. What if Clara found out Robert ripped her off, and she pushed him overboard? Ships are a great place for a homicide, actually. I'm surprised we haven't had more cases involving the cruise lines."

"That's you, Sweets, always seeing more than the obvious. Why don't you look up Wylie Construction, see what you can find out?" Pono had a line between his brows. Lei extracted the Toughbook from its stowage under the glove box, unfolded the retractable arm, and punched up the company. It was time to focus on the task at hand.

Wylie Construction was a big operation, according to their website. They were at the forefront of "gracious, custom, green living" on Maui, and planning a new self-contained community in West Maui, "where everything you need for life and living is in one piece of paradise."

Lei snorted. "Sounds like a petri dish," she muttered.

Pono glanced over. "What's that around your neck?"

"Oh." Lei reached up to touch the ring. It was surprisingly bulky and refused to stay tucked into the neck of her shirt. "Just a gift."

"Uh-huh. It's a diamond ring."

"Yeah. So?"

"Looks like Stevens made his move." Pono shook his head.

"What do you mean?"

"Gotta give the guy points for trying."

"Hey, what if I want to get married? We're good together."

"Then why isn't the ring on your finger?"

He had her there.

"None of your business." Distraction was called for. "Says John Wylie came to Maui ten years ago with a vision to bring 'gracious, affordable, green construction' to the island. Nothing about him being married. I'm trolling through some Google articles—he appears to be a bit of a player. Lots of different women on his arm. Charity events, things like that. Seems involved with the arts."

Wylie looked like a typical middle-aged transplant *haole*: thinning blond hair brushed to look fuller over a weathered ruddy complexion, rugged build. "Look at this one—'Millionaire Developer John Wylie brings Gallery Owner to Opening Night of the Maui Film Festival.' Seems like a real high maka-maka type." Lei used the pidgin expression for society. She swiveled the screen so Pono could glance at the photo of a striking blue-eyed, black-haired woman on Wylie's arm.

They drove into the outskirts of Lahaina, the "blazing sun" the town was named for already high and hot, the ocean a glittering blue plate glass off to the left. Pono pulled into the Wylie Construction offices in a handsome strip mall off the main shopping area of Front Street. Lei took a minute to put on some lip gloss, straighten her rumpled jacket, and fluff her hair, which had seen more cooperative days. Too long to be short and too short to pull back, her curls were really driving her crazy.

"Enough with the fussing," Pono said, hopping out of the cab. Lei gave one last pat to her hair, to no visible effect. The detectives walked into a beautifully appointed reception area.

Wylie Construction's stylized logo hung over the glossy desk of a decorative receptionist. Original oils and sculptures stood out from neutral gray watered-silk walls with skillful lighting.

"We're here to see John Wylie." Lei and Pono held up their badges. The receptionist inspected them carefully, looking flustered, and picked up the interoffice phone. Apparently the great man was in a meeting.

"If you could wait a few minutes, please."

They sat. The furniture was exquisitely comfortable and simple, silver suede couches arranged around a square coffee table covered in a fan of magazines. Pono found a golf magazine and settled in with deceptive ease. Only Lei knew his ears were tuned to anything unusual and his eyes were checking unobtrusively.

Lei browsed an *O* magazine, terrified herself with a brief foray into *Parents*, and finally stood up and paced. Went back to the receptionist.

"Tell Wylie to wrap it up or we're going in. I guarantee that he'll be embarrassed." Lei's tilted brown eyes must have said she meant business, because the woman picked up the phone and shortly thereafter, a gaggle of golf-shirted *haoles* exited, giving curious glances. Lei led the way into the inner sanctum.

Chapter 8

*J*ohn Wylie got up from a traditional red leather, tufted office chair. "Aloha, Detectives. What can I do for you?"

Lei opened her mouth, and Pono put his hand on her arm, stepping in to shake the man's hand. "Pono Kaihale of Maui Police Department. This is my partner, Lei Texeira. We are investigating a homicide."

"My goodness, that sounds serious." Wylie's wind-chapped cheeks went a bit paler. He stayed ensconced behind his vast walnut desk. "Please, sit."

They took the supplicant chairs in front as Wylie resettled himself.

"How can I help you?"

"Well, the young woman in question is still unidentified. The focus of our investigation is finding out who she is." Wylie nodded, a furrow of faux concern stitched between his brows, and Pono went on. "She was recognized by someone from a 'lineup' of women procured for escort services. By you."

This bombshell was delivered in calm, measured tones. Pono could still surprise Lei.

Wylie shot up. Color flooded up his neck like mercury rising in a thermometer. "Who said that? I demand to know who would make such an accusation!"

"Not gonna happen." Pono sat back, laced beefy fingers over his muscular midsection, blinked as slow as an owl in the sun. "Not relevant. What we want to know is, who sent you those whores? Who'd you call? We aren't looking to prosecute you for that at this time."

The threat was in the delicate emphasis of the last sentence.

"Well. Well." Wylie huffed. He turned to a decanter on the credenza behind his desk, poured some amber liquid into a highball glass. "It's five o'clock somewhere." He tossed the drink back. "When was this?"

"So you make a habit of calling for a lineup of whores?" Lei's first contribution to the discussion was acidic and seemed to rattle him further, and he splashed more alcohol into the glass.

"I'm just trying to establish a framework for these questions," Wylie said. He resumed his seat. "I have to put it in context."

"It was a construction wrap party a month or so ago."

"Ah." Wylie sipped. "One of the guys talked. Knew I was taking a chance." He set the glass down. "I'd like you to know that calling an escort service is not illegal. What the girls do with the guys they are escorting is their business."

"Of course," Pono said.

Lei rolled her eyes but restrained herself. She could tell this was the kind of guy who kept a lawyer on speed dial.

"I use this service when I want to entertain." He opened a drawer in his desk with a little gold key on a key ring, shuffled a bit, and pushed a card over to them. It was glossy white with a satin-embossed edge and nothing on it but a phone number in crisp black Gothic script.

"Now, anything further and I must insist my lawyer be present." He took his BlackBerry out, finger poised. Yep, speed dial. Lei was irritated to be right.

"One more question—did you know anything about a girl at that party, long red hair, blue eyes, a tattoo of a butterfly on her ankle?" Lei slid the photo of Jane Doe across the desk to Wylie. He did not look at it; instead he pushed a button on the phone and they heard it dialing. He held up a finger toward them as the phone was answered.

"Kevin, this is John. Can you come right over? Some detectives are in my office, harassing me about an escort service. Oh. Okay." He pressed End and looked up with a smile straight out of a denture commercial. "My attorney has instructed me not to answer any further questions until he gets here."

Pono stood up, put the white card in his pocket. "Thank you for cooperating, Mr. Wylie. MPD appreciates it."

Lei had spotted a picture behind Wylie on the credenza. A pair of blond, orthodontia- wrapped teen girls flanked him in a formal portrait. Lei tapped Jane Doe's photo, forcing his eyes down to look at it. "This young girl, same age as your daughters, was murdered, and all you can do is dial your phone and hide behind your lawyer. Nice."

She waited a long moment, but he didn't look up from the beautiful dead face. She stood and turned away, following Pono. Wylie's voice came as she was almost at the door.

"I recognize her. She had an accent."

Lei moved alongside the desk to align with him. "What kind?"

"Well. I don't know. Seemed European." He harrumphed, as if remembering he wasn't supposed to speak, and then said, "I think all the girls are foreign. I've never seen the same ones twice."

"Anything else stand out about her?"

"No. Other than she was a little younger than the others. I didn't see who she ended up with that evening."

"Do you know anything more about the escort service than just that number?"

"No. But I know who I got the card from." He opened the drawer again, took out another card. "I can't be linked to giving you this information in any way, but I want that girl to get some justice." His pale eyes seemed to be trying to convince her what a good guy he was, and hell, maybe he was a good guy, at least by his own standards. He did try to build "green" after all.

Lei picked up the card. This one was printed on opalescent card stock with a name and address picked out in raised silver lettering.

"Thank you." She reached over to shake his hand. "Takes a real man to take a risk for justice."

Out at the purple truck, Pono shook his head. "That last line was laying it on a bit thick, but he seemed to buy it."

"We might need him again, and I don't want to burn any bridges."

Pono snorted. "That's a first." They pulled out as a cream-colored Mercedes pulled in with a squeal of brakes. "Just dodged the lawyer."

They drove back toward Lahaina's main shopping and art route on a busy four-lane, tree-lined boulevard. Lei chewed her bottom lip, fiddling with the opalescent card that listed a Pacific Treasures Gallery with a Front Street address.

"Let's follow up and hit the address, since we're out here— before he has a chance to give this gallery a heads-up."

Front Street had maintained its former whaling-village charm, and the narrow shop-lined street, facing the glittering ocean and a vista of the tiny island of Lana`i, was jammed with tourists and sightseers. Pono squeezed the oversized truck in between a pair of Hyundai rentals with the ease of practice. Lei jumped down onto the sidewalk and turned to her partner.

"Just scope the place, do the happy tourist thing. I don't want to spook whoever it is until we have a little more to go on." She buttoned her light jacket over her gun and slid her badge into her pocket.

"Right on, Sweets. We can be a honeymoon couple." Pono gave her an exaggerated wink and made a pretend ass grab, which she froze with a look. They fell into character, meandering down the sidewalk with the rest of the tourists, leaning to look into displays of Tahitian pearls, racks of colorful pareu, and even a portable stand of parrots that people could pose with.

Eventually they came to the address. Everything about Pacific Treasures Gallery sent a message of upscale elegance, beginning with the pneumatic sliding glass door that ushered them into air-conditioned comfort seasoned with classical music.

Creamy white walls, white marble floors, and well-designed lighting highlighted a range of dramatic artwork. Lei circled around a sculpture inside a block of Lucite that appealed to her, an angel that appeared to float in three dimensions.

A statuesque blond saleswoman in a white Grecian-style dress approached as Lei dragged Pono over to look at the Lucite blocks. "Oh, honey! How do they do that?"

"It's done with lasers," the saleswoman said. "Each one is signed and numbered."

Lighting from below made the angel glow, and Lei suddenly remembered one much like it, wings outstretched, that she'd had as a night-light when she was a child. That angel night-light had failed her. It had smiled a plastic smile as Charlie Kwon came into her room. Her eyes were on it as she begged him to stop, and as she gave up and waited for him to be done with her, his little "damaged goods," the angel watched, and smiled, and did nothing.

Lei felt her chest tighten, her throat close. Her vision telescoped, black encircling the edges, as she focused on the floating angel. Her hand crept down to her side, and she pinched her leg viciously through her pants. Sucking relaxation breaths, she grabbed Pono's big hand. She towed him into the main gallery area. Another Grecian-gowned saleswoman, a redhead this time, watched them from the back of the room. Lei hated it when memories ambushed her like this; she almost preferred the fog of memory loss she'd struggled with years ago.

"This is so beautiful," Lei said breathlessly, the dark around her vision retreating in front of a stretch of canvas crammed with every fantastical ocean creature that could be imagined. She turned back to the saleswoman who had followed them. "We're on our honeymoon. We want something to remember it by."

"Fabulous," the blonde said, sizing them up. "I have some lovely giclee prints over here." She led them toward the back of the gallery, Lei taking everything in. Pono suddenly dug his heels in and turned to Lei.

"Let's get the manager out here," he whispered. Before she had time to respond, he commented loudly.

"Nothing too good for you, baby," he boomed in pidgin. "I goin' buy you anyting you like." He raised his voice after the saleswoman. "You stay showing us these kine because you don't think we can afford one real painting?"

"Oh, no, I just thought…something modest…" The saleswoman sputtered. "Young couple, starting out—"

"So what you mean is, local people can't buy art here? This one *haole*-only kine place?" Pono's voice had begun to climb.

Lei put her hand on his arm. "Now, baby, no make one scene. I'm sure the lady only meant fo' be helpful…"

She glanced up. In the corner were surveillance cameras. Pono continued to agitate. She could tell he was enjoying this on one level and venting some long-simmering frustration on another.

"This land was our land, stolen from us; now we can't afford to even own our home here. You insult me! I like speak to your manager. No, your owner! I like look 'em in the eye, the person who wen' take my land from me!"

A few minutes more of that and the saleswoman fled through a door at the back. The redhead was already gone. A few minutes later, another woman entered, the blonde following. She was tall, with shimmering black hair that contrasted with a cream-colored pantsuit. Dark blue eyes took in the scene. Weighed them up—and found them wanting.

"Jillian, get these newlyweds some champagne." Jillian hurried away.

Pono drew himself up to his not-inconsiderable height and breathed through his wide nose, thick arms crossed on his chest. "Your girl, she one racist."

"My apologies. My saleswoman knows better than to profile our guests; I'll see to it she's disciplined."

Her use of that word struck Lei oddly, and she darted a glance at the woman's face, an inscrutable, beautiful white oval. She extended a hand, which Lei touched with limp fingertips, intimidated by the gigantic sapphire ring on it.

"Magda Kennedy. I own this gallery. And you are?"

"Lani Hale and this is my husband, Kimo. We're on our honeymoon." Lei spit out the first names she could think of. Cool amusement lit the woman's eyes before she turned back to Pono.

"I understand and appreciate your position, Mr. Hale. I value the support of our local people and again, I hope you won't take offense. Congratulations on your wedding, and take this champagne with our compliments." She handed the bottle the saleswoman had brought to Pono.

He looked down at a magnum of Cristal, flummoxed. Police officers weren't supposed to receive anything over fifty dollars' value. Lei stepped in, conscious of the video cameras on them.

"We can't be bought."

She shoved the champagne back into Magda Kennedy's arms and herded Pono out into the hot and crowded street. They hurried down the crowded sidewalk to a scrap of lawn in front of the picturesque Missionary House Museum.

Lei turned and lit into him. "What were you thinking? We were supposed to be keeping a low profile!"

Pono lowered the mirrored Oakleys over his eyes and set his chin. "Thought it would be a good idea to see who's behind the operation there."

"We are totally on their radar now. They're never going to forget the local guy with the chip on his shoulder and his idiot bride. Not to mention, if we have to get more formal and question that Kennedy woman, she's going to be pissed we went in there on false pretenses."

Pono turned and walked away, giving her his back. He'd had enough, but she hadn't.

"Also, I think there was something off about her. Like, she wasn't totally buying the act."

"She bought it. Enough to give me that bottle of Cristal."

"Are you kidding? I saw the way she was looking at us—she wouldn't hesitate to turn us in for taking a bribe if she ever got wind we were police officers, and I still think she made us somehow. C'mon, Pono—you know that went badly."

She could tell by the red on the back of his neck and the way he pushed his way through the street that she'd had her say. The ride back to the station was long and uncomfortable.

Chapter 9

*T*he Steel Butterfly was tied up in a meeting in her office when Lei and Pono got to the station, requesting an immediate meeting to brief her on the day's events. They settled into their cubicle to wait.

Neither of them wanted to look at the other as they booted up their computers and scrolled through departmental e-mails. Lei started in on her notes for the Jane Doe case, writing up their two meetings while Pono called his contact at Kahului Station about the missing Simmons groom off the cruise ship.

He hung up the phone and turned to her. "They haven't picked up anyone of his description off the BOLO or at the airlines."

"Okay."

April Morimoto, the dispatch manager, stuck her head into the cubicle. "The cruise ship bride keeps calling. Wants to know what's happening."

"We just got in and the day's almost over! We don't know anything," Lei said impatiently. April handed her a stack of pink phone call slips.

"Call her and tell her that yourself, then." She disappeared.

"Damn. I need coffee for this." Lei stood up.

"Want me to do it?" Pono reached over and picked up the stack of call slips. Lei sighed with relief at this olive branch.

"Thanks, partner. You know broken hearts just aren't my thing." He did know, and he smiled at her as she left. She headed into the break room and poured a cup of coffee for herself and one for Pono, chipping hardened coffee creamer out of the jar of Coffe-mate and stirring it in until the color had lightened a fraction.

As she headed back, the lieutenant's office door opened and dapper Captain Corpuz of Kahului Station came out. He grinned and reached for one of the mugs. "I could use a little of that."

Lei laughed. "You're not that desperate."

Lieutenant Omura followed him out of her office, spike-heeled slingbacks clipping the floor.

"Get Kaihale. I need to speak to you two."

The captain winked as he put his dress hat back onto a full head of wavy silver hair. He had an almost jaunty bearing, and she'd never seen him irritable. She saluted, wishing, not for the first time, that he was her commanding officer instead of Omura. Stevens spoke highly of how he ran the much larger downtown station.

Lei fetched Pono and they sat in front of the lieutenant's desk. Lei wrapped her hands around the hot mug of coffee. It felt stabilizing, holding her in the chair.

"Report." Omura sat down.

There was a new brass plaque that read "LT. C.J. OMURA" on her pristine desk. Lei wondered what C.J. stood for, not for the first time. The lieutenant opened the drawer of her desk and got out a tube of hand lotion, rubbed it into her hands. It smelled of rich tropical tuberose.

Pono summarized the situation with the cruise ship and the missing groom. He'd contacted Clara Simmons to update her on the nothing they'd discovered and settled her down with soothing male attention.

"Did you check on all the airlines going out since the time of his disappearance?"

"Yes," Pono said. "But he might have made a run for it under an alias."

Eyes sharp as a crow's took in Lei's frizzing hair and crumpled jacket. "You've been quiet, Texeira. Thoughts?"

"I think he made it off the island and it's going to be a dead end. On the other hand, we've had a lot of movement on the Jane Doe."

She filled the lieutenant in on the interview at Kahului Station, the trip to Wylie Construction, and what the developer disclosed about hiring hookers. That trail had led to a pristine art gallery on Front Street.

"So we went there to check it out," Lei finished.

"What happened?" the lieutenant asked after a long moment.

"We were just going to case it, get a sense of who this was, recommending call girls. We're pretty sure Jane Doe was hooking after that slimeball positively ID'd her from a lineup of girls. Anyway, it's a classy place. The owner is a sharp woman."

Lei could feel tension pouring off Pono in waves. She wished she could reassure him that she wasn't about to throw him under the bus in front of the lieutenant—no matter how he'd screwed up.

The woman in question rubbed the scented lotion into her hands, paying special attention to her cuticles.

"I think I'm going to reassign the cruise ship case to detectives Benito and Franco. I want you two to focus on the cockfighting ring and the Jane Doe. I have a feeling there's more to this than meets the eye."

Lei let out her breath in a whoosh. She hadn't even realized she was holding it.

"Thanks, Lieutenant. I think we may be onto something, but we're going to need to do more interviews, really dig in."

"Keep me posted on whatever you find out about this House character. Seems like a tie to organized crime. We have a task force at Kahului Station working on the organized gambling in our area; contact them and liaise that connection, see if anyone else has heard of the House."

She flicked a hand in dismissal. "Keep me apprised. Oh, and there's no overtime, so you're off the clock in a few minutes."

Lei and Pono went back to the cubicle. Lei finally took a sip of her coffee, now cold.

"Thanks," Pono said. "I know I screwed up back there in Lahaina. I don't know where we should go with it from here."

"It's okay. We'll think of something." Lei powered down her computer. "Let's 'liaise' with Kahului tomorrow, find out who's in the organized crime unit. I'll ask Stevens tonight."

Lei hooked her jacket up and she and Pono exited, peeling off to their respective trucks.

* * *

I'm still in my office, but everyone is gone for the day when I use the burner to call my MPD mole. It's unbelievable that Texeira and Kaihale found their way to the gallery—someone must be talking.

He says he didn't know anything, that they must be off the grid on the investigation because they hadn't even shown up at the station that day to check in. He has to lay low, he says, but he thinks they might have gotten one of the men rounded up at a cockfight to recognize the girl and tell them something.

"Cockfight?" This squeezes my chest with a new band of stress. The cockfights are House's thing. He isn't going to be pleased to have our worlds intersect. At all.

"Yeah, they did a raid, brought in a lot of guys. Texeira was showing the photo of the dead girl around. It's been ruled a homicide."

"Why didn't you tell me this?" I keep my voice controlled. "There is a pretty little girl and her mama who are going to be very disappointed to see the activities Daddy really enjoys when he's supposedly at training."

"No need for that. I didn't realize you wanted daily updates."

"I told you I was interested in anything to do with that crash. That certainly includes the fact that they're investigating it as a homicide."

"I promise I'll get you anything I can." He sounds suitably motivated.

"Find out who talked from the cockfight and what they said."

I hang up the burner and make another call—this one to Healani Chang, our connection on the Big Island. I've been wondering if she's run across Texeira or Kaihale, since they're from there. Maybe she'll know something useful or have some leverage on them.

The call is illuminating—turns out there's bad blood going way back between the Changs and the Texeiras. Healani laughs her smoker's laugh and says, "I should have taken care of that girl last year. Call House and tell him I know a guy who gets it done. I'll pay for it myself."

One more phone call to go. The House isn't happy to hear from me. He never is.

"What?"

He has a voice like stones rolling around at the bottom of a well. It makes me hot, always has. I like imagining him hanging from my bondage ring, but he isn't ever going to go willingly. Probably would want me to be the one hanging from handcuffs.

"Giving you a heads-up. I had to take out some trash, and security are on it. They got someone at one of your events to talk. Thought you should know."

A long silence. The House couldn't have gotten as big as he is without being cautious. We have a little code going, using "security" for cops and "events" for his cockfights. Not that anyone can trace these phones…but it doesn't hurt to be careful.

"Healani's going to pick up the tab on dealing with the security—but only one of them needs to go." I've done my homework. With Texeira out of the way, Kaihale couldn't detect his way out of a paper bag.

"Keep me posted. Funny how accidents happen." The House hangs up. God, that man speeds up my blood.

Good luck, Texeira. You're going to need it.

Chapter 10

Morning filled the back bedroom of the cottage with soft gray light. Lei's eyes wandered over the plain white ceiling, lath and plaster that muffled the pattering of rain on the tin roof. It was going to be wet out when she went jogging. Lei had gone to bed early, too tired to do much more than eat leftovers and watch TV with Stevens. She rolled over and looked at the back of Stevens's head, rumpled and dark beside her, his long body still a country of compelling mystery to her. She so seldom could really look at him—they both were people who stayed in constant motion.

Lei put out her hand and touched his hair. The texture of it was springy and alive, the strands a little coarse under her fingers. The feeling of his hair was an antidote to the slippery feel of a drowned girl's trailing black silk. The tragic case in Hilo where she'd met Stevens two years ago still haunted her.

Stevens turned over onto his back. Dawn slanted through the big old-fashioned window with its louvers below. Pearl gray and soft, it gentled his rugged profile. He breathed evenly. The long ferny shadows of his eyelashes clung to deep caves of shadowed eye sockets, calling to her. She touched them with the tip of her finger.

Lightning fast, he grabbed her hand—the pressure crushing.

She cried out, and he turned toward her, springing awake.

"What are you doing?" He loosened his grip. Her bones seemed to moan as he released them. She rolled away and sat up, rubbing her wrist.

"Remind me never to touch you while you're sleeping."

"I'm sorry." He followed her, wrapping his arms around her waist, pulling her in, rubbing his face into her side, his rumpled hair silky against her skin. "War reflexes."

"Two years in Iraq did this to you?" She knew he'd done a tour early on in the war, but he never talked about it. She kept finding things out about him, nuggets he dropped like bread crumbs on the trail of knowing. This was a big one. He scooped her in and pulled her down beside him on her back, propped himself on an elbow to look down at her.

"Between being a cop and a soldier…I've been like that ever since. Attack first, ask questions later."

"Makes me realize it's a good thing I keep my hands to myself."

"Not necessarily." His open hand had begun to wander. Her body woke up, sensation trailing his touch like phosphorescence on the tide. Her nipples tightened, and she shivered under his hand.

"You have really long lashes. It's not fair."

"So do you." He leaned down, kissed her eyelids. Found the ring on its chain at her throat, hooked it up with his index finger.

"I like seeing this on you."

"It's a little bulky."

"It wasn't designed to wear around your neck."

She felt self-conscious and closed her eyes. Even in the dim light, she felt like he could see into her soul—utterly exposed and at his mercy. That vulnerability hadn't stopped being both scary and thrilling.

He explored the stretchy elastic of the soft boxers she wore to bed. Her stomach fluttered and twitched beneath his hand in anticipation. He lifted the cotton tank top and leaned over to string a row of kisses along her sternum, tracing the triangle of her ribs above her abdomen. She bit her lips to stop a moan as he slid the shirt higher, circling her small, tight breasts with his fingers and tongue.

When she reached for him, he caught her hands and covered them with kisses, the faint rasp of his tongue awakening a flood of sensation that rippled up her arms and down into her torso and below, as if her fingertips were plugged into a vital current.

He nibbled and kissed the tender skin of her wrists. "I love you," he might have said before the song of love he played on her body drove all thought from her mind, replacing it with sensation.

Chapter 11

Much later, she rubbed her hair with a towel and reached for her sports bra. He climbed out of the shower behind her.

"Good thing it's Saturday morning. We'd both be late."

He encircled her from behind, nibbled on the top of her ear. "It'd be worth it."

She pushed away with a laugh.

"Insatiable. Thought old guys like you were supposed to be slowing down."

"Who's old?"

"Thirties. That's old." She pulled on her running clothes. "Wanna go with me for a run?"

"I'm surfing this morning." Stevens had taken up surfing and, as a beginner, he got pummeled regularly.

"Well, I want to go back out to Pauwela Lighthouse today. See if I can find out anything more showing the photo of the girl around. I have a weird feeling about that place."

"Doesn't seem like anyone would know anything more out there. Besides, it's the weekend and I know you aren't getting any overtime."

"Who needs the OT? I just want to get out there while the case is hot."

She trailed him into the kitchen. He poured them each a cup of coffee from the automatic coffeepot, set the night before.

"I gotta tell you something. Charlie Kwon is out of jail." She said it fast, spitting the words out.

He turned, leaning back against the counter. "So?"

"So I'm just telling you."

"Why?"

"You know why."

"Don't. Let nature take its course. Scum like that always meet a bad end."

She turned away, took too big a sip of coffee, burned her tongue. "You know I have to deal with him."

"I understand you want to confront him. . ."

"I *need* to confront him. I need to show him he can't fuck with me anymore."

"Sad to say you're too old for him now. Last thing on his mind is fucking with you."

Lei shot him a glare, pushed through the security door at the front to sit on the weathered top step, looking out into the java plum forest across the street. She could just see a sliver of ocean over the tops of the trees, lighting with the first of the day. A fresh, damp breeze blew down `Iao Valley to cool her hot cheeks and the coffee, but she blew on it anyway.

He followed her out, sat on the step beside her. "I'm sorry. That was a shitty thing to say. What I meant was, you aren't that child anymore."

"You got that right. And I need to look him in the eye and put the hurt on him for what he did."

"You've got a career that's going well. Why endanger it for someone like him? What do you have to prove? You're you. Beautiful. Strong. Mine." He'd put down his mug, and his big hands reached out and took her face between them, turning her toward him, tilting her lips up to his.

"Mine," he said again, breathing it into her mouth as he kissed her.

She melted into him, setting the mug down without even noticing. Charlie Kwon was temporarily forgotten, his touch erased by something better, more powerful—more present.

"Let's go out to Pauwela Lighthouse together later, after we work out," he said eventually. "Don't go without me."

"Think I can't handle myself?" As always, the brittle defense leapt to her lips.

"No. I think it's Saturday, and we deserve to spend some time together. We can take a picnic."

She smiled and reached out to mock punch his hard stomach. "Ever the romantic."

"Someone's gotta be."

Lei got on the road in her running shoes, turning in the opposite direction from Stevens's Bronco with its big beginner surfboard lashed to the roof rack. Keiki was in fine form, prancing, waggling, and lunging at mynah birds.

"Guess I need to tire you out, girl." She cranked up the speed, and they pelted down the street, still damp from nightly rainfall.

Her favorite route, a raised two-lane road that ran alongside a creek to the state park at the end, was empty of traffic. The trees, a mixture of tall, dark-leaved java plum and bright green palmate kukui, were topped with fingers of gold. Sun braised the leaves and dropped coins of light on the road ahead. Wild cocks crowed and mynahs squabbled, a background timpani to the rush of the stream. Early-morning air hinted at the rainfall the night before, the kind of sprinkle that kept `Iao Valley lush all year.

She heard a car behind them and slowed, moving onto the shoulder and pulling Keiki in tight. The car had plenty of room to pass them on the narrow road with its steep shoulder plunging down to the boulder-strewn creek. But instead of passing them, she heard the engine roar. She didn't have time to do anything but react as the realization hit—it was gunning for them.

Lei dove off the shoulder of the road, Keiki's leash tight in her fist. She rolled down the stony embankment that ended at the stream, the dog yanked off her feet and tumbling behind her. The car continued on, engine a shriek of power.

She fetched up against a clump of strawberry guava, mere feet away from a boulder. She struggled to suck air back in, the breath knocked out of her. Keiki jumped up, shook off, and planted a warm, wet tongue on her face. She pushed the dog away and sat up slowly, checking for injuries.

The wrist broken a few years ago had been wrenched by Keiki's leash and gave back some jangles. Bumps and bruises chimed complaints from compass points on her body, but she'd been lucky.

She needed to stop that car. It had to turn around; the road was a dead end at the park. Lei crawled and hauled her way back up the road, wishing she'd brought her cell phone—or the Glock. Preferably both. She and Keiki climbed up onto the road. She looked in the direction the car had taken.

It had to pass her to leave the valley. She could flag it down and make an arrest, or at least get the plates and hunt it down later. She could go home and get her phone, badge, gun, and the truck—but he could get past her and escape if she did, and the asshole had almost killed her dog!

Lei and Keiki walked forward on the light-shadowed road in the direction the car had taken. Lei shook out her arms and legs—she was going to have some mean bruises, but nothing appeared broken or sprained. She looked down the incline to the rocky creek bed and gave a little shudder. Yes, she'd been lucky and her dog, equally so. Keiki glanced up at her, intelligent brown eyes worried. She reached down to pat the dog's broad head.

"We're okay, girl."

She picked up speed to a slow jog, heading up into the valley.

Lei looked into the few driveways off the road, but she hadn't been able to get even a glimpse of the car, so short of going up and feeling hoods, there was no way to tell if one of the residents had been their reckless driver. She entered lower `Iao Park, and as always, there were some cars parked in the lot, early visitors or broken-down vehicles that had been left for pickup later. A huge spreading banyan tree marked the beginning of the park, and she and Keiki passed under its canopy into shadow.

That's when she heard the roar of the engine, coming from the left. It had been waiting for them in the lee of the banyan where she couldn't see it.

She recoiled, yanking Keiki back, and turned to run. The road narrowed as they passed over a culvert twelve feet above the creek. There was nowhere to go.

She ran. Ran like she never had before, adrenaline giving her a superhuman burst of speed to clear the culvert before she felt the smack of the bumper hitting her left hip and propelling her out into space. She flew, arms and legs windmilling, and like a bad dream she couldn't wake from, landed with a gut-wrenching thud that shocked through her body. The world went mercifully black.

Chapter 12

*S*tevens pushed the wheelchair to the Bronco. The surfboards were still optimistically tied there; apparently he'd been sitting and studying the waves when the EMTs called his cell.

Lei tapped her head, swathed in a bandage.

"That answers what to do about my hair." They'd had to shave the section on the side of her head where the rock had cut her scalp. "I guess I'm meant to have really short hair."

"That's the least of it." Stevens helped her out and into the front seat, settling the seat belt around her.

"I'm really okay," she protested, but it was feeble. Just moving caused her to hurt in a dozen places. Being run off the road and hit by a car was a good way to find out all the places that could get bruised.

He shook his head. She could sense something powerfully suppressed in the hard, jerky movements he made as he took the wheelchair back to the attendant and strode back to the Bronco. They'd been at the hospital for several hours as she underwent tests and observation. It had eventually been decided that she had a concussion and a lot of bruises but was okay to go home.

Stevens got in beside her and turned on the SUV.

"So much for our picnic." Lei looked down at her blood-stiff-ened running shirt. The head wound had bled a lot before they stitched it.

"So tell me what happened."

"I already told you. It hasn't changed since the last time, ten minutes ago."

"I want to hear it again."

"Police harassment," she said, with an attempt at a smile. Per-haps that wasn't reassuring, because he looked away abruptly.

The hospital wasn't far from their house, so it wasn't long before they had to go through the ordeal of getting her inside. She didn't want to go to bed, so after helping her with a brief shower and then wrapping her in her favorite kimono, Stevens set her up on the nice leather couch they'd sprung for when they moved in. He propped her up with pillows and covered her with the crocheted afghan Aunty Rosario had made so long ago.

Keiki sat beside Lei. The big dog wouldn't leave her side, and Lei found it comforting to breathe her doggy smell. She trailed her fingers through the dog's ruff and down to scratch her chest. Keiki set her big square head on Lei's tummy and gazed at her with soulful brown eyes. Heroine of the hour, the dog had run back and forth on the road, barking nonstop, until she attracted a passerby.

Stevens poured Lei a glass of water. "They said to stay hydrated."

She groaned but took the glass and sipped. "Wish those pain meds would work."

"Tell me again."

"Oh God." She handed him the glass. "The guy was gunning for me, no question about it. Ran me off the road; I knew the park was a dead end and he'd have to come back. So I followed him, wanted to wave him down and do a citizen's arrest, at least get a look at the plates."

Stevens shot up with the coiled grace that was a part of everything he did.

"That's where I'm having a problem with this. It never occurred to you someone wanted to kill your ass? I mean, you're well known. Who knows who might have tracked us since the Cult Killer case? You should have gotten yourself straight home! You were close to the house at that point—you should have gotten your weapon and called me!"

"I know that now. I thought it was just a reckless driver that needed to be stopped. I mean, he almost hit Keiki."

The blow to the head had knocked the sass out of her, and her voice was small. This felt like the repeat of old arguments.

Stevens sat back down. "Yeah, and he actually did hit you, in case you didn't notice. I know I shouldn't be yelling. But you could have been killed, and I don't. . ." He got up and paced again. "I don't know what I would do if I lost you like that."

He went to the kitchen, leaned against the sink, and looked out at the mountain behind the house, rising green and bright with full day. He turned back.

"So you didn't ever see the car?"

"No. Nothing. It came from behind the first time, and I jumped out of the way. Second time, he ambushed me from the side and hit me here. I barely had room to go anywhere." She touched the hip where the bumper had made contact, a purple-black bruise under the robe. "I'm actually lucky."

"Don't you think I know it?" Stevens banged some pots around. "Let me fix you something to eat."

"I don't know. Kinda nauseous." She rested her bandaged head against the couch cushions. "Just gonna rest a minute."

Approaching night was turning the air blue when she woke up. Stevens watched a ball game from the armchair, and a plate of omelet congealed beside her on the coffee table. He must have been watching for signs of life, because he rose at once and came to sit beside her. Keiki lifted her head off her paws and licked Lei's dangling hand.

"How're you feeling?"

"Better, actually. Think I need the bathroom." She was able to totter in and do her business on her own. He'd given the omelet to Keiki and was back in the kitchen.

"Hungry?"

"Yeah." Lei had been dreaming—and in the dream a beautiful red-haired girl pointed into the tent village. The image haunted her—her gut was telling her there was more to find out at the Lighthouse. "Can we still go out to Pauwela Lighthouse?"

"No. Absolutely not. They said a minimum of twenty-four hours of bed rest. You could have a clot or something."

"Tomorrow, then?"

He shook his head, getting out a box of pasta. "Maybe. If you're good."

"Okay." She snuggled into the couch and decided to enjoy being waited on, since she didn't have much of a choice and her head really did hurt.

Chapter 13

Stevens helped her out of the Bronco onto the wind-scored grass on the bluff at Pauwela Lighthouse the next morning. She slapped at his hands irritably.

"I'm fine. I can do it myself."

"God, you're stubborn." He walked away, heading for the deep marks the fire trucks had left at the top of the bluff. She followed, already feeling bad for being so cranky and wishing she could take back her words.

They stood looking down the rugged bluff at the black rocks where the wreck had been. A crew had winched it up the bluff the day before, but glass still added an extra sparkle to the clear tide pools below, and rainbows of oil marked the water.

A blanket of clouds on the horizon threatened rain, and the ocean had gone slate blue snagged by whitecaps. Lei found her eyes scanning for whales and was rewarded by a featherlike spout bigger than any wind-driven wavelet.

A gust caught the big square Band-Aid on her head and pulled her hair. She held it down gently. Stevens had run a clipper on the number five setting over her whole head, and her curls were now evenly shorn, an inch or so long all over her head. She still remembered the intimacy of the clipper running up the back of her neck, the feel of his gentle fingers treating the wound. She pressed against his side, and he put an arm around her.

"Sorry I'm such a bitch."

"Yes, you are." He kissed the top of her head. "Sure you want to do this?"

"We have a photo now. Maybe there was a reason she came here or was brought here."

Stevens turned with her to face the dense underbrush where the tent village hid. "Let's get this over with so we can go home."

They pushed forward through knee-high grass until they found a path and followed it straight to the first tent, the one where the young mother lived.

"Anyone home? Maui Police," Stevens called.

A long moment passed before the door of the tent unzipped and the young woman came out. She was holding the baby this time, its dark eyes wide and serious.

"You called Child Welfare on me, bitch." She gave Lei a hard stare.

"You deserved it, bitch." Lei gave some attitude back, though her head and bruises hurt too much for any heat. "Thought if I called them you might get some more services, maybe a place at the shelter." The homeless shelter was already overcrowded, with a waiting list.

"Yeah, well, it didn't help." The woman sat in the folding beach chair and gestured to a second one. Lei sat gingerly. Her hip hit the arm of the chair, and she winced. Stevens reached down to pat her shoulder and hit another bruise. She flinched again.

"What happened?"

"Hit by a car."

"Shit."

"Yeah."

"So what do you want now?"

"We have a picture of the girl who died in the car." Lei handed the color-enhanced photocopy they were circulating to the woman. "We're still trying to find out who she is, what she might have been doing out here."

The young mother looked at the lovely dead face for a long moment. "I'd remember her if I'd seen her, but I haven't."

"Okay."

Lei took back the photo, stood slowly from the chair. She handed the girl her card. "You have my number, if you see or hear anything."

"Well. There's a girl here who might know something. I mean, she's around the same age as this one, is all, and she's new here."

"Where?"

"She's camping with Ramona." The young woman pointed.

"We know who Ramona is. Thanks. And we'll try to get you some services; I'll make some calls."

The woman laid her cheek along the baby's downy head. "Okay."

Lei and Stevens approached the bluff-side tent of the imposing Hawaiian woman. She was still out in front, this time working a basket. It was an elaborate construction with patterns of dark hala leaves worked into geometric shapes among light golden ones. Seated at the rickety table beside her was a dark-haired young woman. She looked up at their approach and hurried into the tent, zipping it up behind her.

"Don't tell me, the other guy looks worse." Ramona looked Lei over.

Lei snorted a laugh. "I wish. I was hit by a car. Run off the road."

"Someone have it in for you?"

"I don't know." Ramona had a way of bringing out the truth. "Maybe."

"Well, then you know a little about what brings a lot of us out here." Ramona waved a hand. "This camp's for those with nowhere else to go."

Lei gestured to the tent. "Does she have anywhere else to go?"

"I don't know. Probably. She hasn't talked much."

"Can we ask her a few questions? We just want to see if she might know this girl." Lei brought out the photo. Ramona peered at it and shook her head.

"Don't know her." She turned to the tent. "Anchara, come out. Nothing to worry about from these folks."

The door unzipped and a face peered out. The girl knelt in the opening. She was striking, with dark almond eyes set above scimitar cheekbones. Jet-black hair hung in snarls and tangles past her hips. Lei's hand crept up to touch her own shorn head at the sight.

"Hi, Anchara," Lei said. "We just want to see if you know someone." She proffered the photo.

The girl came out a little more, held out her hand. Lei put the photo in it and witnessed the moment Anchara recognized Jane Doe. She dropped the picture and it fluttered to the ground as she withdrew inside and zipped up the tent.

Stevens had a way of reining in his presence so he became like a tree or a stone, there but not threatening—a calm stillness that he could don at will. Lei called it his "cloak of invisibility," and she wished she knew how he did it. He hunkered down by the closed flap, finally speaking.

"You know her? We just want to find out who she was."

No answer.

"We just want to return her to her people, give her a decent burial."

"I don't know name." The girl's voice was heavily accented. Nothing Lei knew, but Stevens's brows knit. Lei picked the photo up off the ground.

"How do you know her?"

Silence.

Stevens prompted. "She a friend?"

"Yes."

"What's her name?"

"I only know her stage name."

"Stage name?"

"You know. For the…men." She stumbled over the words. "Her name Vixen."

"Vixen. Hm." Stevens sounded thoughtful. "So how did you two meet?"

"In the place."

"What place?" Gentle and slow, he crouched beside her, talking to her through the green nylon. The darkness of not seeing him must have felt like a confessional.

Lei, however, struggled with impatience, pacing back and forth and finally sitting in the chair beside Ramona and stripping the thorns off an unworked piece of hala leaf. She didn't have Ramona's sharpened thumbnail, but once she got the end of the tensile strip of thorns, it was easy to pull off.

"The place where they kept us. That place."

"Where was that?"

"The ship mostly, but sometimes we'd be in a living place."

"Ship?"

"We came on a ship. From our countries."

"So you were both in the sex trade?"

Silence. Lei guessed Anchara wasn't sure what that meant. He went on.

"So you both saw men there?"

"No. We went to hotels and met them there. Then we went back."

"Who kept you there?"

Silence.

"Did you run away? Is that how you got here?"

"Yes."

"How did you get away?"

"Vixen. She had taken the key and she let us out. I think they caught everyone else."

Lei felt excitement smothering her, a tight band around her chest. Could the key she'd found lead to this place where the sex slaves were kept? Could there be a connection to the cruise ships, or was it some other ship? She focused on working the hala leaf to let Stevens keep going.

"How did Vixen die?" Anchara's voice wobbled a bit.

"Car accident," Stevens said. "I'm sorry."

They heard a gasp, a muffled sob.

"Can you tell us more? Where did you two come from?"

A bit of a pause while the girl regrouped; then she spoke more firmly. "We told we could be waitress on a cruise ship. They only want pretty girls who want to see the world." Her voice had a rhythmic quality to it, like she was reciting from a brochure. "They picked us, and we said goodbye to our families. It was so exciting getting on the ship. Then they locked us up, and—did things to us."

Lei blew out a breath, and Ramona's sharp, dark eyes pinned her, seeing more than she wanted them to see. She looked down, focused on tearing the long, flexible leaf into four equal-width strips like she'd seen Ramona do. The older woman went on with her basket weaving, impassive.

"Who brought you here to Maui?" Stevens asked.

"I don't know. We never knew anything."

"When you come to the hotels, who's in charge?"

"We have a woman. She helps us get ready for the night. Puts on makeup, gives us dresses. Then there is a man. He drives the car to the hotel and makes sure we get back."

"Do you know their names?"

"They don't like us to know, but I hear the woman's name—it Celeste. The man is Kimo."

"So have you been on Maui long?"

"Not long. We on the ship a lot. We go to different places. I don't know where they are. It doesn't matter where they are."

Her accented voice had a flatness that made the words even more terrible.

Stevens picked up the rhythm again.

"So where are you from? All from the same place?"

"No. All over. I from Thailand. Vixen from Albania. She never want to talk. We all try to help each other. We talk at night in the dark after they turn off the lights. But not Vixen. She wouldn't tell us her name. She wouldn't be friends. She only thought of get away."

"But she was the one to let you out."

"Yes. And now she dead."

"I think we should take you somewhere safe," Stevens said.

"No!" Her voice climbed. "You deport me!"

"Would that be so bad? What about your family? Wouldn't they rather have you back than think you disappeared?"

"It better for me to start a new life," Anchara said. "I won't go with you."

Stevens looked over at Lei. They could take her in by force, but where would they put her? There was nothing to charge her with, and she was an illegal alien. She'd end up locked up and deported, and they needed her as a witness for their case if it was to go anywhere.

Lei looked at Ramona. "Is it okay if she stays with you?"

"Yes. Girl needs somewhere to stay. I look out for her."

Stevens took out his wallet and peeled off several twenties.

"This is for food for Anchara. We don't want to take her any-where she doesn't want to go, but we need her to stay here, be available in case we need to talk to her again. There may be some danger if the people who kept her captive are looking for her."

Ramona took the money and inclined her head. "I'll look after her and hide her if anyone else comes looking."

Stevens turned back to the tent, gentled his voice. "I've given Ramona some money for food for you. This is an okay place for you to hide for the moment. Please stay here. We may need to talk to you again."

"I heard you," Anchara said. "You won't deport me, will you?"

"No. You'll hide and wait here for us?"

"Deal," she said. The door unzipped a bit and her small brown hand appeared. Lei realized she was waiting for something. Stevens smiled as he bent down and shook it.

"Deal."

* * *

There are only a few permanent penthouse suites at the top of the building above the gallery, and I live in one of them. I'm getting out of the shower when my work phone rings—only our contacts have the number. Ugh, it's never good when the work phone rings.

"Yes?"

"It's Healani Chang. Our man is on it, but he wasn't able to finish the project yet." Healani's husky voice has a deep ring to it. I've always liked the Hawaiian matriarch of the Big Island branch, with her rich chocolate eyes and regal bearing. She took over the Chang family operations after her husband Terry's demise, and I thought she ran things better than he ever had.

"Damn. Well, thanks for taking this on. I hope I'm not overreacting, but I don't like the look of this one." It was an effort not to speak Texeira's name. "I don't know how far along her investigation is. My mole in MPD hasn't been able to pick up much. But it worries me that if she pulls the right thread, we're all connected."

"You're right to be worried. The girl's a pit bull when she gets her teeth into something. That's why I'm helping out—I should

have taken care of it years ago." Healani sighed. "It's too bad, really. She'd have done well working for us."

"Thanks for keeping me posted."

"Watch the news. It'll be on there when he gets it done." Healani hung up.

The House hadn't wanted to bring on the scrutiny of killing a cop, but...law enforcement was a dangerous profession, after all.

I rub gardenia-scented lotion into my legs. They're looking good. I just had them waxed and I've been trying a new Pilates workout that's bringing out some extra definition in the calves. I jump when the work phone rings again.

"It's Kimo."

"Yes. What is it?"

"It's. . ." His voice trails off. He's afraid to tell me something. The man is a chickenshit, and it pisses me off.

"What?"

"One of the girls is still missing. The Thai one with the long hair."

"All the Thai girls have long hair. Which one?"

"Anchara. We called her Velvet."

I remember Velvet. An exceptionally beautiful, delicately built girl with good skin and great hair the men love to grab. Good earner, too. I could get three or four tricks out of her a night when the ship was in town. At five hundred bucks a pop, she was worth her hundred pounds of body weight in gold.

"How'd it happen?"

"Well, you remember how Vixen let a bunch of them out of the warehouse. I said we got them all. I said that because I thought for sure we would, but—we didn't. We've been looking all over the island."

"Kimo, don't ever lie to me. Find her; get it done. I'm going to take Velvet's lost income out of your pay."

I punch Off on the phone. I really need to work on my anger;

it's like a cat clawing at my belly. I go over to the deck, open the slider to my exceptional view of the ocean off Lahaina— smooth as blue silk today. Whipped-cream clouds collect over the purple smudge of Lana`i, and a few whales mark the distance with spume. I sit on my yoga mat and assume a meditation pose, cross-legged.

Empty my mind, breathe. Focus.

In the end it's a fantasy of what I'll do to Anchara when Kimo brings her to me that helps me find my center. She's too valuable to dispose of—I've already lost thousands getting rid of Vixen— but there are things worse than death. I'll enjoy teaching them to her.

Chapter 14

Lei's injuries were beginning to yell at her again, so she was relieved to haul herself out of the frayed beach chair and hobble toward the truck with a wave to the inscrutable Ramona, still working her basket. She climbed into the cushy seat of the Tacoma with a sigh of relief, closing her eyes in sudden exhaustion. She took a Vicodin and washed it down with a bottle of tepid water she'd left in the truck. Stevens got behind the wheel, and they bumped out down the long dirt road.

They got out onto the road back to Kahului, going around a series of wide, swooping turns that followed the sculpted cliff line overlooking the ocean. Lei leaned her head against the window, taking in without seeing the views of rugged cliffs, single wings of windsurfers and bright arcs of kiteboarders riding the strong wind and waves. She dozed.

Lei climbed into bed when they got home. The Vicodin had kicked in, and she fell asleep to the sound of Stevens calling Captain Corpuz to report on the recent developments.

She woke to the murmur of voices in the other room. She'd shucked off her clothes and fallen into bed in her bra and panties, so she grabbed her old kimono off the back of the door and wrapped herself in it.

Her head felt a little clearer, though the bruised ribs still talked to her with every breath and the hip was a solid roadmap of purple. She walked out into their living room and stopped in her tracks.

The Steel Butterfly was sitting on her couch, looking immaculate and quite comfortable.

Pono sat beside her with his forehead scrunched, and Stevens sat in the armchair. They all stared at her. Lei reached up to touch the bandage on her shorn head.

"Hi."

"Hi," Pono said.

"Texeira, you look terrible." Omura's voice was unexpectedly warm. "Why didn't you call this in to me earlier? I had to hear it from Captain Corpuz after Stevens called down there."

"I was pretty out of it. I guess I didn't think it was a department matter." Even on a personal call like this, Omura put Lei on the defensive.

"Well. Sorry to drop in on you like this, but we need to know all about what's going on with this Russian girl and this accident that you had."

Lei came into the room, and Stevens gave her the armchair, fetching one of the kitchen chairs to sit beside her.

"I already opened a case on Lei's hit-and-run. That was definitely no accident." Stevens filled in more details.

"Tell us about this runaway out at Pauwela. What made you go out there canvassing on your day off?" Omura's keen eyes wandered over Lei's battered frame and bandaged head, but for the first time, Lei didn't feel like her boss was taking inventory of her shortcomings.

"The girl isn't Russian. She's Thai. And we thought we'd take a picnic," Lei said. Defensiveness was a hard habit to break.

Stevens looked Omura in the eye and shook his head. "You know how she is when she's on a case."

Omura inclined her head, glossy black hair swinging. "I'm beginning to."

"Well, anyway. That homeless young mom I called Child Welfare on told us about Anchara. The girl's an escaped sex slave." Lei filled them in on the overall content of the interview and the arrangement they'd made to keep the girl stashed out there. "If we bring her in, we don't have anywhere to put her."

"The safe house," Pono said. "It's fine. No one's using it."

"The safe house is available only with proper clearance. It may be worthwhile for me to get it for the girl, however. It's going to take some time to investigate and build this case, and I'd hate for this hooker to disappear." Omura was making notes with her fingertips on a calfskin-covered iPad.

"She's a sex slave, not a hooker." Lei felt compelled to speak up on the girl's behalf. "She got on that ship thinking she was going to be a waitress and see the world, and got raped and imprisoned for it."

No one said anything. It was a nightmare scenario.

"So what about this gallery owner who gave the call girl card to the construction company? Think there's a connection? I thought you said that witness Silva mentioned that the girls at that party had accents." Omura looked around the room, taking in the simple furnishings and two vivid paintings, one an abstract and the other an impressionistic landscape of Bali Hai on Kaua`i.

"I don't know if there's a connection. Pono and I blew our cover on that one; we'll have to monitor from outside, send another team to get in with her and find out what her connection with the hookers is. I was thinking maybe Abe Torufu and Gerry Bunuelos from Kahului Station would be willing to do a sting for us. Or we could just bring her in for an interview."

Omura tapped her nails on the glossy leather case.

"If they're willing to help, set it up. The captain said you could use some resources from his department. We're all thinking this case is going to go big. Oh, and take the day off Monday. That's an order."

Lieutenant Omura stood up. For the first time, Lei realized she wasn't in her usual dapper tailored uniform, but wore a pair of narrow black jeans and a scoop-necked silk top. She looked beautiful but more approachable—until she walked toward the door and her high-heeled shoes, laced in colored bands across the insteps, click-clacked on the hardwood floor.

She gestured to the shoes. "Sorry. They're a real hassle to take off at the door. Thought I was just going to be here a minute." Removing shoes at the door was good manners in Hawaii.

"It's fine," all three of them said. Stevens ushered her out and closed the door behind her.

Lei leaned backward in the armchair, and her head throbbed in protest. She groaned. "Never in my wildest dreams did I expect to see Lieutenant Steel Butterfly Omura in my living room. What do you guys think C.J. stands for? She has those initials on her desk plaque."

Pono leaned forward, a twinkle in his deep brown eyes. "I was curious too. Looked it up online. Her first name is Cherry Joy."

"Cherry Joy!" Lei burst into laughter. "I'm never going to be scared of her again."

"Probably why she tries to keep that under wraps."

Stevens went to the kitchen. Evening was slanting orange light across the counters. He took a couple of Longboard Pale Ales out of the fridge, popped the tops, and brought them back to Lei and Pono.

"Say what you want. I think she's a good commanding officer. Got a good head on her shoulders and willing to take action. Not just playing the political game. Soon as I finished talking to my captain, he must have called her. She showed up not ten minutes later. Was concerned about you." He pointed his beer at Lei.

"I'll bet she was concerned that I'm going to put in for Work-men's Comp," Lei answered, but felt good anyway. She was being taken seriously; this threat was being taken seriously. And she was being given some cred and some resources to follow Vixen wherever she led them—be it cruise ship, art gallery, or boardroom.

Feeling good gave her the fuel to do what she needed to about another situation.

Chapter 15

*L*ei waited until the guys went out on the front stoop, still talking office politics, and fetched her cell phone, going back into the bedroom and closing the door. She lay back down on the bed and called the number for Corrections Aftercare Solutions, the nonprofit agency that handled reintegration of ex-convicts back into the workforce.

She asked for the worker who'd helped with her father's reintegration plan.

"Aftercare Solutions, this is Aaron Spellman."

"Hello, Aaron. This is Lei Texeira, Wayne Texeira's daughter, the detective. I'm with Maui Police Department now. Remember me?"

"Yes, how are you? And how's your father? He was such a conscientious participant!" Aaron Spellman's hearty tone grated on her nerves just as it had back on Kaua`i. The man had a radio announcer's voice and a car salesman's manner.

"I'm fine; he's fine—but I need your help with a case. I'm following up with a recent parolee who's probably in your system. Name's Charlie Kwon."

Just saying his name out loud was difficult. She found her lips pulling back from her teeth in a grimace of disgust.

"What's your interest in him?"

She had her story ready. "Some cold cases. Want to find out where he was at the time."

"Sure, lemme look the guy up." Rattle of computer keys. "Yep, he appears to be on Oahu." He recited the address, and she took it down with a stub of pencil on the little spiral notebook she used for personal notes.

"Thanks." Lei closed the phone and set down the pencil and notebook. Just that easily, she knew where Kwon was. It wouldn't be long before she had him where she wanted him. If she could just deal with him, wherever that led, she might be able to do more than wear Stevens's diamond ring around her neck.

Charlie Kwon was the ghost that stood between them.

She shut her eyes and indulged in a daydream involving Kwon, a knife, and a bathtub. It was just getting messy when Stevens opened the door, interrupting.

"Pono went home. Feeling up to some dinner?"

Lei was surprised to find she'd rediscovered her appetite. "Sure."

Monday morning had sent Stevens to work, and Lei, never one to enjoy a day off, found herself grateful for once to be sitting on the front stoop rather than getting in the truck to join the traffic down the hill into Kahului. She'd been forbidden to leave the house without an escort, annoyed when Stevens had clarified, with a tap on her nose: "No. Keiki doesn't count."

She sipped her morning coffee, feeling the pulse and throb of various bruises. Her headache had downgraded from acute to dull roar, and she decided to switch to Advil so that she could develop a murder board for Jane Doe—something she'd been too busy tracking leads to do.

Keiki trotted back and forth against the chain-link fence, barking at wild chickens scratching in the leaf mold across the street beneath the belt of java plum trees, obviously missing her daily run. Lei moved slowly down the weather-beaten stairs to the little shade-cloth shelter Stevens had built against the side of the house for her collection of orchids.

She'd moved so much that she'd had to give them away after each move, first on the Big Island, then Kaua'i, and now Maui. He'd been giving the plants to her throughout their courtship, and when the flowers had fallen, she'd enjoyed trying to get them to bloom again. Lei was misting them with Miracle-Gro and tossing a ball for Keiki when her cell rang. She dug it out of the pocket of her sweats, glancing at the number.

"Hey, Marcella!" She was delighted to see it was her FBI friend, Special Agent Marcella Scott. They'd hit it off on the Cult Killer case—first with competitive sparks, then with an enduring friendship of like minds and interests.

"Hey, Sweets." Marcella still liked to use her Kaua'i nickname, based on the old Bing Crosby song "Sweet Leilani," to tease her. "I'm in town for a case; thought we could get together for coffee or something."

"I'd love to, but I'm injured and confined to quarters."

"What?"

Lei filled her in, and halfway through a description of the situation, Marcella cut her off.

"I'm coming over. Where are you guys living now?"

Lei gave her the address.

That was Marcella, all decisive action. One time, after a few drinks, Marcella had bragged that she could take out a guy twice her size with just her forefinger—and when Lei challenged her on it, it had taken about three minutes before she'd had Stevens on his back with the aforementioned finger poised above his eye.

Lei shuddered a bit, remembering. She knew what it felt like to burst someone's eye with a thumb, and thinking about it still nauseated her. She straightened up the living room and went into the bathroom to see what could be done about her appearance.

Not much. At least her hair couldn't get any worse, shorn to a cap of curls, but her arms were stippled with black-and-blue bruises from rolling down the embankment, and the bandage on the side of her head was a stark reminder of her near-death experience. She settled for a swipe of lip gloss and a little mascara— good thing Stevens said short hair suited her, and her eyes did look big and exotic. Seeing Marcella always made her want to look her best, but there wasn't much that could be done about it today.

It wasn't long before an unmarked shiny black Acura SUV pulled up into her driveway.

Chapter 16

K eiki sounded an intruder alert but settled into slavish whining and cavorting when the dog recognized Marcella get out of the SUV. Lei stood at the top of the stairs as her friend greeted Keiki with ear rubs and a big beef bone, still sporting shreds of last night's steak. Keiki settled down to enjoy her prize as the women embraced.

"Shit, Lei, what are you into now?" Marcella asked, frowning as she held Lei at arm's length.

"Some deep shit, apparently," Lei said, leading them into the house. "Have a seat. I could use some FBI consult on all this."

"When are we ever going to just talk about boyfriends and nail polish?" Marcella's FBI "uniform," a tailored gray suit, seemed to enhance her taut, curvy figure. Shiny brown hair wound into a bun and no makeup—and still her face was beautiful, all flashing dark eyes and pillowy lips. Marcella shrugged out of her jacket and draped it over the couch. A concession to the climate in Hawaii, the shirt underneath was short-sleeved and she wasn't wearing a tie.

"Coffee, please, I beg of you." Marcella fueled her day with nonstop cups of it, black.

"On it."

Lei poured herself a refill and brought Marcella a mug, sitting down in the armchair kitty-corner to her friend.

"I don't know if either of us is much interested in discussing boyfriends and nail polish." Lei sipped her coffee. "I'm much more interested in who might be trying to kill me and a sex slave trafficking ring using cruise ships for transport."

"Yeah. About that." Marcella frowned, blowing on the surface of her coffee. "If there's any evidence of something like that, you're going to have to bump that to us."

"Seriously? With pleasure. I don't get the feeling we have the authority to make those ships do much of anything, and so far the connection's pretty thin, based on a wit we have stashed."

"Why don't you start from the beginning?"

"Well, okay. I might as well get going on my murder board. That's what I was going to work on before you got here."

Lei got up and fetched the portable whiteboard she liked to use for brainstorming. Stevens had already installed a pair of hooks on the remaining blank wall, and she hung the board up and uncapped a marker.

"This all started with a body. A few days ago, we got called out to a crash site—Pauwela Lighthouse, real creepy place. A car had gone over the hundred-foot cliff. Anyway, it looked like a suicide at first—young girl gone over the cliff in an old Plymouth. But there was something off about it from the beginning, and after restraint marks were found on her, the ME ruled it a vehicular homicide. We're still waiting on tox results."

Lei went on to describe the steps of the investigation, drawing a line and marking it with the different pieces of information that had come together.

"The real break was getting that slimeball at the cockfight

bust to recognize the dead girl as someone he'd seen in a hooker lineup. That was also when we heard about someone called the House. We then found another escaped sex slave who's now staying out at the homeless encampment at Pauwela. Along the way, I must have pissed someone off, because some perp tried to run me over on my jog Saturday morning."

Marcella sat forward intently, the mug of black coffee forgotten. Big brown eyes narrowed in thought as the agent mulled things over. She took a sip of coffee and seemed to make a decision.

"I think our investigations are crossing."

"What do you mean?"

"I'm here on a case involving smuggling. I have to talk to the special agent in charge before I tell you anything more, but I think your case could be the break we've been looking for."

Lei bounced with excitement, joggled her sore head and groaned, clutching her bandage.

"Shit, you can't tell me anything?"

"You know. Bureau politics." Marcella waggled her hand in a dismissive gesture. Her Italian heritage contributed to an expressive, dramatic style. "You think over applying for the Bureau? I'd love to have you on my team someday. Clock's ticking, you know."

"Not ready to decide yet." The ring felt heavy as lead around Lei's neck. Was she really ready to settle down and call the Maui Police Department all she was going to experience in her career?

"Keep me posted. I think you'd rock the Bureau and be a big asset over here with your local background. Anyway, lemme step outside and make a few calls."

Marcella strode outside, shutting the door firmly behind her. Lei got up and carried their mugs to the sink, deliberately not letting herself feel slighted. Marcella had, several times, had to keep her in the dark on their case on Kaua`i while milking her for information, but she knew the other woman didn't like doing it. She always said she'd tell her everything if she was just in the Bureau.

At the sink, Lei reached up to touch the ring on its chain around her neck. Suddenly claustrophobic, she took the chain off and slipped the ring into one of the drawers, slamming it shut.

Marcella came back in.

"Yeah, I can give you partial disclosure in return for meeting with your commanding officer and taking over the smuggling and human trafficking part of the case. We're going to do the interagency cooperation thing, baby!" She high-fived Lei.

"I can't wait for you to meet my lieutenant." Lei glanced at the door where Marcella had toed out of her shoes—they were Louboutins, with trademark red heels. Marcella and Omura were bound to strike sparks and might even have a lot in common. "So, you gonna tell me anything now?"

"If I must," Marcella said as she sat. "More coffee?"

"If I must." Lei fetched it, and Marcella went on.

"We know about the House. He's serious organized crime: heroin, coke, meth, pot—the whole range of drugs. Which isn't an FBI focus. He also has a whole gambling network across the islands—cockfighting, dogfighting, parlors with cards, mah-jongg, all that. Still not our focus. Then there are the whores—lots of them. We were already aware there was something going on with some sort of imported hooker ring—but we don't have anything hard on that. Human trafficking is an FBI priority—as are the weapons."

"Wow."

"Yeah. The Bureau's been directed to stay away from any cases local PD can handle, like drugs, hookers, and gambling. But when he started bringing in guns, and now it looks like sex slaves, we're on it. We also look hard at anything that could contribute to domestic terrorism." Marcella sipped her coffee. "I've been thinking the priorities have been screwed up for a while, but ever since nine eleven and all the budget cuts, we really focus on cases that could have terrorist implications."

"What about ATF? Thought they did investigations with guns and armaments."

"Usually, but the agency is small out here, and once we knew this one was leading to the House, we knew that was way too big a case for them. More interagency cooperation." She grinned, a dazzling display. "The House has his headquarters on Oahu, so it's a surprise that Maui is the place where we may finally get some momentum on this case. I want to interview both your witnesses—the witness from the cockfight and the runaway."

"I'll call Bunuelos down at Kahului Station and have him bring in Silva for you. I can take you out to interview the Thai girl. Maybe the safe house will be available and we can kill two birds with one stone and take her there. My lieutenant was going to try and get that authorized today."

"Aren't you supposed to be off today?"

"Yeah, well, this is my case, and with you here, I'll be well escorted."

"I think we're going to find that the art gallery owner is a little more than she at first appears. What we've been observing is that the House has cultivated contacts in some of the most affluent levels of society throughout the islands. They never get their hands dirty, but they help him launder all that gambling, drug, and hooker money through shell corporations."

Lei shook her head at the magnitude of the case, instantly regretting it. She touched the bandage again. Marcella leaned over, concerned.

"You okay? I never asked."

Lei showed her the bruises on her legs, arms, and hip. "Car hit me here, and I rolled off the road twice. Concussion. Bumps and bruises otherwise."

"Damn." Marcella extended her left arm, pushed up her sleeve. A deep red mark transected the exterior of her biceps. "Got shot for the first time six months ago."

"Nice. You'll have a good scar from that. How'd you get it?"

"Bank robbery. You'd be surprised the shit they get up to on Oahu. This idiot robbed the downtown Waikiki branch of Bank of Hawaii. Took a shot at me as he was running away."

"Holy crap. Did you get him?"

"Stupid dude ran right into a newspaper kiosk. I was so hopped up on adrenaline, I didn't even know I was shot until blood got on my hands as I was cuffing him."

"War stories. One for every mark." Lei clinked her mug against Marcella's. "Better than nail polish any day, right? Let's make some calls, get this thing going with the witnesses."

Lei called Stevens from the back of the Acura SUV as Matt Rogers, Marcella's partner, drove them out to Pauwela Lighthouse. Rogers's broad shoulders filled the cab as he drove. He hadn't changed his military style, sporting a buzz so short she could see that his scalp was a little freckled. The SUV had a Plexiglas panel up between her and the agents.

Stevens wasn't pleased to hear the plan. "You were supposed to be off today. Lieutenant's orders. You have a concussion!"

"I feel fine," Lei lied. Actually, she felt queasy, and the headache was calling for Vicodin again. "Anyway, how is Marcella going to find this girl without me?"

"You could have called me. I'd take her out there."

"True. But where's the fun in that? Lieutenant knows I'm going. I'm just going to direct them to the camp and stay in the car. I'll ride in the back with Anchara and reassure her she's not in trouble. The safe house has been cleared for us to stash her there."

A long silence. Lei rubbed the black stone in her pocket as

she looked out the window at the passing scenery. This was the part she didn't like about being in a relationship—always having to account for her actions and whereabouts. "Well, anyway. Just thought I'd keep you posted."

"Thanks." He hung up.

Marcella glanced back, pushed a button that lowered the panel. "Everything okay?"

"Fine."

"Good." Marcella turned back. "Not much room at the Academy for the ol' ball and chain."

"Hey, Stevens is hardly a ball and chain!"

"I didn't mean him in particular, just relationships in general. They only hold you back."

Rogers snorted. "Don't listen to her. I'm married and the Bureau life is fine, as long as your spouse doesn't mind long hours, frequent moves, and a few PTSD symptoms on the weekends."

"It's just that while you're a field agent there's so much to do, and you don't want anything to get in the way of your cases. I stay out of entanglements—but I don't say no to a little bounce now and again." Marcella smiled at Lei over her shoulder. "A woman has needs."

Lei looked out the window at the lush, rugged coastline. The ocean was bright and sparkling today, and she gazed at it unseeing. She preferred to let things unfold and try to make the best of them—making plans too far in advance only led to disappointment, in her experience as the child of a drug addict. She had to consciously work to make her mind assess the future, and dealing with the engagement ring, deciding about the Academy—it was just too scary to try to figure out.

"There it is." Lei pointed to the narrow, unmarked turn into ten-foot, waving guinea grass, and Rogers cranked a hard left.

The black Acura SUV bounced down the rutted road, red dust rising around them to coat the shiny finish. "Yeah, Hawaii Land

and Pine stopped working this field about ten years ago, but the irrigation system was still in place. After the field went to seed, the homeless found a place to get shelter in the brush on the bluff, and they tapped into the irrigation system." Lei held on to the back of the panel for support as the SUV crawled along.

"At least they're not right in your face, living in the public parks. We have quite an issue in Honolulu and nowhere to put them." Marcella hung on to the dash and sissy handle.

"Not very picturesque for the tourists," Rogers said as they bumped to a halt in front of the unprepossessing steel light tower with its glorious ocean view and grim human aspect. Lei got out of the Acura as the FBI agents did a quick survey of the area. Marcella took 360 degrees' worth of reference photos, clicking the tiny, high-tech camera no bigger than her thumb as they approached Ramona's tent.

The older Hawaiian woman stood up when she saw them coming but didn't speak until the three of them faced her.

"She's gone."

Chapter 17

"When? How?" Lei stammered, as the two FBI agents immediately approached the tent, unzipping it.

"After you left, that afternoon a man and a woman came. I saw the car they were driving, looked too rich for this neighborhood; I hid her in a place we'd talked about. They searched every tent in the camp. They had guns." She shook her head. "They show no respect. They left when they didn't find her. Everyone said they hadn't seen her. They asked about you, too."

"What do you mean?"

"They asked if any cops came out here, showing a photo of the dead girl. We said yes, cuz what else was we supposed to say?"

"You did right," Lei said, even as the agents spread apart and began looking all around the tents.

"So then what happened?"

"I went back to get her, and she was gone. She must have run."

Lei's heart squeezed. Where could the young Thai go to hide? "Why didn't you call us?"

Ramona pointed to her swollen ankles. "Long walk to the

phone, and my feet were killing me. Beside, what could you do?" Ramona sat back down, picked up a hala leaf, gesturing to the agents. "Who these people stay?"

"Special Agents. They want to help Anchara, keep her safe." Marcella and Rogers had begun systematically canvassing the encampment. To Lei, their buttoned-down efficiency reminded her of a pair of Dobermans in work mode. Lei settled in beside the older woman to work the hala leaves.

Marcella eventually came back, stood in front of Ramona. She gentled her voice and extended her hand to shake the older woman's weathered one.

"Special Agent Marcella Scott. It's very important we find your young friend."

"I know, and I don't know where she is."

"Can you show me where her hiding place was?"

Ramona pulled herself up carefully, leaning on a gnarled kiawe staff, and hobbled to the edge of the nearby cliff. A rope tied to a good-sized guava bush dangled down to a ledge several feet below.

"There's a little cave down there. I hide stuff there when I need to."

Marcella grasped the tree and the rope, swung herself down onto the ledge in a couple of quick hops. She looked back up at them.

"Nope. Shallow declivity here; no room to do anything more than hunker down out of sight of above."

They did one more sweep through the camp. As they headed back to the SUV, Lei swept her arm to gesture out over the acres of long grass. "She could be hiding anywhere out here."

"We'll have to rely on Ramona to let us know." Marcella dusted a little red dirt off her black pants.

"You saw her feet. She's not going to hike a mile up to the community center to use the pay phone."

"Just might have something for that." Rogers rummaged in a duffel bag beside his seat and pulled up a burner phone, still in its package. "Agents are like Boy Scouts—always prepared. Let's preprogram this with our numbers and leave it for her."

Marcella took the phone and removed several bills from a wallet she kept in her shoulder pack.

"A little insurance money to make it worth her while." She strode off with the phone and money to ensure Ramona called them if Anchara came back. They got on the road to Kahului Station shortly after.

"Let's get this interview with Silva going and get a BOLO out on the girl and the car the people were driving," Marcella said. "We need to find her before they do."

Chapter 18

The gallery's always busy on weekends, so Monday is my day off. I usually exercise, shop, and train some of the merchandise.

This morning I sit on the balcony and sip my coffee, reading the paper. I like the way the sun on the horizon lights my paper from beneath, and the far blue-purple smudge of Lana`i on the horizon, dressed in cloud, keeps me company. Waxing lyrical. It's my creative side, the part that has built the business and knows beauty is worthwhile for its own sake.

John Wylie, that golf-loving scumbag, called me Saturday, wanting to go to some Rotary Club mock-gambling function. The one time I bent my rules and slept with him (though you couldn't call what we did sleeping) keeps him coming back, hoping for more.

It's always the people you least expect who like a taste of the whip.

I turned him down, but in the course of his bumbling begging he told me he'd given out my card to the cops—he'd been the leak to my gallery. He's been cut off from goodies of all kinds for the foreseeable future.

I scan the paper, looking for the demise of Texeira, but there's nothing. Surely the accidental death of a cop would make the paper. The job must not be done yet, but why?

Healani is usually more efficient. Well, perhaps arranging the right accident is taking some time. I need to call House and make sure he's okay with all of this.

Calling House is a double-edged sword. It might piss him off, and then it could as easily be me falling ten stories off my own railing. That danger makes calling him irresistible. I settle myself on the lounge chair, coffee and papaya on the little glass table beside me, and dial the work phone.

"Hello, House."

"Why are you calling me?"

"Do you say that to all the ladies?"

His voice. Just that makes me reach down between my legs. I don't have anything on but my white silk robe.

"I know why you're calling me. You want to know why the trash hasn't been taken out."

"Well, yes. Just checking that you're okay with Healani's arrangement?"

"Accidents happen, as they say."

I smile. I love listening to that rough voice. My hand moves faster, imagining all I'd like to do to him. "You know how to make me hot."

First time I've taken a chance like that, letting him know he affects me. I part my legs, naked under the white silk robe, the wind off the ocean ruffling over my skin. I'm getting there, can feel it building, a coiling deep inside punctuated by stabs of pleasure almost like pain.

"What are you doing?" He sounds suspicious, and best yet, curious.

"Wouldn't you like to know. I told you, you make me hot." I'm panting a bit.

"Describe it."

"I'm on my deck. Only wearing my robe, nothing underneath. I'm ten stories up, so unless someone's in a helicopter, no one can see what I'm doing. You already guessed what I'm doing."

"Take the robe off."

"Why?"

"I told you to."

He's into this. Arousal sweeps over me in the first mini wave of what promises to be a very nice orgasm.

"Okay. Because you're telling me to. Because it's you, House." I usually don't like taking orders, but I slide out of the robe. It puddles on the floor, and I stretch out on the lounge chair, enjoying the sun, the breeze, and the pleasure building.

"Oh, this is good," I pant. I haven't been this turned on by any of the merchandise, no matter how good they look. It's power that turns me on. Mine. His. Ours together.

He gives me more directions. I do everything he asks, including something inventive with the papaya and the spoon.

When I come, it's explosive, mind-bending. I'm sure he's with me.

Sweat cooling on my skin gives me a shiver a few minutes later. I still hold the phone, and I can hear his deep breathing. I shrug back into the robe. My delicate skin's picking up a touch of pink, which won't do. I go back into the penthouse, walking across the white carpet. It feels wonderful to sensitized nerve endings.

I feel amazing, and amazed. I didn't know there was anything sexual left for me to discover, but House has taken me to a whole new place, just with phone sex.

What could he do to me in person?

"I want to meet you." I know my voice is small. I hadn't done anything but give orders for more years than I can count. I don't like asking, but I can't seem to help myself.

"When you've earned it," he says. The phone goes dead.

I feel bereft, abandoned. A puppy dropped off at the curb of *nowhere. These feelings make me angry, and I need to get rid of that unhealthy anger. I take a shower and go downstairs to find someone to take it out on.*

Chapter 19

L ei and Captain Corpuz sat in the molded plastic chairs outside a window into the interview room at Kahului Station.
Gerry Bunuelos and Abe Torufu had been officially assigned
to help with the investigation and sat with Lei to observe the
interview. Inside, seated at a shiny steel table, hunched James
Silva.

He was wearing a toupee, and he stole a finger up to scratch
under the rug. A Primo Beer shirt, weather-beaten Dockers, and
rubber slippers on feet that could have used a wash completed
his ensemble.

"He didn't want to come in," Bunuelos said. "I had to threaten
to press charges on the cockfight, which we'd let him off of
before in exchange for info on the girl."

"Don't really blame him," Lei said. "Now that I'm hearing a
little more about the House."

Marcella and Rogers, in full buttoned-down FBI glory, entered
the interview room.

"Hey, who are you? What's going on?" Silva cried. They didn't
answer as they set up a video camera on a tripod (they'd declined

to use the station's equipment) and an audio recorder. They took seats across from Silva.

"What's going on?" he asked again.

"What do you think is going on?" Rogers flipped open his cred wallet. "Special Agent Rogers, FBI."

Marcella opened hers as well. Silva, not handcuffed this time, jumped to his feet and ran to the door, yanking at the handle—locked of course.

"I suggest you have a seat, Mr. Silva." Marcella patted the table invitingly. "You aren't in trouble. We're just looking for some information."

"I don't know anything!"

"MPD seems to think you do. We're investigating who's behind the gambling and cockfights and hear you know a little something about betting against the House. You have a little bit of your own thing going, don't you?"

Silva's pallor went gray, and he sat abruptly in the remaining steel chair, clutching the back of it for support. Lei glanced at the guys. "What's she talking about?"

"Don't know," Bunuelos said. The captain shook his head.

"How did you know?" Back in the hot seat, Silva scratched under the toupee, which slid to the left.

"You can bet that if we know, the House knows. You might as well help us take him down."

"I just do a few local fights on my own. No threat to his operation. He won't bother with me."

"How do you know? We can help you. Protect you. He's already put a contract out on a police officer who's investigating."

Lei flinched, and her hand crept up to fiddle with the bandage on her head. The guys swiveled to look at her.

"Yeah. Someone's trying to kill me," she said to Bunuelos and Torufu, who looked at her wide-eyed. "Don't know if it's the House, though. Seems like the Feds sure have a lot of intel."

"The Feds have a lot of confidential informants. They're in a position to pay them a lot more than we can," Captain Corpuz said.

In the interview room, Silva appeared motivated by this information. "Okay, I'll tell you what I know—but only if I can have protection."

"Done." Marcella pushed a pad and paper over to Silva. "Who does the House run over here? Names and contact numbers."

Over the next hour, they pried much more information out of Silva than Lei had imagined the man could possibly know. Apparently, he was running his own small-time cockfights and resented and feared the stranglehold the House had on the underground industry.

"What do you know about the House and guns?" Marcella asked.

"I know he brings them in. Supplies several pawnshops and dealers with whatever people want. That's another reason I want to take him down," Silva said, sucking in his paunch in righteous indignation. "Guns and drugs are bad for our community."

They pried more names out of him—local gun and drug distributors. Captain Corpuz looked satisfied as Lei glanced over at him, and Lei knew Rogers and Marcella were doing this for their benefit—the information was exchange for pulling Silva in and using their facilities. You scratch my back and I'll scratch yours, the secret to interagency cooperation.

Silva finally left, half-moons of sweat darkening his shirt under the arms, and Bunuelos met him in the hall to tell him police protection was going to be a patrol car doing hourly sweeps by his house.

Lei, whose head had begun to throb in earnest, could hear him yelling that it wasn't enough all the way down the hall as they escorted him to the front of the building. She rested her head on her arms as the interview room light went out and waited for Marcella to be done.

Stevens woke her with a hand on her shoulder.

"What're you doing here?" His voice was cold. "You're supposed to be home in bed."

"Waiting for Marcella and Rogers. They did an awesome interview with that slimeball Silva. The FBI thing scared intel right out him like shit from a goose." Lei got up with a boost under her arm from Stevens.

Marcella appeared in the doorway.

"There you are. Hey, Stevens." They embraced. "Sorry, I had to borrow your girlfriend."

"Some day off. She's supposed to be resting," he grumbled.

"Well, you know how she is—refused to be left home, and I figured I could keep an eye on her." Marcella poked him in the chest. "Getting pretty attached, I see."

"It's a sickness," he said, and gave Lei a little swat on the butt. "Get home and rest."

Chapter 20

Lei lay in the dark beside Stevens, listening to his even breathing. It annoyed her how, no matter how mad they were at each other, he could always just get in bed and go to sleep like flicking a light switch, while she tossed and turned. They'd gone through a whole evening without saying much to each other.

For the first time, Lei wondered if it was a good idea for them to live together. Back when they had their own places, they'd just take a few days apart, start missing each other, and come back together. Now she felt trapped in an orbit, circling him, circling, circling, unable to get away when she needed to, unable to stop disappointing and irritating him, and vice versa. No point in talking about it anymore—this was the same fight they'd had a dozen times.

She studied the ceiling. The house, built in the thirties, had tongue-and-groove wood covered with plaster lining the ceiling. It was raining lightly outside as it often did in `Iao Valley, and the patter of water on the tin roof was a song she'd learned to love in Hanalei on Kaua`i, a place with more rainfall than most anywhere in the world.

Keiki slept at the foot of the king-sized bed she'd hauled to three islands, on her ratty old quilt. She'd been agitated when Marcella dropped Lei off that evening, running the fence and barking at nothing, but when Stevens got home and played with her a bit she'd finally settled down.

He was even stealing her dog.

Now Lei could hear a doggie version of a snore fluttering past Keiki's wide black nose, and she couldn't help smiling and giving the dog a little prod with her toe. Keiki sat up and looked around.

"Come here, baby." Lei patted the comforter and Keiki belly crawled over, stretching out beside her. Lei stroked the big wide head, remembering the terrifying moment she'd almost lost the Rottweiler, shot on the Big Island. Lei stroked the deep groove of the scar where a bullet had exited Keiki's shoulder and scored down her side, leaving a hairless line that would always remind Lei of how close she'd come to losing her companion.

Keiki whipped her head up and growled deep in her chest, a bass rumble.

"What's the matter, girl?" Lei whispered, patting the dog as the animal's ruff rose under her hand.

The big Rottweiler leapt out of bed. Lei heard a muffled *whump!* that sucked at her eardrums.

The dog ran into the living room, barking, as Lei reached over, shaking Stevens.

"Wake up! Something's wrong!"

She grabbed her Glock out of the bedside table as he rolled up, reaching for his gun as well. The smell of smoke hit their nostrils.

Lei looked at Stevens. "Fire!"

They ran out of the bedroom into the living room, where Keiki stood, barking stiff-legged at the wall of flame engulfing the front door.

"Shit!" Lei ran to the phone on the kitchen counter and lifted it. Dead. She fumbled in her backpack for her cell phone, flipped it open. No signal.

Lei snapped her fingers and Keiki retreated to stand beside her, trembling and whimpering, ears flattened.

"Phone's out. Cell signal must be jammed," she yelled at Stevens, who had gone to the back door and was wrestling with the handle.

"Something's wrong. It's not opening," he yelled back over the roar of flames that moved in a sheet, unbelievably fast, across the ceiling. "There must be some sort of accelerant. This shouldn't be spreading so fast. Let's get in the bedroom and break a window!"

They chased the dog back into the bedroom as the kitchen filled with choking smoke and billowing flame, glass bursting from the heat with shattering pops.

Lei shut the bedroom door to buy a few more minutes as Stevens yanked the comforter off the bed. She stuffed the rag rug into the crack under the door.

"Old house—it's a tinderbox even on a rainy day," she yelled back. "I don't like that the cell phones are jammed. Think he's still out there? Whoever set the fire?"

"Only one way to find out." Stevens wrapped the comforter over the straight chair from the desk and swung it up to hit the bedroom window, a plate-glass insert above a lower set of louvers for circulation.

The glass shattering was drowned out by the roar of the fire in the other room. He wrapped his fist in the comforter and knocked remaining shards of glass outside. They still had to get up to the chest-high window and jump out, a drop of ten feet or so with the elevation of the house. Stevens put the chair back down in front to use as a step to climb into the frame.

"Let's put Keiki out first. Maybe she can flush him if he's out there." The dog was whimpering with terror and had crawled under the bed, so they wasted valuable minutes coaxing and dragging her out. By the time they got her onto the chair, the paint on the door was blistering and fingers of smoke had worked their way under the door, weaving a hypnotic spell against the bubbling paint. The fire was moving so fast there wasn't much smoke, but breaking the window caused a sucking draft of oxygen that only fed the beast roaring in the other room.

"Hurry!" Lei screamed. They forced the big dog onto the sill by hauling her up by the scruff, boosting her haunches, and shoving her out. The framed picture on the wall behind Stevens seemed to explode and they both ducked.

"Just a second," Stevens said, as Lei started to climb into the window. He pushed her back and grabbed a dark shirt out of the closet, throwing it over one of the pillows. He moved it up into the window and waved it.

The shot couldn't be heard over the roar of the fire, but there was no mistaking the puff of back-blown feathers that floated down on them as he tossed the pillow out.

"Shit!" Lei cried, coughing. They hunkered down below the sill. Lei's lungs burned. Every breath felt like she was sucking in fire. She reached up to yank a sheet off the bed, but she was getting too weak to rip it. Instead, she pulled down the other pillow and handed Stevens the pillowcase. They wrapped makeshift masks over their faces.

"What do we do now? He's going to keep us in here until we burn!" Her voice was muffled but frantic. Stevens's eyes tracked around the room as he looked for a solution.

"I doubt there are two of them. Let's try the other side."

They could hear Keiki's frantic barking as they crawled across the floor to the opposite, mountain-side window and, staying out of sight, removed the glass louvers and one final barrier, the screen on the lower window.

Lei's throat was so raw that she couldn't speak. They used the comforter again, to beat out flames that had burned through the rag rug stuffed under the door. They wadded it against the door, but the roar was all encompassing and the heat blistered. The air was so hot it seemed like it would spontaneously combust.

Stevens yanked open the closet and shoved the clothes aside. Bolted to the back wall was what he called his "weapons locker," where he stored spare guns and a collection of early American pistols. For a second, his eyes flashed blue mischief above the cloth mask as he spun the combination and took out three pistols, tossing her a Glock. He stuck a full clip of extra ammo into his waistband.

"Let's get out over here and distract him." He gestured to the mountain-side window, away from where the shooter had fired.

Lei got in position beside the window as he ripped the sheet off the bed, dropped it over the straight chair, and heaved it through the front-side window, just as the entire bedroom door burst into flame with a roar.

They were out of time.

Lei clutched a pistol in each hand and jumped out the back window.

Chapter 21

*L*ei landed and rolled, forcing rubbery legs to carry her to cover behind the white propane tank that was surely too close to the fiercely burning house. Stevens was right behind her as she ducked behind the metal tank. She could hear the wail of oncoming sirens.

Her ears rang; her eyes burned. She scanned the yard lit by the fiercely burning house for her dog. She heard Keiki barking somewhere to the front.

"Let's look for the shooter," Stevens croaked. His eyes gleamed with a fierce warrior light—maybe it was just the reflected flame—but Lei nodded, energized by his confidence though still unable to speak. They circled the pyre of the house, covering each other and keeping to the clumps of banana and plumeria trees at the edge of the fenced yard.

Keiki stood barking at the north corner of the yard, where a stand of guava trees leaned out over the six-foot fence. Stevens got there first and used one of the guava saplings to boost himself over, setting off down the road. Lei ran to the front gate and unlatched it, following him.

She heard the roar of an engine, and muscle memory tightened her whole body with the traumatic threat of an oncoming car. Her heart thudded as Stevens stepped into the road and shot out the windshield of the speeding sedan, throwing himself to the side as the vehicle barely missed him. Lei got off a few shots at the passenger-side window and the tires. The sedan kept going, weaving wildly, and swerved to avoid hitting an oncoming yellow fire truck, plummeting off the shoulder and into a ditch.

Stevens and Lei ran over, weapons drawn. The car, a tan rental Taurus, was hubcap deep in the irrigation ditch, the shooter slumped against the steering wheel. The airbags had failed to deploy.

Stevens hauled the unresisting suspect out by the armpits, laying the stocking-capped man in a black coverall in the road. He patted down the body and removed a Glock and a couple of knives as one of the firemen approached.

"This man need first aid?"

"Eventually. This man set our house on fire and tried to gun us down. Police on the way?" Lei asked, as Stevens scooped up a little ditch water and splashed it on the man's camouflage-painted face, slapping him briskly. No response.

"Hey!" the fireman exclaimed. "Don't hit a man with a head injury!"

More sirens, and a couple of uniforms approached on the run, recognizing Stevens. Amid exclamations and a heated exchange with the emergency medical technician, Lei felt her wobbly knees give way. She folded up onto the side of the road, reaching to feel her singed head. She tried to breathe in the fresh air and ignore the crackling roar of the burning house, but coughed uncontrollably instead. Moments later, she was in the back of the ambulance wrapped in a blanket, an oxygen mask over her face.

"Good thing you already had short hair." Stevens hopped up into the ambulance, reaching over to give her a hug.

"You don't have any eyebrows," Lei said, touching his reddened skin with a gentle forefinger. He winced.

"At least we're alive—but on that note, I talked to the captain. He's going to put it out that we're dead. That might buy us some time to interview the gunman and see who put him up to it. Suspect wasn't looking too good, though."

As if to punctuate this, they heard the wail of the other ambulance pulling away.

Chapter 22

*L*ei huddled on the corner of the sofa in the police safe house, wrapped in the green army surplus blanket she'd arrived in. She should get in the shower, wash off the smoke and grime, but she didn't have anything to put on afterward—no clothes but the filthy boxers and tank top she'd worn to bed the night before.

Her hand crept down to caress Keiki's head, playing with the triangular silky ears as the big Rottweiler slept curled on the floor. She might not have anything else, but she still had her dog. Keiki could easily have been shot or perished in the flames.

Voices in the kitchen—Stevens retelling the tale to Rogers and Marcella. Lei was too exhausted to go through it again and had opted out. Having repeated the story several times, she just didn't think she had the energy to deal with the agents' machine-gun questions. Lei felt profound gratitude covering her as warmly as the blanket. "Thank you, God," she whispered, and closed her sore eyes to rest them. The voices went on out in the kitchen, a low rumble punctuated by laughter.

Lei found herself smiling as she sank lower into the couch, her hand on Keiki's ruff as the Vicodin she'd taken carried her off into darkness.

Lei woke up to instant coffee, a peanut-butter sandwich, and a bag of clothes Pono had brought over—some of his and Tiare's castoffs. After a shower and dressing in an outsized muumuu, she felt strangely disembodied but at least clean.

"Sorry—Tiare thought it would fit because it says one size fits all," Pono said, eying the way the tentlike dress hung on Lei's slim frame.

"It's fine. Thanks, Pono. I'm in disguise anyway."

"Yeah, on that note, I picked up this wig for you." He handed her a long red wig. "The kids had it left over from Halloween."

She set it on her head and heard Stevens snickering.

"Shut up, Eyebrow Boy," she said to him. Stevens's dark hair had singed patches and his eyebrows were completely gone, his face red. "I'm never gonna live this down."

"Actually, everyone feels really bad for you," Pono said. He came over, gave her an awkward side hug. "Nobody's going to say a word."

They turned Keiki loose in the fenced yard and piled into the purple truck. He drove them to Kahului Station for a debrief meeting. The air-conditioning was turned up high in the conference room, and seated around the long table were Lieutenant Omura, Pono, Bunuelos and Torufu, and Captain Corpuz. Lei adjusted the wig on her singed head, reaching up to scratch her scalp with a pencil. Stevens wore one of Pono's Hawaiian-print shirts and sat kitty-corner to her.

"You two definitely have made an impression on someone," Captain Corpuz said. "The fire investigation team said there was some sort of incendiary device set in your house, probably on a timer or with a detonator."

"Maybe that's why Keiki was so agitated," Lei said. "She was all riled up that evening. Wonder how the guy got past her."

Stevens's reddened face looked odd without eyebrows. He rolled his Styrofoam coffee cup back and forth in his hands. "Any news on our hit man?"

"Still in a coma. We want to keep you two on the downlow and put out the story that you're dead. That'll buy us some time to figure out who's behind this," Captain Corpuz said.

"We really need to find the Thai girl. Did you guys put out a BOLO? She's the key to the case right now." Lei wanted to get up and pace. She missed the black stone, then remembered it was burned, along with all of the contents of her little koa box—each item an irreplaceable loss. She pinched the web between her thumb and forefinger and that helped, but not much.

"Done," the captain said. "It's been out ever since the FBI came in yesterday and interviewed Silva."

"I want to know more about this art gallery owner," Omura said. She looked fresh and immaculate in a navy uniform whose brass gleamed. A skirt that hit her above the knee showcased toned legs ending in a pair of pointy-toed slingbacks. Lei was pretty sure she'd left a trail of tiny pockmarks all the way across the station. "Let's bring her in for an interview. Since you and Pono blew your cover, we'll have Bunuelos and Torufu bring her in."

"On what basis?" Captain Corpuz asked. "She seems like one of those uptight *haoles* with a lawyer on speed dial."

"She's our only lead to the hookers, and the hookers are our lead to Jane Doe's identity and this whole sex trade ship thing," Omura said impatiently. Her tone implied she wasn't all that convinced the idea had merit. "In the meantime, I want Lei and Stevens to lay low at the safe house."

"I don't think they're after me," Stevens said. "It's Lei who someone tried to run over with a car. I'm just the lucky boyfriend." The room erupted in chuckles, and Stevens glanced over at Lei.

She saw, by the widening of those blue, blue eyes, vulnerable without lashes or brows—that he realized she wasn't wearing the diamond ring around her neck. That same moment, she remembered where she'd left it—the ring was in a drawer, in a kitchen that was now a pile of ash. Her hand crept up to her throat, as if wishing could make the ring reappear.

"I can do more with the cockfighting ring," Pono volunteered. "I can go reinterview all the names we got and look for connections to the girls or the House."

"Why don't you do that." Omura inclined her shining head. "Try not to get the boys all riled up, though. Just do some casual fishing and we'll feed anything you find to the FBI for their investigation of the House."

"Why don't I go with Pono? I think the 'contractor' was looking for Lei, and now that we're both dead, I can get back out there," Stevens said. He didn't look at Lei again.

"Hey! I'm going to go crazy sitting around that box of a house!" Lei exclaimed.

"You look like you've been hit by a car and burnt by a fire and you need another day off. For now you can do some online research for us and work with Kendall, the sketch artist, on a picture of the Thai girl for that BOLO. Get that done so Pono and Stevens can take it out canvassing; then go back to the house and rest." Omura had steel in her voice.

Lei frowned and scratched her head again. "Okay. Dammit. But I want to watch the interview with Magda Kennedy."

Chapter 23

*L*ei sat in the booth behind the mirrored window looking into the interview room. Stevens and Pono had gone out on their assignments and there was some delay in the hall. Waiting for Bunuelos and Torufu to bring Magda Kennedy in, Lei looked down at the copy of the sketch Kendall had worked up on Anchara, the Thai girl.

Wide, dark almond eyes looked startled above those scimitar cheekbones. He hadn't gotten the mouth quite right—it looked puffy and pouty, and Lei remembered it as full but decisive, a set to the lips that said she would do whatever she needed to, to be free. Lei respected that and found herself saying a little prayer that the girl was safe until they could find her and bring her in.

The metal door with its little safety glass insert opened. An imposing bearded man in business casual walked in, followed by Magda Kennedy. Regal in a creamy halter dress, long black hair that had to have been flatironed shimmered under the harsh neon lights as she sat and crossed spectacular legs ending in a pair of gold sandals.

Bunuelos and Torufu followed. Lei could tell they were intimidated, as Gerry Bunuelos combed an overlong sheaf of hair out of his eyes repetitively. Abe Torufu hoisted his belt as he sat, relying on his size. Lei knit her brows, concerned they might not be up to the task of interviewing such an intimidating witness.

Captain Corpuz, jaunty as usual, joined her in the booth. He'd brought a pair of Styrofoam cups of coffee and handed her one with a wink. "We have bad coffee too."

"Thanks." Lei didn't have time to express her worry before the show got under way.

"I'm always happy to support Maui Police Department in whatever way I can." Magda fired the opening round. "If you check, you'll see I am a regular supporter of police charities. How can I help you today?" She held herself stiffly upright, as if touching the back of the steel chair would dirty her dress—and it probably would.

"We appreciate that," Bunuelos said. Before he could go on, the lawyer interrupted.

"Why is my client here? Her time is very expensive, and mine almost as much. Let's get this over with before I have to send the county a bill for it."

Bunuelos, rattled, spoke too quickly. "Thank you for coming in, Ms. Kennedy and Mr. Chapman. We appreciate that your time is valuable and we just want some information. About this." He gestured, and Torufu produced the satiny calling card that Wylie had given them with the number for the hookers on it, sliding it over in front of Magda.

"I was given that by a friend."

"Do you know what it's for?"

"I was told escort services. So I imagine that's what it's for."

"Who is this friend?"

"I'm not at liberty to say."

"That's not good enough!" Bunuelos tried to generate some heat, but it withered in the face of Kennedy's and Chapman's contemptuous stares.

The door opened and Lieutenant Cherry Joy Omura walked in, slingbacks rapping the floor. She made a flicking gesture, and Bunuelos gave a relieved glance at the surveillance mirror and withdrew, leaving Torufu behind for bulk.

"Where did you get this card?" A red nail tapped the item in question.

"And you are?" The lawyer tried some attitude, but Omura never blinked.

"Above his pay grade. I'll be conducting this interview."

Magda Kennedy stood suddenly, apparently scenting trouble. She picked up her little purse, a flat clutch painted in scarlet designs. "I don't have time for this."

She made for the door.

Faster than Lei could have believed, Omura blocked the exit, grabbed Kennedy's wrist and twisted it up behind her back, horsing her onto the hard metal chair. She sat the woman on it, slapping on a pair of cuffs. The lieutenant then locked them on to a ring on the metal table.

The lawyer burbled objections, but Omura's voice cut through them. "I'm placing you under arrest for suspicion of procurement."

"That's ridiculous!" Magda snarled. She yanked at the cuffs, and Lei could see that it hurt. Gold bangles jangled against steel.

"You can't make those charges stick," Chapman said.

"Probably not, but in the meantime I get to hold her for twenty-four hours. Or she can cooperate with our investigation."

"Is this legal?" Magda asked the lawyer.

"She hasn't been Mirandized," Chapman finally said.

Omura simply repeated the Miranda catechism. A moment

passed in which Kennedy and Omura exchanged stares. The lieutenant shrugged.

"I'll leave you to think about your choice." Omura gestured to Torufu, and they left the room.

Captain Corpuz broke into a grin almost as big as the one on Lei's face as Magda Kennedy gave a shriek of rage and cursed the lawyer with more fluency and imagination than Lei would have believed. Omura came into the peanut gallery, took a seat. Aimed hard dark eyes, sparkling with the light of battle, at Lei.

"I want a full background workup on her. Dig up everything; make phone calls. Something doesn't smell right about her."

"We already ran a quick one—she's clean. Not even a parking ticket. And I don't want to miss the interview!"

"What interview? I'm leaving them in there." Omura looked at her watch. "For two hours. After two hours, they can launch a civil complaint, so get me everything you can. I imagine she'll need a pee by then—and in the meantime, cut the air-conditioning to the room. I find that woman annoying."

Lei hurried to obey. She wondered what Omura was capable of when she was more than annoyed. Torufu showed Lei to the computer lab—a dim, cool room equipped with a row of high-speed flat screens. Lei logged in and began searching for Maui art maven Magda Kennedy.

The woman appeared to have moved to the island sometime in the last ten years, and a search pulled up reams of information on her. Media appeared to be in her pocket. Lei scrolled through articles on her busy social life, where she always appeared immaculately dressed in signature shades of white.

But prior to 2000, the trail went cold.

The magic combination of birth date and social security number generated very little—Magda Kennedy, born in Westport, Massachusetts. No schools, no early life that Lei could find with either of the search programs the MPD used for background. Her criminal record was clean, not so much as a parking ticket. She moved on to researching Pacific Treasures Gallery, and the lawyer, Robb "Keoni" Chapman.

Bunuelos stuck his head in. "Anything?"

"Not much. She moved here and started Pacific Treasures in 2000, apparently had connections to New York and East Coast galleries that helped open doors for the enterprise in Lahaina."

"Anything earlier?"

"Not really. I'll try to figure out where she went to school. She doesn't appear to keep in touch with anyone from her past—no Facebook or LinkedIn or anything. That's weird for someone of her type—it's all about who you know in that world."

"Maybe she just needed to drop the Kennedy name around and that was enough."

"Yeah. But not all Kennedys are 'the' Kennedys. It's actually a pretty common name."

Bunuelos disappeared and Lei went on digging. It seemed like only a few minutes had passed when Omura rapped on the door frame.

"Got anything for me?"

"Nothing tying her to prostitution," Lei said regretfully. "What's more interesting is that she seems to have so little history prior to moving to Maui."

"When was that?"

"In 2000. That's when she started Pacific Treasures Gallery and really hit the map."

"Well, that's about when everything started to be available online. Prior to that, most things were written records, so I'm not surprised. Anything on the lawyer?"

"Yeah. He's one of Maui's priciest defense lawyers. Belongs to the golf club, the country club, all the right memberships in Rotary and such. Works the Hawaiian angle by doing some work for Kamehameha Schools. Guy's well connected and has probably been working his cell phone the whole time we left them in there," Lei said.

"Damn cell phones," Omura muttered. She narrowed her eyes. "Okay. Probably going to have to let her go anyway, I haven't been able to get the DA to sign her warrant."

"Too bad," Lei said. "I was really hoping to see how that white outfit held up in the drunk tank."

"Me too." Omura cracked a smile, spun on her considerable heel. "Oh well. I'll get her next time." She clacked down the hall. Lei hurried after her, carrying her notes, and ducked into the peanut gallery. She grabbed a seat next to Captain Corpuz, who barely glanced up, intent on the drama taking place inside.

Omura was once again at the table, and she tapped the white business card. The click of her shiny nail echoed through the speaker on the counter into the observation area.

"Let's start again. Who gave you this card?"

Magda had chewed off some of her red lipstick, but her mouth was set in a stubborn line and arctic-blue eyes hadn't warmed in two hours. She glared at Omura, refusing to answer.

"Lieutenant Omura. Yes, I know who you are." Chapman stood up, sucking in his paunch and thrusting out his beard. "I have the mayor on the phone, and he'd like to know what possible grounds you could have to hold us in this hot box without even the courtesy of a restroom." He held out a squawking cell phone to the lieutenant.

Omura reached out with one of those nails and punched the Off button.

"Need the restroom? Torufu will take you. We aren't Neanderthals here."

Abe Torufu lumbered to his feet and cocked his head at the door invitingly.

"I don't need the restroom," Kennedy said. "You're harassing me. We'll be pressing a civil suit."

"We are within procedural rights," Omura said, as the lawyer's phone chimed. He read the ID, answered the phone, and then held it out to Omura.

"This is the district attorney. You might hang up on the mayor, but this one makes your cases. I think you want to take this call."

She took the phone and left the room. Everyone in the peanut gallery sighed as Chapman leaned down to his client, patting her shoulder and whispering in her ear.

Captain Corpuz said, "I think the show's over," just as Bunuelos returned to the interview room with Torufu and a handcuff key. Bunuelos uncuffed Magda Kennedy.

"You're free to go."

"Where's that bitch lieutenant?" Kennedy said, lips barely moving and face bone white as she stood up, rubbing her wrists.

"She had other business. Said to pass on her apologies for the inconvenience," Bunuelos said with a straight face, holding out the cell phone to Chapman. The gallery owner's teeth bared in rage as she tossed back her shimmery hair and cocked her arm. The lawyer caught it, pulled her in and held her against his side.

"Your department will be hearing from our firm regarding this outrage," he said, marching Kennedy through the door and down the hall.

"Conference room," Captain Corpuz said. "Find Lieutenant Omura."

Lei and the other detectives spread out. Lei went straight to the women's room, where she guessed Omura was holed up, hiding from the rest of the team and hoping Kennedy would need to make a potty stop.

Sure enough, a pair of pointy toes were visible from under the stall.

"She took off," Lei said. "She waited to pee somewhere else."

"Dammit!" Omura slammed the door open and put her hands on her hips. "I was hoping for one last word."

Lei almost liked her at that moment.

"Captain wants a confab in the conference room."

Omura stalked off. Lei followed, feeling like a remora following a tiger shark.

Chapter 24

The conference room was hot, its AC on the same circuit as the interview room, and Torufu, Bunuelos, Pono, Stevens, and Captain Corpuz appeared in various stages of overheated. Omura was immaculate as usual—the woman hardly had a pulse. Lei sipped a bottled water, feeling itchy in the ill-fitting muumuu and wig.

Captain Corpuz opened the discussion.

"We need something more to tie this whole thing together. So far we have a dead Jane Doe prostitute, a runaway Thai girl, a business card with a procurement service number on it, and someone so pissed off they're trying to kill Texeira and Stevens. Or at least Texeira. This is a random collection of maybes, not a case. Omura? Opinion?"

"That Kennedy woman is involved," Omura said. "We have to keep digging. We'll find something on her. Her past is sketchy."

"So maybe we find she left a sketchy past behind. So have a lot of people who end up in Hawaii; that doesn't make her a madam or a murderer. Besides, she's connected. We aren't going to get anywhere without some hard evidence."

"So what about getting the coast guard involved? Make a few calls through our FBI connection and get them searching those ships for sex slaves, money, and drugs. Or, hell, maybe even prizefighting cocks." Stevens plucked Pono's overlarge aloha shirt away from his body. "I want to bust not just Magda Kennedy, but the House. Who else has brass ones enough to torch a house where two detectives live? And what's happening with our injured hit man?"

"Still out, unfortunately. I have a uniform outside the door," the captain said. "Oh, and the tox screens on Jane Doe came back—she was four times the legal alcohol limit."

"No big surprise there. Someone went to a lot of trouble to make that scene look like suicide. I agree with Stevens's idea about the coast guard," Omura said. "Captain, we don't have any authority on those ships, and I think we have a viable tip that there's something illegal going on."

The captain inclined his head in agreement, and Omura turned to Lei. "Call your FBI friend."

Omura was showing qualities Lei respected. Decisiveness. Skill. Persistence. Just because she was tiny, perfect, and wore fancy shoes didn't mean she wasn't a good cop. Lei hurried into the chilly computer lab, closing the door to make the call on her cell phone.

"Marcella? We need your help." She described the team's conclusion and the fruitless interview with Magda Kennedy.

"I know the commander of Maui Coast Guard Station," Marcella said. "I was hoping you guys would give us enough to move on."

"Well, we still don't have anything totally solid. The captain is requesting assistance based on some reliable info." Lei crossed her fingers at the idea that Silva was reliable, but the man had implicated the House, and so had Anchara, if indirectly.

"I'll call and see if they can search everything currently in harbor."

"How about getting a schematic map of the ships and looking for false compartments or mislabeled rooms?"

"Yeah, the coast guard know all those tricks. I'll give them a call. Commander will probably call back and look for a formal request from the captain."

"I can get that," Lei said. Her fingers were still crossed. She hurried back to the conference room, where the team meeting was breaking up, everyone with assignments.

Lei reported to the captain, who agreed to fax over a request for sweeps looking for weapons, drugs, money, and human cargo on all ships docking anywhere on Maui—and a general alert to all Hawaii ports.

Omura ran an eyeball over Lei. "You can't be seen in public, and I don't just mean that outfit."

"I don't have any clothes." Lei suddenly remembered the ring, left in the kitchen drawer. That, and everything else she owned, burned to ash. Her eyes filled and she sat abruptly. "I don't have anything to wear."

Omura blanched, either at the prospect of losing all her clothes or of Lei crying.

"I think we better get you back to the safe house. Someone can pick some things up for you. You've put in enough of a day."

"Guess it's catching up with me." Lei blinked hard, still surprised by Omura's kindness. The tears receded. "My headache's back. Stevens and Pono able to shake anything loose?"

"Yes. Sounds like they've got some confirmation on Silva's story about the House. No apparent connection between House and the Kennedy woman, though. That must be through the smuggling and human trafficking."

"That's good." Lei yawned, her jaw cracking. It really was all catching up with her. Omura stood up. "I'll have Larson drive you to the safe house and keep an eye out. He's not directly involved with the investigation, but he's offered to help."

"Okay." Lei trailed Omura out and met Detective Jed Larson in the bull pen area. Larson, beefy with a receding hairline, had a forgettable but kind face that helped in law enforcement.

"Sorry to hear about your bad luck," he said as he led her to the unmarked Bronco he drove.

"Nothing lucky about it." Lei's eyes darted around the parking lot, looking for threats, but she felt suitably invisible in her disguise. "I hope we get some breaks on this case soon."

"Yeah, I heard. I offered to help if your lieutenant or the captain wants any more manpower. We gotta look after our own."

He turned the key of the Bronco, and the roar of the engine drowned out his voice as she glanced at him.

"Seems like someone's got a hit out on us. We have an idea who, but nothing to pull it all together," Lei said, leaning back in the bucket seat and indulging in another jaw-cracking yawn.

"Who are you thinking?"

"Organized crime on Oahu, guy they call the House."

He whistled. "He's deep. Good luck getting anything on him."

"I'd be happy with just getting a good night's sleep, at this point."

Lei shut her eyes and leaned back in the seat. In no time they were pulling up to the steep driveway bisected by the six-foot chain-link fence that surrounded the modest ranch "safe" house. Keiki ran back and forth in front of the gate, making sure they knew she was on the job.

Lei got out. "I can take it from here."

"I've got to keep an eye on you until the uniform gets here. Let's go through the house, do a quick security check."

Lei opened her mouth to object, to say that Keiki would have kept out any intruders, but someone setting the fire at their house had been able to get past the guard dog, so she shut it again and punched in the code for the gate.

Larson followed her up onto the porch as she unlocked the front door. She took her Glock out of the canvas shopping bag from Tiare, and they did a quick room-by-room check of the house.

"All clear," Larson said, holstering his weapon.

"Thanks." Lei put the Glock back into the canvas bag and set it on the gimp-legged Formica kitchen table—the house was furnished with police department castoffs. "This has to pass for both my purse and shoulder rig right now. Pretty sad."

"Fires are tough." There was an odd note in Larson's voice. "I'll be outside until the patrol unit gets here."

"Okay. Appreciate it."

"Least I can do."

She locked the front door behind him and leaned against it with a sigh. Keiki bumped her thigh with her head.

"Yeah, girl. We need a snack and a nap, don't we?" She went to the fridge. It was kept stocked with a variety of soft drinks, water, and the basics.

"How about some eggs?"

She scrambled some up, fed herself and the dog, and then went to the back bedroom and fell onto the cheerless gray spread on the bed. She was asleep in minutes.

Chapter 25

*L*ei woke to the feel of something wet on her ear.

"Keiki!"

She lashed out and Stevens yelped, rolling away. "Sorry. I thought you were the dog."

"So much for the romantic stealth approach." Stevens wore only a towel. "I guess it's not any better to sneak up on cops than on ex-soldiers."

"Come over here. Let me make it up to you."

"I do need something to distract me from that muumuu—like getting you out of it."

"Not a problem."

She shucked it off. She'd thrown the wig over the back of the retired office chair squatting in the corner of the room. "I have to admit, it's comfortable."

Stevens snorted as he dropped the towel and crawled across the bed, growling playfully. He stopped at the sight of her bruises. They hadn't improved much in the days since the hit-and-run— just picked up a few more colors.

"Are you okay?" He traced the dinner-plate-sized purple mark on her hip. "These are scary-looking."

"Kiss them and make them better."

And so he did.

Later, Lei got out of the shower and reached for her old kimono robe, realizing it was gone, ash. She'd had that robe since high school. She wondered, wrapping up in a towel, when the multitude of little losses would stop hurting. She tucked in the ends of the towel and went into the kitchen, where Stevens was contemplating the bare refrigerator.

"How about eggs for dinner?"

"Already did them."

"Toast, then. And there are some cans of chili over on the shelf."

"Sounds like my cooking night.Speaking of, how'd it go with you and Pono today? Flush out any new leads?" Lei leaned on the counter as Stevens applied the can opener to the chili can.

"Nothing new. It was a lot of rattling the same bushes. We did locate the Simmons bridegroom, though."

"Oh yeah?"

"Yeah. He tried to get on a plane out of Oahu, and the new facial recognition scanner at the airport picked him up, even under another name. So he's busted...But it's hard to make a charge stick—that property was jointly owned and they were legally married. DA's going for fraud."

"Poor lady. How's she taking it?" Lei gave a little shiver, remembering the cry of mortal pain the woman had uttered when she heard the bank account was empty. Lei never wanted to feel that kind of pain. Ever.

"Not well. Son from her first marriage came to take her home. Nice outfit, by the way." He tweaked the corner of towel sticking out under her arm.

"Why, thank you, kind sir. Terry cloth is back in among the homeless."

"It's missing something." He tapped the dip at the base of her throat. "My grandmother's ring."

"I know. I'm just sick about it. I'd taken it off to take a shower." It was bad enough that she'd taken it off at all—a little lie couldn't hurt. Her stomach clenched with guilt.

"Bull. You weren't wearing it when I saw you at the station after you went to Pauwela Lighthouse with the agents and you guys lost the girl."

"I didn't lose the girl. You saying we did something wrong?"

"Don't try to distract me. You took the ring off, all right—probably when you saw Marcella, because you didn't want to hear shit from her when she saw it. Were you ashamed of wearing it?"

"Is this an argument we're having?"

"Where in the house did you leave my grandmother's ring? Where should I look for it when the rubble's fucking cooled off?" Stevens's voice had risen, his face flushed.

"The rubble's cool, drama king. Do you want to go now and look for your precious ring? It's in the kitchen drawer—not that the kitchen exists anymore."

"In the kitchen. That doesn't sound like you were taking a shower."

"I don't see that it much matters. I took it off, and now it's burned. Along with everything else." Lei tightened the towel. Her palm actually itched with the loss of her little black stone— so much less valuable than a diamond ring, but much more valuable to her. All she had left of a precious friend, dead on the Big Island. The ring could be that meaningful to him. "I'm not hungry. I think I'll go to bed now."

"It's six thirty p.m."

"So what? We already did all there is to do in this fucking house."

She stomped down the hall, but bare feet on the tatty carpet didn't do much for sound effects. That called for a good door

slam, which she did, and felt a bit better. And when she got into
the hard bed with its cheap pilly sheets, she finally cried—cried
for her lost four-hundred-thread-count sheets on the comfortable
king-sized bed she'd hauled to three islands, her old kimono, her
little black stone, and most of all for losing the antique ring she
hadn't really wanted to wear.

"Lei." He got in bed with her, hauled her stiff body into his
arms, smoothed her ruffled, shorn head. "I'm sorry. I was an ass.
It's not your fault."

"It is. It is. It always is. There's something wrong with me.
You have to get out while you still can." Damaged goods. That's
what she was. D.G. for short, and unlucky as the day was long.
Kwon had made her that way, and she owed him for it. Payback
was coming soon.

"No. Not that old shit. Come on. This kind of thing is part of
the job. It could happen to anyone."

"But it doesn't. It happens to me, and to you because you're
with me."

"Then I'll take it. The salt with the sweet, because you're
Sweets."

"Corny." She sniffled and blew her nose on the towel—which
had come off.

"That can be my 'handle.'"

"You're such a glutton for punishment. Really. Adult child of
an alcoholic, doesn't know a lost cause when he sees it."

"I won't dignify that with an answer, since you've just been telling me what a case *you* are, and I'm not about to argue with that."
His hands had begun to wander, and they were distracting her from
her misery. His fingers trailed down her side, slid along her hip, as
he pressed a necklace of kisses around the nape of her neck.

"Corny," she said again later, breathed on a sigh.

Chapter 26

I open my wall safe. I haven't made any particular effort to hide it—just hung a luminous landscape by local Maui artist Michael Clements over it. If someone is going to the extreme of breaking into my penthouse, they're pretty determined to get something, and I don't keep much around—most of it's safely in overseas accounts. All I have in there are some new identities and ten thousand dollars in walking-around money.

I look through the identities and pick one that appeals. A red-haired beauty named Dr. Aurora Middleton, expert in identifying art forgeries. I take the passport and dossier out to peruse later. I don't often indulge in alcohol, but after the debacle at the police station and where it's headed, I need a drink and something more. A lot more. I pick up the phone.

"Celeste, send someone up. I'm thinking that guy from the Czech Republic. He needs some manners lessons. Oh, and a scotch on the rocks."

"Yes, ma'am."

I go back on the deck, lean on the scrollwork railing. Gaze out at the purple flag of Kahoolawe, a tiny island to the left, and Lanai off the coast, floating on the turquoise sea. Wind ruffles my hair, and I close my eyes.

My mole at MPD called earlier and Texeira's alive. They know there's a hit out on her. I find myself flushing with rage again, just in time for the knock on the door. I stride over and yank it open.

Celeste and Kimo push the new merchandise in. He's hand-cuffed but awkwardly carrying a tray with my drink on it. He's a tall young man, well muscled. Rumor has it he's some sort of boxer. His knuckles are scarred and his eyes dark with unbroken pride. They've dressed him in some sort of ridiculous loincloth patterned in leopard print.

I'm not amused by the lack of taste.

I take the drink and the tray, incline my head. "Thank you."

He nods. Maybe he understands that much English. I go to the wardrobe where I keep supplies and get him a plain white pair of boxers, gesture for him to take the loincloth off. He gives me a grateful look and retreats to the bathroom to change.

It'll be the last time he ever looks at me that way. I smile a bit, anticipating the shock, betrayal, and humiliation that are coming next as I mix up his drink.

* * *

Celeste and Kimo escort my new favorite back downstairs. I'm tired but mellow, sore even—he really was a boxer at one time, and I've taken some licks, but after the masseuse spends an hour rubbing gardenia-scented oil into me, I'm ready to forgive him for the defiance.

He deserves another session or two. These silly young people, thinking they're signing up for a glamorous job traveling the seas. They end up getting a lot more than they bargained for—but they do get to see the world.

Well, at least a small, locked part of it.

After the massage, I'm relaxed enough to call Healani Chang. I get one of my burner phones and punch in the number.

"What now, haole girl?" Not an auspicious beginning. Healani needs to work on her people skills.

"Trash is still not taken out."

Long pause. *"My man didn't report in, but I saw in the news the job was done."*

"That's what the police put out there, but they got out of the building somehow. And MPD knows there's a contract out, and they've got her stashed somewhere. I want to call off the hit. It's drawing too much heat."

"This isn't like canceling room service."

"It is to me."

"We'll see."

"I'll talk to House, then."

"You do that." The phone went dead. Well, with any luck the assassin would die anyway—only I hadn't been having any luck lately. I made another call.

"You're a piece of work." House's dark, raw voice is working its magic. *"Good thing I like you. I'll talk to Healani."*

"Security's also getting close to the gallery."

"What grounds?"

"The business card. One of my johns passed it on. It's thin. They've got nothing, but I'm getting itchy feet." I finger the dossier on my new identity. *"'Dr. Aurora Middleton' has a nice ring to it."*

"Hang tight. You've worked too hard building the business to chuck it at the first sign of trouble."

"What is this? A pep talk from the House?"

"I don't like the hassle of building new relationships. Our partnership is working nicely."

"Yes, it is." I savor the words. *"Very nicely. Well. I'm going to monitor the situation, but just know I'll pull the plug if I have to."*

"Will do. So—what are you wearing?"

The first time he's initiated anything. I feel a hit of heady power that goes straight to my core.

"Not much. Gardenia oil. The masseuse just left."

I hear his mind working.

"You alone?"

"Now. I broke in a new guy off the boat a little while ago, got a good workout. Czechs are sturdy stock."

"You're incorrigible. I like it. What did you do to him?"

I tell him in detail.

We end the call a long time later, and I know I want to hang on to what I have as long as I can. Texeira and that bitch lieutenant have nothing on the gallery—and if they do make me run, I'll make them pay.

I put the dossier and passport back in the safe and spin the dial.

Chapter 27

Lei and Keiki watched Stevens pull out of the driveway in the Bronco the next morning. Lei reached up to itch under the wig, back to wearing the voluminous muumuu.

"I can't last long like this, girl," Lei muttered to the dog, sitting alert beside her. "Nothing to do, nothing to wear, nowhere to go."

Keiki cocked her big square head, sympathetic, leaning heavily on her mistress. Lei looped an arm over the dog, noting the patrol car parked a block away. Surveillance detail was in place. She heard the roar of the black FBI Acura. It pulled up to the gate, and she hurried down to unlock it for Marcella.

Her friend got out of the vehicle, turning back to pull out a shopping bag.

"Where's Rogers?"

"On the job. Came to give you a sit-rep—and these." Marcella opened the back door of the vehicle and pulled out a welter of bright shopping bags. "Apparently, your lieutenant and I do have something in common—we've both been wanting to give you a makeover for ages. She helped me with the shopping."

"No way," Lei said, hefting another few shopping bags and following Marcella into the house.

"Yeah. All this is courtesy of a nonprofit, LawVictims. Special fund for replacing personal items of service people who lose it all in the line of duty."

Lei held up a tiny, bejeweled pair of kitten heels from one of the bags. "Really? This counts as replacement apparel?"

"You bet. Never know when you'll need the right pair of shoes for the job."

"I've found tennis shoes cover almost every situation."

"Shows what you know."

Over the next hour or so, Marcella made Lei try on every outfit from lingerie to evening wear.

"At least you got me a couple pairs of jeans," Lei said, wriggling into the aforementioned, ignoring the complaining of her bruises. Even the jeans were fashionable, dark with a flare at the ankle.

"You'll like this." Marcella broke out a new shoulder holster and a wallet with replacement creds, cards, and ID. "They put a rush on them down at the station."

"Oh, this feels good. I'm not Jane Doe anymore." Lei took the items and stowed them in a new leather backpack purse. "Seriously, thanks so much. This is amazing."

"I know. Got any more coffee? My caffeine level is subpar after all this shopping."

Lei filled her friend a mug of inky brew. "'Nuff of this girly stuff. What's the word on the investigation?"

"Boot up that new laptop I brought you. It's got a wireless satellite uplink. You won't ever be out of wireless range again."

Lei turned on the device and Marcella went on. "Coast guard's begun their searches. They're going top to bottom with schematics and looking for compartments. They are also checking tickets and IDs in case the sex workers are disguised as regular employees or passengers."

"Be pretty easy for them to make fake IDs," Lei said. "Especially with all the foreign countries they could be from. Aren't the cruise ships having a fit? They weren't happy with the search for a missing person we had to do."

"Most of them are offloading the guests at port and putting them in a hotel for complimentary poolside play and just screening as they get on and off the ship. Then, while the guests are off the boat, the teams search. And no, they aren't happy."

"Anything happening in Maui?"

"Not today, but tomorrow the *Rainbow Duchess* is due in port. The coast guard is standing by."

Lei's pulse sped up. Searching ships, banging down some doors would be so exciting. It was killing her to sit here idle. But—maybe this was the perfect time for that other errand. The idea took hold and galvanized her.

She hugged Marcella. "You're such a good friend. I can never thank you enough."

"Yes, you can. Let me take you away from all of this. Come to the Bureau with me."

"I'm thinking about it." Special Agent Lei Texeira. The world to police, all the assets and resources she would have access to—not to mention a whole different kind of crime to bust. "I don't know what to do about Stevens."

"He'll wait for you. Couple of years and you'll be back in Hawaii, if all goes like I hope it will."

"Let's talk after this case wraps up."

"I'm taking your word for it. Forward me your CV."

"My curriculum vitae's not much. Oh, and it was on my old laptop, and that's burned."

"It'll be a good project for you to re-create it. Okay, hon. Grow some hair and get it done."

"Will do." She hugged her friend goodbye.

Marcella always seemed to bring both sunshine and storm into a room—one of the things Lei liked about her. Once the agent had pulled out, she got online and looked up Hawaiian Airlines.

"No time like the present," Lei murmured aloud as she charged a round-trip ticket to the new charge card in the replacement wallet. Now she just had to ditch the officer on the corner.

She looked up the map and located an address a block away, far enough to be out of sight and close enough to seem within response distance, looked up the occupant and called the house.

An elderly voice answered.

"Hi, I'm calling because I think I see someone in your yard. They might be trying to break into your house. You should call the police!"

Querulous thanks, and only a few minutes later the Crown Victoria outside the house fired up and pulled away down the street.

Lei strapped on her Glock and filled her backpack with a few essentials, put on her new running shoes (size eight and her favorite brand) and put on the blond wig Marcella had included as a joke. Her tilted brown eyes looked big and mysterious under the platinum bangs—even more so when she put on wraparound silver sunglasses. She shrugged into a hot-pink jean jacket—an item of clothing she shook her head over.

She looked like an anime cartoon come to life.

Guilt was a familiar twist in Lei's gut. But she'd be back before anyone knew she was gone, with any luck, and this was something she had to do. Something she'd promised herself she'd do for years. Something she needed to do to be free, and healthy, and whole.

At the last minute, she stashed a pair of rubber gloves from under the sink in her backpack. She would need them where she was going.

Chapter 28

*L*ei got out of the taxi in front of a condo building in downtown Honolulu, just up from the Ala Wai Canal with its brackish scent of paradise gone wrong. Wash lines flapped across the balconies of the dingy Pepto-Bismol-pink complex, and tired bougainvillea in cement pots failed to brighten the entrance. She took a couple relaxation breaths on the sidewalk, gathering her resolve as she looked around.

No one was in sight on this dilapidated side street with its smell of dead end. She glanced at the sky, the same brilliant blue as Maui—but she could have been a world away with the skyscrapers of downtown crowding it out, squeezing her chest with claustrophobia. Still, she wanted to do this. Needed to do this.

Lei glanced at her reflection in the window to make sure the blonde wig was straight. She wore her sunglasses, and her mouth was painted bright red. No one would recognize Lei Texeira, tomboyish cop from Maui. She climbed the aluminum stairs on the outside of the building to the fourth floor, paused in the hallway, and glanced both ways. No one around. Sleepy afternoon sunlight slanted through bars across the concrete aisleway that fronted the building.

She put on the rubber gloves, tucking them into the sleeves of the pink jacket, pulled the Glock, and walked quick and light on the balls of her feet down to 4C. The door was peeling plywood with a peephole and a grilled iron screen, an extra layer of security she hadn't considered. The worn rubber mat spelled WELCOME.

She pushed the bell.

Approaching footsteps—someone was inside. A pause. Must be checking the peephole. The wig and sunglasses would be intriguing. Sure enough, the door opened and he stood in the doorframe, the grille casting a barred shadow over him.

"Yes?" He was smaller than she remembered, blurred around the edges, black hair gone mostly gray. An ordinary man who had done terrible things.

"Charlie Kwon?"

"Who's asking?"

"I have business to discuss. Can I come in?"

"I don't think so. What's this about?"

She brought the Glock up, aimed it at his head. "I can't miss at this range, even with the security door. Open up."

A long moment while he weighed his options; then he slowly pushed the door open. She grabbed it and whipped inside as he backed up, hands in the air. She kicked the main door shut with her heel.

"On your knees."

"I thought you had business to discuss." Kwon tried to keep his voice steady, but it wobbled into soprano.

Lei kept waiting for the heady power of having him at her mercy. It didn't come.

"On your knees!"

He obeyed, put his hands on his head. "What's this about?"

"The past catching up with you."

His angular face went even paler.

She still didn't feel what she wanted to feel. Instead she felt a creeping shame—using her weapon issued in good faith this way, using her training meant to serve and protect to subjugate.

"I've done a lot of bad things in my life. I'm sorry for whatever I did."

"Not good enough. You raped me when I was nine. You used me." The gun wobbled in her hand as she spoke. "You made me damaged goods."

"Who are you?"

"You don't know?" A hot wave of rage blew over her. "You had so many victims, you don't remember me?"

"I'm sorry! I'm sick and wrong, and I deserve to die!" His voice was anguished.

"Are you fucking kidding me? The Charlie Kwon I knew never gave a shit who he hurt. He just took what he wanted."

"I've gone to treatment, and I've changed, but I deserve to die for what I've done. So just do what you need to do."

"You pervert. Messing with little girls. Prison isn't good enough for you." It suddenly occurred to Lei that she might actually kill him. That made the gun wobble more. She'd never been less in control of it. "I came to see you and tell you…you'll never be able to touch another little girl again."

"Just do it! Do what you came to do!" Kwon swayed, his eyes ringed in white, staring into the bore of the pistol.

"I don't know what I came to do," Lei whispered. This was all so hollow. He closed his eyes, bowed his head.

On his knees before her knelt a gray-haired Chinese Filipino man in need of a shave. Smaller than average, wearing a blue T-shirt emblazoned with HALEIWA SHAVE ICE and a pair of baggy cargo shorts. His legs were startlingly white, feet bare.

He still didn't know who she was. But maybe it was the disguise.

"My name is Leilani Rosario Texeira, you sick son of a bitch."

He looked up at her blankly.

His lack of recognition was an icy blade. Her arms shook; her finger tightened—and she stepped forward and pistol-whipped him so hard he flew over sideways, sprawling in the graceless pose of the deeply unconscious. She looked down at him for a long time.

Nothing here could fix the past.

Chapter 29

*L*ei was in a taxi back to the safe house when her cell rang.
She glanced at it—Marcella. She let it ring. Blue shadows of
evening wove patterns on the road. She got out a block away from
the house, paid off the cab, and boldly walked down the sidewalk,
the sunglasses, wig, gloves, and pink jacket in her backpack. The
uniform, back in his car on the corner, did a double take as she
tapped on his window.

"I had to get some air."

"How'd you get past me?"

"You'd gone out on a call." She strode on and let herself
through the locked gate.

Keiki greeted her rapturously, whiffles of joy mixed with much
bouncing and wagging of her cropped tail. Lei knelt and hugged
her. She sat on the steps, letting the dog's rough tongue sponge
off tears she hadn't known were on her face. Finally, she patted
Keiki and led her up into the house.

She went straight into the shower, shedding her garments in
a crumpled, sweaty heap. With the water pouring hot absolu-
tion over her, she cried—cried for the child she'd been, for the

revenge she'd dreamed of for years that had been so empty. Cried for all the little girls Charlie Kwon had made damaged goods.

The water ran cold by the time she got out. She was done with Charlie Kwon. She felt empty. Empty and very, very clean.

Lei dried off, slathering scented lotion onto her body. The lurid bruises were fading at last. Marcella and the lieutenant had even remembered hair gel—and Lei worked it into her hair, the short curls coiling up instead of frizzing, thank God.

She noticed that, though her eyes in the mirror looked the same, she was different. Changed. Lighter. With the confrontation with Kwon behind her, life could only improve. Maybe it was better he'd never remembered her.

Stevens was rattling pans in the kitchen when she walked out in the new yellow terry-cloth robe she'd found among the shopping bags. She rose on tiptoes and hugged him from behind.

"Mm. You smell good." He nuzzled and snorted into her neck and turned back to chopping bell peppers. "Looks like someone went shopping—I hope it wasn't you."

"Nope. Marcella and the lieutenant bought all this stuff for us—some fund for officers who lose their homes in the line of duty."

"Wow. That's above and beyond—and I'm trying to wrap my head around Marcella and the Steel Butterfly cruising the aisles together. Terrifying."

"I'm sure it was. But they got good stuff. Seemed to want to do a makeover on me. The clothes aren't what I usually wear."

"Wonder what horror they bought me. Probably polyester pants and golf shirts."

"Anything breaking on the case?" Lei asked. "I'm planning to go back into the station tomorrow, now that I'm feeling fine and I've got some new clothes."

"Yeah. I was meaning to tell you. The Thai girl turned back up. She's down at the station and she's going to be spending the night with us, since this is the safe house. The Feds are bringing her here to interview her."

"You should have called me!"

"I did, but your cell was off. Anyway, I wanted you to get some more rest."

Lei felt a stab of guilt—she'd hardly been resting. "Well, at least we'll get to listen in on the FBI interview. How'd you find her?"

"She was hitchhiking, had her thumb out when a patrol car was passing and they picked her up. The BOLO worked, for once."

"She was probably terrified."

"She should have stayed where we left her." Stevens dished up the food, a tasty stir-fry. He'd kill her if he knew she'd gone to see Kwon. Guilt, her familiar, twisted her guts. She wished she could tell him—but he'd be so angry at the danger she had put herself in. Sometimes she just had to do what she had to do, and he'd never totally understand that.

After dinner they went into the bedroom and unpacked the rest of the shopping bags. The choices for Stevens were what he usually wore—jeans and khaki pants with subdued aloha shirts, the Hawaii business-casual uniform. Stevens put the last of his new socks away as Keiki barked, letting them know someone was in the driveway.

The black Acura SUV Marcella drove had pulled up. The agent and her partner escorted Anchara up to the locked gate. Lei punched in the code and made Keiki sit and greet the visitors politely.

The girl looked exhausted and unkempt; skeins of long black hair tangled down her back, and her cheekbones were sharp and her eyes sunken. She shrank back from the Rottweiler.

"Can I make you something to eat?" Stevens took Anchara's arm and walked her past Lei and the dog and into the house.

"How's it going?" Lei asked her friend. Marcella looked tired, shadows under her eyes and a droop to her mouth, lush hair straggling out of its ponytail.

"Putting together some good connects on the House. We think his organization is spread out across the islands and run by substations. Could be a thread tying him to your old friends the Changs on the Big Island—we're tracking the network through some CIs we've been developing."

"Now, that would be sweet." Lei followed Marcella, as Rogers, carrying a duffel of recording equipment, walked up the steps into the house. "Why did you want to interview her here?"

"She's close to collapsing. Thought the homey atmosphere might help," Rogers said over his shoulder.

The girl was already seated at the little Formica table, and Stevens had filled a plate with more of the stir-fry, setting it in front of her.

"Smells good in here," Rogers said. "Got enough for a couple more plates?"

"Give me a few more minutes and I'll whip up some more."

"Lei's out of the kitchen. Good choice," Marcella said as she and Rogers set up their equipment in the living room area.

"I can chop vegetables," Lei grumbled, going to the refrigerator to take out the bags of stir-fry ingredients.

"That's all I'll trust her with," Stevens said, turning up the flame under the frying pan as he tossed in more chicken strips.

In the midst of this swirl of activity, Anchara sat, eating efficiently, her head bent. Tangles of long hair shielded her face from view. Lei was reminded of the feral cats that were a part of life on Maui—thin, bedraggled, and blazing with intention to live. She'd seen them eating the food local residents brought to the parks with the same focus and speed. Stevens filled her plate a second time with the last of his and Lei's meal. A slender brown hand picked up the glass of water Stevens had brought her, and the girl drank it down.

Lei finished chopping more bell peppers, celery, and onions, and Stevens added them to the pan. Marcella came in and sat beside Anchara. "Nice place."

"No, it isn't. But it gets the job done." Stevens was generating a lot of good smells and sizzling sounds. "Why don't you get started. This will be ready when the interview's over."

"Okay. Anchara, do you mind coming in and sitting on the couch, where we can record you?" Rogers leaned on one of the kitchen chairs, muscular shoulders bunching as he grasped the chair back. His blue eyes were kind. "We'd like to get it over with so you can take a shower and rest."

Anchara nodded. She ghosted past them with the silent, graceful way of moving she had, and sat on one end of the old tweed couch.

Chapter 30

Marcella and Rogers seated themselves, Rogers in the armchair across from Anchara and the battered coffee table and Marcella on the other end of the couch. Lei brought kitchen chairs and set them back from the seating area while Stevens turned off the stove after giving the savory-smelling meal one last stir and covering it with a lid.

Marcella turned on the video recorder set on a tripod beside her and recited the date and time and the names and positions of all parties present.

"State your full name for the record, please."

"Anchara Mookjai."

"Your age and address?"

"I am twenty-three. My address is village outside of Bangkok. It not important."

"How did you come to the United States, Anchara?"

"I came on cruise ship. They put up signs asking for waitress. I go because. . ." She took a deep breath, sighed it out. "My husband. He beat me."

Lei took this in. Anchara was older than she looked, which

was no more than twelve. She was curled up with her knees under her chin. She'd wrapped tawny arms around them, and her hair spread over her like a cloak.

"What happened next?"

"I go on board and apply. They say papers not important because we in international waters. I think it strange, but I go because I want to get away. Then we all go below in many beds in one room, and they lock us in." She pushed the skeins of hair behind her ears. "I know something is wrong then."

"How many other women were there?"

"There are ten in each room. The beds, they—how you say?" She made a gesture with her hands. "They on top each other."

"Bunk beds. You speak English well. How did you learn?"

"I always want to come to United States. I am a teacher in Thailand; I study English for when I hope to come."

"So then what happened?"

"We are cleaned up. They make us exercise in other room with machines. The food good. I think it not so bad; then we arrive in port. We get in dresses, and they drive us to hotel. Then I know it not so good." She closed those big, expressive eyes for a long moment. "I read little bit, other languages. I see the signs out the window of van. That first port, Singapore. I know what we are now. Whores."

Lei felt her heart constrict, and she had to speak up. "Not whores. Slaves. You were taken. You were forced."

Marcella shot her a look for interrupting the flow. "What was the name of your ship?"

"We changed ships two times." She told the names, neither of which were American. "Then we get on *Rainbow Duchess*. We go around through Hawaii. Now I trying to escape because I'm in America."

"How long did this go on?"

"I think almost one year before Vixen help me escape."

"How did you get away?"

"Vixen. She from Albania. She never talk much, she never be friends, but we both trying harder than other girls to get away. She hardly speak English, but we communicate how we can. We locked in...what you call...storage room in this island when we come after we...work." Anchara's eyes had become wide, the pupils dilated as she tried to find words in a foreign language and remember traumatic events at the same time.

"Kimo and Celeste, they move us and watch us in this port. The guard, Kimo, he pick us sometimes after we done. He like her; he take her outside. She do something for him. Then she hit him and take the key. She let us all out." Anchara sighed a shuddering breath. "Most girls, they cry; they not want to leave. They scared of being beaten, no English. But we go." She wound to a halt.

"Then what happened?" Gentle prompt from Rogers this time.

"We run. They chasing us in car. They catch Vixen. But I small, and I crawl between fence they can't follow and hide until next day. Then I go along road, looking for where people hide. I find the camp with Ramona." She closed her eyes again. "I think I know they kill Vixen because she make trouble. She never stop trying to get away."

"Did you ever hear any other names here or on the ship?"

"They not talk to us. But I know English, and I listening. I know who in charge of Celeste and Kimo—the boss named Kennedy."

Lei stiffened to attention, and so did the agents. "How did you hear this?"

"They talking about her. She come look at us when we first get in. She tell them how to make us pretty. They scared of her. Sometimes she take one of the men and she beat him."

"Men? Where were they kept?"

"Only a few of them. They kept in different room in storage and on ship. They treated same as us. Only Ms. Kennedy, she like to beat them, do things to them."

Lei suppressed the need to get up and pace—the description of the sadistic madam was getting to her. She pictured the arctic-blue eyes, the fury the woman had barely kept in check in the interview room.

"Did you ever hear any other names? Anything that would help us find them?"

"Ms. Kennedy, she have boss, too. He called the House."

Marcella pounced. "How did you hear this? What was the situation?"

"Celeste and Kimo, they talking. They did the…what you call? Doctoring with the men when they come back from her. They working on this boy. He only a boy, he crying, and he all torn up outside our door in the warehouse. They grumbling. They say maybe they call the House and tell him she damaging the merchandise." The last words had a memorized quality. Lei could imagine Anchara latching on to this nugget of potentially useful information and committing it to memory.

They all vibrated with attention—this was big, the first solid confirmation there was a connection between Magda Kennedy, the House, and the cruise ships. "Did you ever hear that name mentioned again?"

"Yes. About the safe."

"The safe?"

"In the room on the ship—a big black safe. When we come into port in Honolulu, they make us go to the workout room and they move things in and out the safe. I always trying to see what is inside. I pretend to go back and get something. I see an Asian man, he putting money and bags inside the safe. He yell at me and I run out." She closed her eyes as if remembering. "I keep watching. I try to see. And I hear them one day talking about the

House. It his money going in the safe, his drugs in those bags. Then it come out at the ports—but not Maui."

Magda Kennedy must be laundering the money for him, Lei thought. An art gallery would be a great venue for that.

"What about the other islands?" Marcella asked.

"It all come into safe from Honolulu and go back out to Kaua`i, Big Island. Then money go in from other islands, I think from the drugs. But not go in from here. Only go out to Maui."

Marcella and Rogers exchanged a look, and Lei considered— this accounted for the drugs and prostitution money, but what about the purported guns?

"Did you ever see anything else being loaded on the ship?" Rogers asked.

"No. I always watching, but the room we in have no windows."

"How did they get you on and off the ship?" Marcella picked up the thread.

"Late at night we go off the cargo exit. We get in van. We go to the place they keep us. There is one for us on each island." Anchara lay her head down on top of her knees. "I tired. I can shower now?"

"Yes. Thank you, Anchara. You've been amazing." Marcella smiled her luminous smile. "We'll need to talk with you more, but that's great for now. Get clean and get some rest." The young woman nodded, unwound from the couch, and padded off to the bathroom. A few minutes later, they heard the rush of the shower.

"Think that stir-fry's past ready," Stevens said, getting up to return to the kitchen. "Wow, is all I can say." He scooped rice out of the cooker and layered stir-fry over it.

"Hot damn, that girl's going to be gold on the stand," Rogers said, carrying the chairs back into the kitchen and sitting at the table.

"Yeah, she's a gold mine, all right. More important than ever that we keep her safe and sound. I'm still worried—we don't have anything on the guns, and we don't have anything hard. We can't make a case this big on the word of an illegal immigrant hooker—sorry, Lei. Human trafficking victim." Marcella accepted her plate of stir-fry and rice from Stevens and sat down beside Rogers. Lei brought them some Aloha Shoyu and glasses of water and sat down with them.

"We've got solid grounds to search the *Rainbow Duchess*, though. And we've got Anchara and the key to the warehouse, if we can find it. It must be somewhere not too far from the encampment on the bluff," Rogers said between bites of stir-fry.

"Yeah. I'll call the coast guard again with this latest about the safe and confirmation that the *Duchess* is carrying human cargo. We should do a joint raid on the *Duchess* as soon as it gets into port, before they have a chance to move anything." Marcella, as efficient an eater as Anchara, shoveled up the last bite of her stir-fry. "Stevens, you're welcome to join us."

"Hey, what about me?" Lei exclaimed.

"House arrest. You still have a hit out on you, and we need you to keep an eye on Anchara. Can't have her giving us the slip at this stage."

Lei sulked as she followed the agents out. Marcella was already working her cell phone. She locked the gate as the Acura pulled away, high beams slicing through the velvety plumeria-scented dark unique to Hawaii. She went into the light of the kitchen as Stevens put the leftovers away.

Lei could hear the shower still running. Anchara must be a prune by now, but Lei knew how good a hot shower could feel.

"Poor kid. She looked really wiped out." Stevens gestured toward the bathroom.

"Me too." Lei gave a jaw-cracking yawn. The confrontation

with Kwon was catching up with her. She went to the cabinet and took out sheets, heading for the second bedroom. A plastic grocery bag with the girl's meager belongings had been placed inside the door.

Lei resisted the urge rifle through it and made up the mattress. She was fluffing the flat polyester pillow when Anchara appeared, a towel around her midsection and another one wrapped into a turban on her head. With the grime off her face, Lei could see the beauty that had made the girl a victim of human trafficking— long-lashed doe eyes, a rounded little nose, full, cushiony mouth. Her skin, the warm gold of honey, was marked only by the shadows cast by a tracery of pleasing bones.

Anchara unwound the towel, draping it carefully over a chair, and used her fingers to comb out waist-length hair.

"Do you have anything clean to put on?" Lei asked.

Anchara shook her head.

"I've got some new clothes—I might have something that fits you." Lei brushed past and went into the master bedroom, pulling out a set of sweats and bikini underwear that looked small enough for the petite woman to wear. She handed the bundle of clothing to Anchara and went on into the kitchen. They turned on the TV and eventually Anchara returned. Lei gestured to the couch beside her.

"Come, join us."

The girl obeyed with obvious reluctance, curling up in a ball with one of the cushions against her chest, combing her hair with her fingers again.

"Where'd you go after Ramona's campsite?" Lei asked.

A shrug of the skinny shoulders. "I ran because someone was coming for me. I hid and camped wherever."

"Well, we're glad you're here. We'll keep you safe until we can close the door on these people."

"Are you sending me back to Thailand?"

"I don't know." Stevens answered that one. "Do you want to go?"

"No. I don't want to go back."

"We'll talk to the district attorney and see what he says. You help us bring in this case, we're going to owe you something, that's for sure."

Anchara nodded, lashes drooping in dark fans against her cheek.

"Why don't you get some rest?" Lei asked. The woman nodded again and trailed off to bed. Lei indulged in another yawn. "I think I'll go to bed early, too."

"Yeah. I imagine you're tired from wherever you went today."

Lei sat upright, a jolt of adrenaline hitting her like a slap. "What do you mean?"

"You know what I mean." She glanced over at his narrowed blue eyes.

He was fishing. He knew she'd left the house, probably heard it from the uniform watching them—but he couldn't know where she'd gone. Still, she hated lying to him.

She took a breath. Said it. "I went to Oahu and saw Kwon."

"What the hell!" He stood, looming over her, hands on hips. "You never cease to amaze me."

"I told you I was going to see him. You'll be happy to know I left him alive, just gave him a little love tap upside the head with my gun." Her stomach roiled at the memory—there was much she couldn't put into words about seeing Kwon again.

"Thank God. Jesus. And I mean that like I'm praying."

Lei got up and took the recently restocked emergency vodka bottle out of the freezer, splashed a portion into two glasses, handed Stevens one. "Medicinal purposes." She tipped her head back and tossed the shot, burning and painful, down her throat. "I'm not losing one more day of my life over him."

"I should have known you'd find a way to go over there. It's so dangerous, with whoever has a hit out on us still out there, and you. . ." Stevens drank the shot, set the glass down on the coffee table with a thump. He pushed his hands through his hair, leaving tufts of unruly distress. "I want to put you over my knee, dammit."

"You can try."

"I'm going to. It's a promise, when we're not sharing close quarters with a traumatized sex slave."

"Don't be mad. I needed to see him, it's over, and I'm fine. Unfortunately, he's fine too, but I'll let someone else deal with him. My father said these guys tend not to live long, either in the joint or once they get out."

"Sounds like a threat. Don't let Wayne do anything stupid either—you both have a lot to lose."

"Don't worry about that—my dad's favorite saying is from the Bible—'Do not take revenge. I will repay, says the Lord.'"

"What did Kwon say to you?"

"Begged me to kill him, actually. Said he deserved it."

"Doesn't sound like the Kwon you told me about." Stevens was pacing.

"Said he was rehabilitated, but that he still deserved it. I was never going to kill him, just scare him straight—but the gun got pretty wobbly there for a minute." The bomb of warmth from the drink loosened the tightness of her fingers around the glass, but she shuddered, remembering.

"Jesus, Lei." He ran his hands through his hair again. "That's the last thing we'd need—you getting investigated for murder."

"You're freaking out for no reason. I had to see him, I did, and now it's done."

"Don't ever fucking ask me to cover for you."

"You don't need to say that to me. I know what the law means to you—I just don't think it always works like it should. Kwon out in five years because of crowding is one of those times. But like I keep telling you, nothing happened."

He came to a stop by the sink, staring out into the darkness. Turned to face her, his long, muscled arms braced wide on the edge of the counter. "Don't do this shit to me, Lei. You're killing me."

She walked toward him, ran her hands up those arms, pulled his head down to her, whispered into his ear. "I'm sorry. That's the last thing I want to do. I love you."

He pulled her into his arms. It wasn't gentle, and her bruises protested. She ignored them.

"You're a piece of work, Lei," he whispered, as he took all she offered and more, drawing her up against himself. She gave a little hop, ignoring a twinge from her ribs, and wrapped her legs around his waist. He boosted her up against his hard crotch, holding her ass as he walked them down the hall.

"I told you. I warned you," she said. "I don't want to break your heart."

"You already did."

Then there were no more words.

Chapter 31

*L*ei woke to the combined buzzing and toning of both of their new cell phones. Lei got hold of hers first. Lieutenant Omura's voice was clipped with suppressed excitement.

"Coast guard turned up a hidden room on the *Rainbow Duchess* in Kahului Harbor. Get down there and represent ASAP. Wear a wig and a vest."

"On it." Lei hauled on her discarded jeans from the night before as she closed the phone. So much for Marcella's order to stay home. Stevens was doing the same on the other side of the bed and looked over at her. "What're you doing?"

"Lieutenant called me in. You'll just have to make sure I don't get shot."

"So much for laying low."

"Thank God. I would hate to miss this." Lei loaded her Glock into the new holster and clipped a shiny new badge onto a belt she still hadn't removed a price tag from. She hauled on the red wig from the day before, covering it with an MPD ball cap.

Anchara stuck her head out of her bedroom as they hurried down the hall.

"Go back to sleep," Lei said. "Police business. An officer is still watching the house."

The girl nodded and withdrew.

They trotted down to the Bronco, and Stevens fired it up. Lei made sure the gate was locked and shot a salute to the uniform watching the house. They pulled out in full lights-and-sirens glory, and Lei Velcroed herself into an extra vest.

White-knuckled minutes later, they pulled up at the harbor. The cruise ship loomed in the early dawn, lights twinkling from stem to stern, a floating city. Marcella and Rogers were conferring on the dock with several uniformed coast guard officers and the captain of the ship. The captain, resplendent in gold-braided white, gestured wildly as the two of them arrived at a run.

"I had no knowledge of this! I'm telling you, I never would have permitted such a travesty on my ship!"

Marcella, hair tumbled down her back and shirt buttoned askew under a bulletproof FBI vest, spotted them. "Lei, what are you doing here?"

"Omura sent me."

Stevens finished securing his vest. "We couldn't keep her back anyway."

Marcella rolled her eyes and jerked her head toward the gangplank. "Let's go take a look." She led Stevens and Lei up the steep ramp onto the ship and down halls dimly lit, inner doors closed as passengers slept on in blissful ignorance.

Lei poked her from behind. "Do something about your hair."

"You're one to talk." But Marcella bundled the fall of curls into a knot as they strode down the hall. "Crack-of-dawn raid, and I had trouble sleeping last night."

Instead of down into the bowels of the ship as Lei had expected, they entered the grand foyer, ascending a curving staircase past glowing blown-glass Chihuly chandeliers to a second story. Marcella led them down a wide hallway to a polished wood door crowned by a beveled-glass insert. "There's a service elevator at the end of the hall they must have used to bring the girls on and off the ship."

Two uniformed coast guard officers with rifles stood aside as she opened the door.

Lei stepped inside and drew her breath in sharply. The stateroom was bare except for a double row of five bunk beds. A cluster of young women dressed in short white satin robes huddled in a corner.

Against one wall was a handsome carved armoire. Without a word, Marcella led the way to the armoire and threw it open. A big safe squatted inside, its matte black surface seeming to absorb all the light in the room.

"Anybody able to get this open?" The safe looked serious to Lei.

"Not so far."

"Someone on the way?"

"Yes. Homeland Security's got a safecracker deployed."

"So what was the MO here?"

"Hide in plain sight," said Marcella. "A lot of people had to be involved to keep this room secret. Now that you're here, the Maui Police Department can take the women into custody for interviews."

Stevens was already working his cell phone, getting transport arranged.

"We're taking the captain in for interviewing, but he's adamant he didn't know about the smuggling," Marcella said. "We've got the ship on lockdown; nobody leaves until we interview all the crew."

"Sounds like you have things under control," said a new voice. Lei turned to see Lieutenant Omura, looking sharp even at five a.m., enter with Pono and Jed Larson from Kahului Station. "Nice work."

"Coast guard found the room and secured the scene before they called us," Marcella said. "We're just coordinating agencies and looking for connections to the House."

Lei approached the group of women huddled in the corner. "Anyone here speak English?"

In ports on all the Hawaiian Islands, Duchess cruise ships were boarded by coast guard troops and searched stem to stern as the sun broke over the shoulder of Haleakala on Maui. Marcella, Rogers, the coast guard captain, and several Homeland Security agents continued interviewing the crew on board. Lei stood by the Bronco as Pono, Larson, and a couple of uniforms helped escort the women from the stateroom onto a transport bus going to Kahului Station. An Immigration and Naturalization official took down each name as they climbed onto the bus.

Lei's stomach clenched at the sight.

Many were in tears, dreams of a glamorous cruise ship job having ended in sex slavery, with deportation imminent. At least the familiarity of their home countries would be returned to them even if their innocence was lost.

Her eyes wandered down the dock—and she spotted movement in the shadows of the bow of the ship. A giant chain anchored the cruise liner to the rubber-padded dock, and a shadow moved precariously down it.

Someone was escaping.

Chapter 32

Stop! Police!" Lei bellowed. A man dropped off the giant anchor chain and glanced back. Ignoring lingering tightness from her injuries, Lei pushed off from the Bronco and sprinted down the dock, dodging vehicles, boxes, and piles of rope. The man broke into a run, tearing down the dock.

"Stop! Police!" This was that moment she'd trained for, bruises or not. She poured on more speed and cleared a low stanchion like a hurdler, using the extra momentum to hit the fleeing man in the back with an extended elbow. He flew forward and provided with her a nice landing pad. She straddled him, hauling his arms behind his back to cuff them.

He was still trying to drag in some air from having the breath knocked out of him as she sat back on her haunches. Adrenaline had obliterated the voice of her bruises, but they threatened a dull roar in the future from all of this activity. Pono jogged up from where he'd been helping load the women onto the bus.

"Who's this?"

"Dunno, but he was sneaking off the ship."

A compact square of a man, dressed in nondescript sweats

and running shoes, he had the fresh-scrubbed look of a midlevel executive. His lips folded into a hard line now that he'd got some oxygen back in his lungs.

Larson had joined them, and he hauled the man up by an armpit. "C'mon down to the station, buddy, and tell us why you were taking the rat's way off the ship."

Lei followed them and dug her cell phone out of her pocket, where it was none the worse for wear. She pushed down the speed-dial button for Stevens.

"Where are you?" His voice was brusque.

"I called to ask you the same thing. I caught someone getting off the ship, and I want to interview him. Can you get another ride down to the station?"

"Never mind that. I'm on my way."

Lei shut the phone and put it back.

Larson hauled her prisoner toward the transport bus, and she stopped him with a hand. "Put a guard on the anchor chain, and I'll take him in."

She led the man to the Bronco and put him in the backseat, then got in front. Stevens appeared at a run and jumped into the passenger side. Larson stood by the transport bus, frowning as they pulled away.

Lei decided to let Marcella know after she'd had a crack at the guy—after all, finders keepers.

* * *

My latest burner rings. It's an unknown number. Maybe it's the House. My heart picks up speed.

"Hello?"

"Didn't think you'd pick up." My MPD mole. Today his voice has got a touch of steel. Guy's getting an attitude.

"Didn't think I'd hear from you again." I match the ice in his voice.

"Did you send out that dirt to my wife? 'Cause if you did, I'm hanging up and you won't get this tip."

I sit up straighter in my chair at the gallery office. It's early to be behind my desk, but I get some of my best work done before the doors open and the phone begins ringing.

"As a matter of fact, I haven't gotten around to it."

"Good. For you. Because I thought I'd let you know busts are going down on all the Duchess cruise ships. We've got the women and whatever's in the safe on the ship in Kahului Harbor."

My heart begins doing heavy pounding thuds. I touch my throat, and it helps keep my voice steady when I speak. "So what? There's no connection to me."

"That's not all. They found the Thai girl. Lei Texeira has her."

Lei Texeira. A thorn in my side, if there ever was one.

"Where do they have her?"

"Safe house. My job is done. Send the usual to my account, but this is my last job for you—and, I suspect, your last job, too."

The line went dead.

Screw him. I'm not paying him one more dime, and for good measure, I take the envelope with the photos in it, preaddressed and stamped, out of a locked drawer and put it in my Out box. My secretary will post it when she comes in. That parting gesture helps with the sting of what I have to do next.

I take a deep breath, let it out on a whoosh, and activate the encryption program that I embedded months ago on the gallery's computers, all networked together. I can retrieve the information remotely, but it will take months for anyone else to do so. The computer sighs into permanent silence as I spring up and hurry to the elevator.

I have to warn the House. I make the call on my burner as I ride up to my penthouse for the last time.

"Yeah?"

"House, it's me. We're blown."

"I already heard. Pull out."

"I'm on it." I get out of the elevator and hurry inside to the wall safe, setting the beautiful Clements painting aside with a little inward sigh of regret. Oh well. I can buy others. "You bailing?"

"They've confiscated our stash on at least three ships now, and it's going to lead back to my operation. I've had a good run, but it's time to execute my retirement plan."

"Want to meet up?"

The words trip off my tongue before I can stop them. I take the passport out of the safe along with my Sig and the bundled ten thousand dollars. I hold my breath and find myself hugging the gun and the cash. His response means more to me than I could have imagined, and my stomach knots. Damn, I should have let him take the lead—but that's never been my style.

A long pause.

"Where are you going?" A tentative note in his dark voice. I don't remember ever hearing it before.

"Moving around for a while. I'll decide on the way. Dr. Aurora Middleton, art forgery expert, is doing some international traveling."

"Get going, then. I'll find you." He clicks off.

I feel something hot and hungry shoot through me. He's going to find me. We'll finally meet—and now I can't wait to get on the road.

I toss the safe's contents into a capacious Coach bag and strip out of my signature white, putting on chinos and a lavender polo shirt. Dr. Aurora Middleton is conservative, even on vacation. I go into the bathroom and get out the haircutting kit I keep handy. With a few quick, brutal snips, my long hair falls into the toilet, leaving a choppy bob that's pretty fashionable, if I do say so myself—I've always had more than a few fall-back skills, and haircutting is one of them.

I put on a ball cap with PEBBLE BEACH on the front and a pair of plain flat white sandals and then head out.

I have only one more thing to do before I say goodbye to this chapter of my life.

It's time to get my hands dirty again.

Chapter 33

Lei clipped the prisoner's cuffs to a metal ring on the aged steel table in the interview room at Haiku Station. The room was small, lined with nailed-on foam waffle insulation. A rectangular mirrored viewing window punctuated the wall, and three molded plastic chairs completed the decor of the claustrophobic space. Lei switched on the hidden video camera via its switch by the door. She knew the lens was aimed at the pale, sweating face of the ship's escapee.

Stevens sat down across from the man, giving his best grin and blue-eyed twinkle.

"Great way to start the day, right? What's your name?"

"Rodney Farrell. I didn't do anything."

Lei glanced to the window, where Pono sat on the other side at a counter with a phone and computer. He'd run Farrell's name for any priors.

"If you didn't do anything, Rodney, why did you climb down the anchor chain like a fucking monkey? And don't tell me it was for the exercise." She gave a contemptuous glance at his broad midsection.

"I—owe money for a gambling debt," Farrell stuttered.

"Well, we're doing a completely unrelated investigation," Stevens said. "You've got nothing to worry about."

"Yeah, well, you don't know who I owe money to," Farrell said. "I didn't want to get caught up in something. I took the chance to get out."

"What's your role on the ship?" Stevens asked. Start off slow, Lei thought. Lull him into complacency. She was having trouble with that and got up to pace.

"I'm the purser. I keep track of all the guests' bills, accounts, and activities." With that job, he'd definitely know whatever was going on. Lei swiveled, paced past him. Stevens went on.

"Do you know anything about some girls being kept in a stateroom on A-Deck?"

"What do you mean?" Beads of sweat popped out on Farrell's forehead; he tried to swipe them away and the cuffs clashed.

"Bullshit. The purser knows everything that goes on." Lei leaned in to his face. "Purser takes care of all the accounts, right? I bet you kept track of the girls' fucking billing—and in this case, I mean that literally. The guy you owe money to happen to be the House?" Lei pressed in.

Farrell's face whitened further. "Holy shit," he whispered. "I'm not saying another word. I want a lawyer."

Pay dirt. Lei made another gesture to the observation window. "My associate is going to call one for you unless you have someone local. Do you have your own lawyer?"

"No."

"Get the public defender," she said to the window. She turned back. "Too bad it's the weekend. This could take a while. Mind if we go on?"

She nodded her head as she said this, and like an automaton, he imitated her.

Stevens picked up the thread. "Good. You're small potatoes

in all this, and if we get the House, your gambling debt would be canceled as a bonus. So what can you tell us about his operation?"

"I want my lawyer," Farrell said. His nostrils flared, a rabbit smelling wolves.

"The lawyer's on his way. Now talk."

"What can you give me? Witness protection? A plea bargain? I'm not doing time—that guy has a long arm."

"Tell us what you know, and I'll tell you if it's worth anything," Lei countered.

Stevens cut in. "We know you are taking your life in your hands with a character like the House. We'll do all we can."

"Well." Farrell sat back. "I'm counting on that agreement."

"You'll have it," Stevens said, blue eyes sincere. Lei tapped her toe, keeping up the pressure. "Assuming you have something worth trading for."

"The girls were kept on the A-Deck, nice accommodations. We'd get texts from the madam on each island for their bookings when we got into port."

He described a well-organized operation. The girls were taken out in a van to various hotels for parties and service when in port, and kept in a warehouse on each island. This confirmed Anchara's story. Farrell had overseen the overall operation and coordinated the girls' schedules.

"They were treated well," he said virtuously. "I had the medic up to check them out whenever they got back, and they had cable TV and healthy food. We even had them work out in the gym every day."

"They were sex slaves!" Lei burst out. "They thought they were getting jobs on the cruise ships to see the world. Instead, they spent their lives locked in a room and on their backs for variety!"

Farrell recoiled, covered his face with his hands. "I never

would have agreed, but I owe the House money, and he'll take it out of me however he can!"

Stevens shot Lei a repressive look and leaned forward sympathetically. "Detective Texeira's taking this a little seriously. We both know those girls never had much of a future, and you did what you could for them. So who was the Maui connection when they went out?"

"I only ever saw the handlers, Celeste and Kimo. But sometimes the guys came back in bad shape. Kimo said the Maui madam, Magda, liked to work them out. She had a bondage thing." Farrell's eyes skittered around as he blinked rapidly.

"Magda? Magda Kennedy?"

"I never got a last name."

Lei halted her pacing. "So we didn't find everyone, since we only got the women."

She made a phone gesture at the window for Pono to call Marcella and make sure the male prisoners were found.

"So what about the safe?" Stevens asked. "What are we going to find in there?"

"The House used it to launder money. He'd send a lot over here from Oahu. The madam here did something with it. All I know is, the Oahu guy would bring it on and Kimo would take it out in boxes. That safe is pretty tough." He'd obviously checked it out to see if it could be broken into. "I think Magda, whoever she is, cleaned the money for him. He didn't have that going on the other islands. I know, because even though we ran the whores in all the ports, we only moved the money from Oahu to Maui."

The art world was a perfect place to launder money. All those expensive paintings and sculptures that could be bought and sold—not to mention Magda Kennedy's connection to the real estate sector. Perhaps it was the House's money that was powering Wylie Construction even in the current economic downturn.

Pono's broad brown face appeared in the little mesh window in the door. He was holding up a cell phone.

Lei opened the door, and he handed it to her.

"Texeira. What the hell are you doing?" Marcella didn't sound happy.

"Just a little interview of the ship's purser. Caught the rat climbing off the ship. I'm recording the interview, but you'd better get here fast because he's asked for his lawyer."

"Son of a bitch!" Marcella exclaimed. "Why didn't you tell me you caught someone?"

"Why should you have all the fun? Besides, finders keepers. He's got a lot to say. He's a credible witness, and he's making our case against both that snooty bitch Magda Kennedy and the House. Now we'll have two witnesses, with the Thai girl." Lei couldn't help the satisfaction that had crept into her voice.

"He got a name for the House? 'Cause it's hard to generate a federal arrest warrant without a name."

"Let me get back in there and see. Did you get the message about the men?"

"Yeah, we already found them at the bottom of the ship behind a false wall. They had a tanning bed, a Bowflex, and a lot of pipes in the ceiling. They're on their way to the station."

"Do they know anything?"

"Most of the poor dudes can't even speak English. Nothing good from them so far. Anyway, I'm on my way." Marcella hung up.

Lei shut the phone and handed it back to Pono. "What's up with the public defender?"

"It's Fujimoto on call. He wasn't happy getting out here on the weekend, but he's on his way."

"Crap. Okay."

Lei went back in. Sat down. Gave Farrell her best narrow-eyed stare.

"Got a name for the House?"

"I want something in writing on my witness protection and immunity deal before I tell you anything more." Farrell seemed to have used the break to find his backbone, and try as she might, Lei couldn't get him to budge.

Public defender Al Fujimoto, Lieutenant Omura, Marcella, and Rogers all arrived, all black suits and badges, and relegated Lei and Stevens to the peanut gallery with Pono. Omura had the DA on the line and an immunity agreement and protection order faxed over in less time than Lei had ever seen. Marcella slapped the document down in front of the purser, who'd begun licking his lips compulsively, a nervous tic.

"We've got you what you want. Now give us what we want."

"I've only ever heard him called the House, but I know his money guy on Oahu. He's an accountant in Honolulu, and his name's Ken Taketa. He must know everything about the House's operation. He brings the cash on board and loads it in the safe for the delivery to Maui."

He went on to describe in detail all he'd already given Lei and Stevens. Marcella came out of the interview with a signed statement.

"I forgive you for cutting me out on this witness, but we're even from that Kaua`i thing, now and forever." Marcella gave Lei a hug.

"Okay. That Kaua`i one stung, you know—you took my intel and tried to make my bust without me. I just had a crack at a witness first."

"You know it would be different if you joined me at the Bureau. I'm on the next flight to Oahu. I've already alerted HPD to send a unit to pick up Taketa. I'll be in touch."

"Good working with you again," Lei said, squeezing her friend back. Marcella socked her in the arm and glanced over at Stevens, who was intently watching the wrap-up in the interview room.

"Time's a-wasting," Marcella stage-whispered. "Quantico wants you."

"Quit bugging me. I'll call you."

Rogers gestured, and Marcella set off after him at a jog—they had a plane and a crime lord to catch.

Omura appeared in the doorway of the observation booth. "Go get Magda Kennedy."

"Yes!" Lei said, breaking into a grin echoed by Omura. Lei, Stevens, and Pono headed out at a jog.

Chapter 34

*I*n no time, they were on the road to Lahaina, driving fast, cop lights on as the purple truck followed Lei's Tacoma—singed in the fire but still functional. Pono radioed ahead to have a patrol unit watch the gallery since the drive was over an hour. They careened along the swooping curves of the Pali above the crystalline ocean.

Just to be back in her truck, something familiar and totally hers, felt great to Lei, especially with her adrenaline up to catch the Kennedy woman. She glanced over at Stevens and matched his grin. The two-lane road cleared before the siren, people pulling off on the shoulders, and she put the pedal down just to remember how fast her truck would go.

She glanced in her rearview mirror. Pono's truck was hard-pressed to follow, so she eased up on the gas. They eventually pulled up in front of the Pacific Treasures Gallery, double-parking against the busy sidewalk behind the patrol unit, who reported no movement.

Lei jumped out, instinctively touching her gun, making sure her badge was in plain sight and her cuffs tucked into her back pocket. Pono slammed the door of his vehicle and joined them on the sidewalk. They strode to the doors, which slid open with a whisper and a draft of cool air-conditioning.

Lei hurried past the Lucite sculpture that had distracted her last time, keeping her eyes on the woman across the gallery, a tall, bottled blonde in a white Grecian-styled gown.

"Where's Magda Kennedy?"

"Who may I say is asking?"

"Maui Police Department." Lei tapped the badge on her belt, and Pono and Stevens held theirs up.

"I'll see if she has time to speak to you."

"We'll show ourselves up," Stevens said, heading past the burled desk for the back wall, where an elevator was semi-concealed behind a shining silk screen.

"Wait!" exclaimed the woman, punching buttons on the phone.

Lei got into the small elevator beside Stevens. He punched the button marked OFFICES.

"She's sounding the alarm."

"I was thinking the same thing."

The elevator slid open in mere seconds. Gleaming black marble floors led to a hallway with several doors marked SCULPTURE, WALL ART, CERAMICS, or TEXTILES. Lei headed for the one marked OFFICE and didn't pause to knock. She just hit the door with her shoulder as she turned the knob and ended up staggering a few steps into the luxurious room, surprised to find it unlocked. Pono and Stevens followed, guns drawn.

A bank of windows looked out at the ocean, a sparkling turquoise contrast to the polished ebony desk and sweep of velvety dark carpet. A black Mac computer decorated the desk like a sculpture, with three small Japanese porcelain cups beneath it. Not a paper marred the surface of the desk except a single tray marked OUT with a manila envelope in it. MRS. CORPUZ was written on it in block letters with a Kahului address.

"No one here," Stevens said.

"She could be hiding."

"I'll check the other doors," Pono said, and headed out.

Lei went behind the desk and spotted a door set flush in the silk-covered walls, with nothing but the crack of an outline marking it. There was no apparent door handle. She and Stevens felt up and down the expanse.

Lei put her hands on her hips.

"I bet this has an 'open sesame' somewhere. The desk?"

She and Stevens pulled at the drawers—all locked. Lei took a paper clip from one of the little porcelain cups under the monitor, opened it, and inserted it into the main desk drawer, wiggling it around until she heard a click.

She opened the drawer and felt along the top under the smooth polished black wood until she felt a button. Pushed it.

The door in the wall whispered open, and a bluish glow beckoned from inside. Stevens stood to the side, gun out, waiting. He gestured with his head.

She pulled the Glock and took the other side of the doorway, Stevens covering as she sprang in.

"Police!"

A bank of computers ringed a cockpit-like half-circle table, and there, face lit by the glowing reflected technology, sat Magda Kennedy.

"It's gone. All gone." She looked up at them, blue eyes cavernous, seemingly unsurprised by their intrusion and drawn weapons. "She's wiped me out."

Chapter 35

C hapman, the lawyer, handed Magda a bottle of water. The woman sipped like an automaton. She hadn't spoken a word as they took her out in cuffs and brought her back to Kahului Station, except to tell the fluttering blonde to call her lawyer as they walked her across the gallery. She'd conferred with the lawyer in private for a moment upon his arrival, and now Chapman said, "My client would like to make a statement."

"By all means." Lei gestured to the notepad on the table. Stevens turned on the video camera, and he came and sat beside Lei. Pono had taken up his post in the observation booth along with the captain and Lieutenant Omura.

"I am missing an employee," Magda said, each word distinct. She ignored the notepad. "My gallery manager. She's been my right hand."

"Who is this?" Stevens asked.

"Her name's Karen Walker—I count on her to run the day-to-day operations. She didn't come in today—or if she did, she left the office early. I got a call from the gallery downstairs when she didn't show up, which is highly unusual, as she lives in the same building as the gallery, on the top floor. I went up and checked her apartment—I have a key, as I rent the unit to her as part of her salary. Anyway, a suitcase and some clothes were missing, and it looked like she'd left in a hurry. I got worried and went down to the office. She's done something to the computers. All our inventory is on them, and they are all just...blank."

"Wow. That sounds serious." Lei let skepticism into her voice. This was Magda Kennedy's story? But—it was so far-fetched it just might be true.

"That's not all. She cleaned out the safe." The pride had seeped out of Magda's voice and it trembled. She twisted one of the gold bangles around and around her wrist. "I was trying to see what she'd done when you showed up. I think she must have been doing something illegal."

"What do you know about this?" Lei slid the white satin card over to her.

"I told you. I passed it on for a friend. It's an escort service."

"We've been through this before," Chapman huffed.

"It's a prostitution operation with ties to organized crime, being run by someone called Magda. We have two witnesses who can corroborate." Lei watched Magda's pale face go a shade whiter. She tossed back her silky black hair, a nervous gesture. She wore a dark green T-shirt and jeans, face bare of makeup, and she was still stunning. She glanced at Chapman.

"This is a nightmare. Karen set me up."

The interview went on as they quizzed Magda on the connections to the ships, the girls, the money. She denied it all.

Omura appeared at the little wire-lined window that looked into the room and gestured. They got up.

"We'll be back. We're going to check a few things."

Lei and Stevens stepped out into the hall. "Yes, Lieutenant?" Stevens asked.

"This is Karen Walker." She held up two printed color photocopies. A head shot, professionally done, of a woman in one of the Grecian-styled white dresses worn on the floor of the gallery. Tilted green eyes under straight brows stared haughtily down a blade of a nose, contrasting with a full, sensual mouth. An artful tumble of red curls framed a stunning, porcelain-skinned face. Lei suddenly remembered that face, standing at the back of the gallery the first time she and Pono had visited. She shut her eyes to remember—but the image was blurry.

She'd been so upset by that Lucite angel.

"What a looker," Stevens said, perusing the photo. Lei elbowed him as she took her copy.

"Someone needs to take these to the two witnesses and check if this is the 'Magda' they know. Stevens, you take this shot to Maui County Correctional, where we have the purser, and Lei, you go to the safe house and show this to the Thai girl. I'll take over for a while."

Omura had a smile lurking around her mouth as she headed into the interview room. Lei sighed—she hated to leave the interview, but it was actually a miracle Omura hadn't gone in sooner. She felt almost sorry for the gallery owner as she headed for her truck. The woman's bewilderment and betrayal had seemed genuine, and going into another round of interviews with Omura was enough to give anyone a cramp.

Lei got on the road for the safe house, glancing over at the photo of Walker on the seat beside her. They'd been so sure it was Magda all along…but in a few minutes they'd know for sure.

She drove out of Kahului on the winding country road that bordered a ravine plummeting into `Iao Valley, ascending the ridge. Lei realized that she hadn't eaten anything all day; her stomach rumbled loudly as she popped open the glove box, leaning over and fumbling with one hand for her emergency granola bar.

The truck lurched suddenly and she banged her head on the steering wheel.

"What the hell?" The Tacoma veered dangerously close to the steel girder that was the only thing between her and space, and she yanked the wheel the other way, overcompensating, glancing into the rearview mirror.

That view had filled with the looming black shape of an oncoming SUV.

Lei straightened up and put both hands on the wheel, punching down the gas pedal as her adrenaline surged. Apparently, the hit on her was still out, even with the last assassin in the hospital.

The truck leapt forward, and Lei concentrated on the narrow, winding road, thinking ahead to the turnoff into the subdivision where the safe house was located—but she couldn't lead the hit man there. She had to get far enough ahead to be able to pull over and get her weapon out. Even as she glanced in the rearview mirror, the SUV hit her again.

"Shit!"

This time her truck's fender scraped the girder as she yanked it back into the proper lane, still trying to accelerate. The SUV had to have a pretty potent engine to outrun her truck, and as she spared a glance in the rearview, she saw the distinctive grille of an Escalade. Damn.

Still, she knew the road and, hopefully, the assassin didn't. She pulled ahead, thanking God that the road continued to be empty of other cars. She was able to gain a little ground by angling straight across curves she knew were ahead, but the Escalade began gaining again as they wound down into a gulch. A turnoff was on the upside of that. Lei kept the gas pedal down, but as the truck juddered, she finally had to brake, and that's when the Escalade hit her for the third time.

She felt the precise moment she lost control of the vehicle in the sudden looseness of the wheel. Time stretched out, each separate nanosecond recorded without meaning.

A kaleidoscope of colors. The scream of dying metal blocking thought. An impact crushing her forward, whipping her back, smothering her in white oblivion. A sense of flying. Then tumbling whiteness, followed by dark.

Chapter 36

I barely see the silver Tacoma hit the guardrail because the momentum of its impact transfers and hauls the Escalade in its wake. I fight the wheel in the other direction. All I hear is the shriek of rending metal and the wail of the Escalade's fender scraping along the girder. I wrestle it away with all my strength—too much. The big SUV rocks onto two wheels and spins back, jerking to a brain-jarring stop facing back down the road. The Cadillac's engine stalls and dies with a shudder and a burp.

I squint through webbed fragments of broken light. The windshield's broken but holding. I focus on the ragged gap in the railing straight ahead where the Tacoma went over.

That'll fix her wagon.

A hysterical laugh bubble chokes me at the memory of a stupid saying my late unlamented mother used to use. The engine ticks, cooling, and there's silence. My heart's still roaring in my ears, and the fierce exaltation of taking a life surges through me.

God, I love that feeling.

I turn the key and the Escalade starts after a grind or two. Thing's built tough; no wonder the gangsters like them. Magda's going to miss this vehicle and report it, and I need to ditch it as soon as possible—but I want to make sure Texeira's really gone. I pull the SUV up onto a shoulder area and step out, pulling my Sig Sauer with the silencer already screwed on out from under the seat.

I roll my shoulders. That impact's going to hurt tomorrow. I'd felt it shudder through my body and snap my head back, enough to need a massage, at least. My legs are a bit unsteady as I walk back along the road to the gouged, torn hole in the steel girder.

I look over. The Tacoma is upside down about fifty yards down the precipice, one side of the cab wedged against a huge orange-blossomed African tulip tree. The truck's passage has gauged and hacked a meteor-like path through the underbrush, and the vehicle is crumpled and twisted.

I feel a rumbling in the road before I see the car coming toward me, too fast, and I hug the remains of the guardrail. A shiny red Acura brakes and the window rolls down. An Asian businessman in a suit addresses me.

"You okay? What happened?"

"Looks like an accident. There's a car down there!" My voice comes out breathless and terrified.

"Did you call nine-one-one?"

"No. I was just looking over to see what happened."

"I'm calling it in." Too late, I see the Bluetooth in his ear. "I'm reporting an accident. Someone's gone off the cliff on Haulani Road."

My exit line. I make my rubbery legs walk back to the Escalade, gun flattened against my leg where he can't see it as he gets out of his car, running over to the cliff and exclaiming into the Bluetooth.

I get in and fire up the Escalade and pull away, leaving the businessman staring after me. He's sure to report me now; it must seem odd that I'm leaving the scene with the drama just beginning to unfold—not to mention the crumpled front bumper, scrape marks, and broken windshield.

I hope I've succeeded in getting rid of Texeira—I know it's just spite, but spite is underrated. It's kept me going many a time. I hate losing so much that I always find a way to win in the end. This crash wasn't as sure a thing as Vixen had been—pushing that car off the cliff in such a remote location with the ocean to finish her off was sure thing, and I like sure things.

This whole disaster began with Vixen. Stupid little whore. I'd kill her again if I could.

I need to ditch the Escalade as soon as possible.

Chapter 37

Lei felt consciousness gathering, pulling her back from somewhere far away and much less painful. Her eyes popped open and all she saw was white. She screamed, or thought she did—something was off with her hearing too. Another few seconds later, her brain interpreted the white as a smothering cloud of airbags deployed all around her.

Lei was upside down. She fumbled for the seat belt cutting into her shoulder. Her hand and arm responded clumsily, getting hold of the buckle and pushing it down. She dropped onto the ceiling of the cab, semi-folded around the steering wheel. Thank God for those airbags. Her brain supplied her with images of the red-haired girl who'd started it all, crushed in the sedan off Pauwela Lighthouse, and her heart still squeezed at the memory.

Miraculously, that hadn't happened to her. But whoever had run her off the road might still be coming.

The airbags deflated as she pushed at them. She eased her body over to the side and got onto her hands and knees, hunching in the confined space. None of her bones seemed to be broken, another miracle. She pawed through the side-door airbag to the handle, but couldn't budge it. The window was still up and intact, blocked by some dark surface. She pushed aside the front airbag. The windshield had buckled, bent, and cracked outward, though safety glass held the gemmed, starry fragments in place.

Lei reversed herself and kicked. And kicked again. With a protesting tinkle and screech, the windshield popped out of the frame. Two more motivated kicks, and it lifted away enough for her to wriggle out, scraping her hands on glass that had fallen to the ground. She squeezed out from under the upended hood, sitting up.

Lei looked up the impossibly high incline above, the path of the truck's trajectory marked by gashes of red soil in green growth blanketing the slope. Sirens were blaring. She hadn't noticed them before. Clustered heads looked down at her from the blown-out gap in the guardrail.

"I'm okay," Lei yelled, and was surprised to find she actually was.

Lei sat semi-upright on a pile of firm pillows on the threadbare couch of the safe house in the dimming light. Anchara held out a mug of tea to her.

"Thanks." Lei sipped it, and found the dark brew surprisingly tasty—strong, milky, and sweetened heavily.

"They didn't have any Thai kinds of tea, but I tried to make it like we do in our country." Anchara sat at the far end of the couch, curling slim legs beneath her. "I feel bad. This my fault."

The woman's soft voice hitched, and she ducked her head so a curtain of long, shiny hair slid forward.

"Not your fault," Lei said. "Someone's been trying to off me since the investigation started. This was just their latest attempt."

She was a bit fuzzy from painkillers and exhaustion; she'd spent some hours at the hospital for observation and repairs and a debrief with the police team. She had nothing more from this latest adventure than cuts, bruises, and whiplash, and they'd put her in a highly annoying foam collar. She reached up to scratch underneath it.

Her phone kept ringing with calls as the "coconut wireless" word-of-mouth relayed this latest attempt on her life through the cop world.

She glanced at the number on the buzzing device and picked up. "J-Boy!"

"Sweets!" Jack Jenkins, her former partner on Kaua`i. "I hear someone's been trying to kill you. They should know better—you're tougher than a boot and luckier than a cat with nine lives—though you must be down a few by now." Under the jocular note, she heard concern. "You okay?"

"Well, this has been my worst case in a while—we think there's a contract out on me. Been hit by a car, had my house burned down, and now run off the road." Listing the events made her stomach feel hollow, and she realized she now no longer even had her truck, totaled at the scene. As if to remind her, Keiki sat up and licked her hand. She played with the dog's ears.

She still had her dog, at least. "The net's closing, though. We have a suspect, witnesses, and the perp's apartment's being searched as we speak."

Omura had triumphantly flourished the signed search warrant at Lei's debrief before setting off for Lahaina with Torufu, Bunuelos, and Stevens.

"As long as you're safe. Anu wants to know if you need anything." The Kaua`i girl had made a move on Jenkins, and it appeared they were still together.

"Nope. Doing fine," Lei said, ignoring the twinge of loss she still felt for all that had been burned in the house fire.

"Well, don't be such a stranger. They give you some time off, come recuperate with us on Kaua`i."

"Will do." She said her goodbyes and turned on the TV, scrolling through until she found a news station, curious to see if her accident had made the evening broadcast.

The newscast appeared, and Lei felt a punch to the gut as she recognized the worn apartment edifice behind the reporter. Its bedraggled bougainvilleas didn't look any better on television. She turned up the volume as the woman spoke.

"Neighbors reported a loud exchange in this apartment in downtown Honolulu and a day later called police when the apartment's resident failed to appear."

The camera zoomed into the familiar grilled doorway, crossed with yellow crime scene tape. Lei couldn't see the worn rubber WELCOME mat, but her mind's eye supplied it.

"Investigators arrived to find the body of a man identified as Charlie Kwon, age fifty-three, who had been shot. Investigators refused to comment, but this station has discovered that Kwon was a recently paroled registered sex offender."

The camera switched to a short, round Filipino lady in a lurid purple muumuu. Her hands trembled as she touched the tight bun pulling black hair away from a square-chinned face.

"He was real quiet, real nice," she said. "We never expected nothing like this in our building."

"Why did you call the police?"

"I heard fighting over there, words exchanged. Then it was quiet, real quiet. Charlie, he never come out, and he always took a walk in the morning." The chin wobbled.

The camera panned back to the reporter, brows knit in faux concern.

"Investigators refused to confirm whether this brutal murder could have been revenge for, or by, any of Kwon's several victims."

Cut to the lead detective, a tall, well-built Hawaiian with folded arms and the requisite mirrored Oakleys in place. "Detective Kamuela, do you have any leads?"

"No comment except this: Kwon paid his debt to society, and all the resources available to the Honolulu Police Department are being deployed to find the killer."

A wide, meaty hand came up to block the camera's money shot of the black-bagged body being wheeled out of the apartment on a gurney.

Lei hit the button for the TV and turned it off. Forgetting the foam collar, she dropped her head into her hands. Instantly, a lance of red-hot pain shot up her neck. She moaned, and tears welled again.

She never used to cry this much.

She'd endangered herself and her career with that stupid trip to see Kwon. But at least she wasn't the one to have put him down. She could only hope no one had seen her, could identify her. She felt soft hands rub her shoulders, and someone handed her a dish towel.

"Thanks," she snuffled, mopping her face with it. Anchara helping again—the Thai woman was so kind and sensitive. She cried harder.

"Can I help?"

"No. It's nothing." Lei put the towel over her face, pressing her eyeballs.

"Someone shot that man. Was he a friend?"

"No. Not a friend. But I did know him."

It was all just too damn much. Anchara rubbed her shoulders.

That's how they were when the front door locks clacked open. Keiki made sure the visitor knew Lei was well guarded until she saw Stevens, eyes ringed with fatigue. Lei gave her wet face one last wipe and put the dishcloth down as Anchara padded to the bedroom and went inside, closing the door softly.

"Hey. You okay?" Stevens came over, kissed her forehead.

"'Course. Just blowing off a little stress. Pull up a chair. What did you find?"

"We have a BOLO out on the Escalade that hit you, which turns out belongs to Magda and according to her is missing, stolen by Walker. Our girl Walker has a few aliases at least; she left behind a fake passport in the safe in the apartment. So we have a screening out for any departing air passengers with Walker's description, but I'm not too hopeful, since she seems good at changing her appearance."

"Shit."

"I said worse at the scene when I saw some of what she left behind. From what we can tell, she left with plenty of cash, a false identity, and a good number of contacts who owe her favors. Omura thinks Magda Kennedy's in on it, but we have to find a solid connection to her, which we still haven't."

"Be nice for Kennedy to have Walker take the fall."

"Well, we can make the case if our witnesses identify Magda as the Magda they worked with. I wasn't able to make it to see the purser before I got the call about your accident." He stroked her arm. She turned up her hand and squeezed his as he went on. "Walker had what they call 'unnatural tastes.' There was a whole S&M room decked out in DNA evidence and drug trace in her safe. That could tie her to the drug money the coast guard intercepted on the *Duchess*."

"Wow," Lei said. She felt a reluctant tug of admiration for someone so devious, clever, and deadly. Wished again they'd met face-to-face. Maybe they had; maybe it had been her behind the wheel of the Escalade. She'd never seen anything but a shadow behind the tinted glass.

"Did you show Anchara Walker's photo?" Stevens asked.

"No, it was still in the truck when I got out of the wreck."

He pulled out his folded copy of Walker's photo from an inside pocket, set it on the coffee table, and made as if to get up.

"Wait. I have to tell you something private." Lei set her jaw. "Kwon. He's dead—shot. I saw it on the news."

"Shit!" He stood up, a surge of graceful motion. Even distracted by distress, she was drawn to Stevens's power of movement, the directness of his piercing blue gaze. "Did you do it?"

"No." She plucked at the dishcloth in her lap. "Of course not. Just like I said, I gave him a knock upside the head—but he was alive when I left him."

"Anything tying you to the scene?"

"I don't think so. But with nosy neighbors like I saw on the news, it's good I got rid of what I was wearing."

"Tell me."

"Never mind. It's gone now. I told you I wouldn't ever make you choose." Lei knew he loved the law—and he loved her. Participating in a cover-up, no matter how justified it might seem, would eat away at that love. "I'll cooperate if anything gets back to me. That's all you need to know."

"We're so screwed." He shook his head, moving down the hall. She heard the shower start. She slung her feet over to the side of the couch. She really did need to get rid of the disguise she'd worn.

Lei checked that Anchara was still in her room and took the clothing items out of the backpack she'd set by the door. She put them in a ziplock bag. Stepped out into the warm darkness, Keiki by her side. Went to the toolshed on the side of the house and stashed the bag in a hollow metal ceiling beam.

She'd get rid of it properly later.

Lei went back in the house, rubbing sweating palms on her new jeans. A shower was what she needed, too. But she wasn't about to join Stevens in his present mood—or hers, for that matter. Charlie Kwon was a blight, a disease—and, dead, he might be able to fuck up her life even more.

Eventually, she had her shower and, feeling marginally better, limped back out to the couch wearing the yellow terry-cloth robe, rubbing her short hair gingerly with a hand towel. Anchara and Stevens generated tasty, exotic smells and cooking noises in the kitchen as Lei punched in the last phone call she needed to make.

"Hey, Sweets!" Her father had latched on to Jenkins's version of a nickname. He couldn't know about the accident, she remembered. "How you stay?"

"Not so good, Dad. I was in an accident today."

"What! You okay, girl?"

"Some bumps and bruises, whiplash, but I'll be okay."

"Oh, honey. I'll tell your auntie."

"That's fine, but that's not why I called. Do you still watch the Hawaii news?" He'd kept up with it in the past, even in California, living with her aunt.

"Not today. What's up?"

"Charlie Kwon was shot."

She stared blindly out the window at the high chain-link woven with plastic privacy fencing. Her vision dimmed with familiar dissociation, and she put the side of her finger in her mouth, bit down on it. Pain anchored her in her body. The black ebbed, leaving the cheerless view.

Silence from her father. A long pause filled with an ocean of unspoken.

"No shit," he finally said. "Bastard had it coming."

"Dad. Did you have anything to do with it?"

"Did you?"

"'Course not. I'm a cop, Dad." She shut her eyes, thinking of Charlie on his knees in front of her, the Glock in her hand—and how close she'd come to pulling the trigger. If she had, she'd never have known if it was an accident. "You, on the other hand, have already killed someone."

"Self-defense," he rapped out. He'd never said anything else of his prison killing of Terry Chang, Hilo crime boss. "I think that pervert deserved putting down. I might even imagine killing the man who raped my little girl, but I know better than to get involved with God's justice. You don't believe me? I'll alibi out on this. Been working in the restaurant all day and with your auntie the rest of the time."

"What about yesterday?"

"Same thing. I'm in California, for Christ's sake!" His volume climbed, then went low as he seemed to catch himself. "God, give me strength."

She heard him murmuring. Praying. Lei remembered his fervent Christianity, a "new life" he'd gained in prison. It seemed to have stuck, even two years out. Her father wouldn't commit murder. Lei envied his certainty, his conviction.

"Okay. Sorry. Must have been someone else."

"Thanks for the vote of confidence." He hung up.

Lei closed the phone, settled it in her lap. Wondered for a moment if he hadn't been just a touch *too* defensive, if that attitude of outrage was to keep her from asking the next question on her lips—had he sent someone else to do it?

She pressed Redial, and this time it went to voice mail. She didn't leave a message.

Chapter 38

S o *ono*, Anchara," Lei said, scraping the bowl for the last of the chicken curry Anchara had made for dinner. "That means delicious, in Hawaiian."

"Yeah, I could get used to this," Stevens said.

Anchara ducked her head with a smile. "Thank you."

She got up as if to clear their places, but Lei waved her down.

"No. Sit. You've done enough. We have to show you something."

Stevens got up and went to the coffee table, picked up the folded photo and brought it to Anchara. He unfolded it in front of her, smoothing the creases. Karen Walker's green eyes looked up at them, haughty and beautiful.

"Have you seen this woman before?"

The girl's eyes widened with fear and recognition. "That's Magda."

Lei and Stevens exchanged a glance. "When did you see her?" Lei asked.

"She came to look at us when we got off the van the first time, our first time on this island. Celeste and Kimo made us strip at the warehouse. They had us do beauty treatments." Anchara hid her face behind her hair. Her voice trembled. "When we were all clean and had no hair even down there"—she made a gesture with her hand—"they put us against the wall. Took pictures of our faces and bodies. Then she came in." She pointed to Walker's photo.

"What did she do?"

"Looked at us. Said things to do to us to make us prettier. Said to Celeste what kinds of parties to send us to. Then she got out white satin robes and had us put them on."

"What else?"

"It was the way she did it. Like we weren't even there. Like we weren't even people."

Lei found herself reaching to stack the dishes, clearing the table for something to do as Stevens took another folded color photocopy out of his back pocket. Smoothed it out in front of Anchara.

"What about this woman?"

"No. I've never seen her."

"You sure?"

"No. I would remember."

Anyone would remember the pale oval of Magda Kennedy's face, ice-blue eyes contrasting with ebony hair.

"All right," Stevens said. "We've got some confirmation Walker might have been setting Kennedy up. I'll call Omura with this, and I want to get back over to the jail, see if I can get a confirmation from the purser." He stood and headed for the door.

"Thanks," Lei called after his retreating back. "Thanks for understanding." Her words were rich with meaning, pleading forgiveness. Kwon was still a shadow between them. He strode back and leaned over to kiss her, a little too hard.

"Don't mention it."

Those words were a warning.

Chapter 39

*L*ei sat with the rest of the team the next morning around the big conference table at Kahului Station, a big pink box of sugary malasadas from Komoda's Bakery as the centerpiece. A whiteboard on the far wall was cluttered with a hand-written timeline, and a series of color photocopies were clipped to the top, beginning with Magda Kennedy. Morgue shots of Jane Doe and Lei's attempted assassin, deceased in the night, were on the opposite wall. A final, blank sheet ended the row with "THE HOUSE?" printed on it in Stevens's block writing.

"All right, everyone, let's begin." Omura pulled the group to order, and Abe Torufu set down a malasada he'd been about to consume in one bite. Lei scratched under the foam collar and, suddenly frustrated, pulled the Velcro open and eased it off into her lap, earning a sharp glance from Stevens.

Captain Corpuz turned on the video screen on the opposite wall, adjusted the volume on the triangular pickup feed on the table, and in a moment Marcella and Rogers appeared via video-conferencing, nursing Starbucks cups and looking FBI in white button-downs and black jackets.

That outfit must get hot in Hawaii. Lei chalked up the outfit on the mental tally of minuses she was keeping on a move to the FBI.

Omura stepped up to the whiteboard. She used a laser pointer to put an unnerving red dot in the middle of Jane Doe's forehead. "Let's do a recap. It all started here. This girl is still unidentified except for a stage name, Vixen, and her Albanian nationality, which she shared with Anchara, our witness in protective custody. We've sent inquiries through the INS and Interpol to Albania to see if anyone comes forward to identify her, but so far no-go."

Lei felt a deep tug of compassion for the anonymous girl who'd died trying to be free.

"Jane Doe's murder investigation led us to this man." The red dot bloomed on Silva's greasy-looking mug shot. "He identified her as one of several 'escorts' provided by this man, John Wylie, at a construction job wrap party." The dot found its next target. "Wylie led us to this woman, gallery owner Magda Kennedy. We brought her in, but we didn't have anything on her but a business card and Wylie's say-so, and she's well protected. Silva also implicated the House." The dot moved to the blank paper. "That brought in the FBI, who have been working to bring down the House's crime organization. They were hopeful we could help make a connection, and we began working together." Omura seemed to have an easy time taking credit for Lei's work, with a royal "we." Lei pinched the web of her hand to help stay calm.

"Around that time, attempts were made on Texeira and Stevens's lives by this man." The dot pinned the gray face of the dead assassin. "We still don't know who he is or who he worked for—he never woke up from that coma, and his prints aren't in the system—but we suspect he's an agent of the House, who must have decided they were getting too close. Torufu and Bunuelos are heading up the John Doe assassin case."

The hypnotic dot moved on, zeroing in on Anchara. "Anchara

Mookjai, the runaway that escaped with Jane Doe, resurfaced. Her intel gave the go-ahead for the coast guard sweeps that have turned up a cache of girls and money on the *Rainbow Duchess* in Kahului Harbor and two other ships on the other islands. Texeira was able to capture the ship's purser, Farrell, who has turned out to be the key to making a connection to the House and to Magda Kennedy, the gallery owner on Maui who ran girls and laundered money for him."

Omura paused to glance around as if for input or questions, but no one chimed in. She aimed the red dot at the photo of Walker. "When Kennedy was apprehended, she implicated her business manager, Karen Walker, who'd skipped earlier. Walker appears to have set Kennedy up to take the fall, by conducting all her business with the House and his connections under Magda's name.

"In fact, when we apprehended Celeste Anderson and Kimo Emmanuel, they identified Walker as Magda, their boss. Rodney Farrell and Anchara also both identified Walker's photo as the Magda they knew," Omura concluded.

"Celeste and Kimo also led us to the warehouse in Haiku where the girls originally escaped. We found the current crop of girls there. They're being processed by INS. The key Texeira found at the original crash scene fit the door and confirms Anchara's story," Marcella said, voice tinny in the feed.

"So is Magda Kennedy involved or not?" Captain Corpuz asked.

"Apparently, she was more of a socialite than a business-woman and let Walker run most of the day-to-day operations. Walker, or Kennedy, encrypted the computers that would have led to the money trail. Farrell, the purser, indicated 'Magda' was the money launderer for the House. We have IT division trying to reconstruct something, but it doesn't look good—and Kennedy is doing a good job of pleading ignorance. We're still digging."

Omura's sniff indicated what she thought of the gallery owner, and she went on. "Then, to top it off, Walker stole Kennedy's Escalade and ran Texeira off the road with it."

"How do you know it was Walker?" Lei asked.

"We recovered the Escalade, abandoned downtown with trace on it from Texeira's Tacoma and prints from Walker inside. We're beginning to wonder if Walker's just another alias as well," Omura said.

"Why would she bother? She was on the run; her cover was already blown," Lei said.

"Don't know. Maybe she's just a sore loser," Pono said. "She should've known you've got more lives than a cat."

Lei shook her head. "Been hearing that too much lately," she said.

Omura clicked off the pointer and gestured to the monitor. "Agents, what's up on your end?"

"We brought in Ken Taketa, House's money man." Marcella's voice was amplified oddly by the feed, and wavy lines emanated from her dark hair like a demented halo. "He gave us an identity on the House—a prominent businessman in Honolulu, Joseph Millhouse. We did a raid on his mansion last night, but Millhouse had skipped."

Silence met this bald statement.

"Maybe he and Walker ran off together," Bunuelos said, and the room erupted in tension-breaking chuckles.

Stevens added, "Probably on Duchess Cruise Lines," and the chuckles erupted into guffaws.

Omura clapped manicured hands for order. "Not a bad idea. Did we do a BOLO for passengers matching their descriptions for all the cruise ships?"

"Just the airports, I think," Stevens finally said, and just like that the meeting was over as Captain Corpuz bellowed, "Get the word out to the coast guard NOW!"

The feed cut to the FBI as the agents disappeared. The other detectives scattered.

Lei, still on admin leave for the investigation of her accident, was left sitting at the table contemplating the malasadas with Pono, who had his Oakleys down and a line between his brows.

"Shit. I think they're going to fucking get away with it all. Probably got a fortune banked in the Bahamas." Lei sighed and put the foam collar back on.

"Looks that way, but the Feds are after them, coast guard, Interpol...Someone could still bag them." Pono rubbed his bristling mustache with a forefinger. "When you coming back to work? We got other cases, you know. I miss my partner."

"I know. Doctor I saw at the hospital said at least a week off work. They're worried about complications from the concussion I had and then the whiplash. I'm also supposed to start looking for another house for us." Lei couldn't put into words how that depressed her and made her head ache. Setting up a home from nothing while Stevens got to go to work seemed like the height of unfair. She'd picked up the morning paper on the way into the meeting and tapped the classifieds. "This is what I'm supposed to be doing."

"Have fun with that. I'll run you back to the safe house."

They got up and headed down the bustling hall through the bull pen together. Lei blinked as they emerged into the unrelenting Maui sunshine of the parking lot. Pono led her to his truck. She hopped up into the cab with the help of the chrome step.

"What's going to happen to Anchara now that the case isn't going to trial anytime soon?" Pono asked, turning on the engine with a roar.

"I'm working with Omura on a special circumstances visa application. I think she deserves to stay in the States after all she's been through and how she's helped with the investigation."

"I hope she gets it. Poor girl deserves a break."

"Yeah."

He dropped her at the gate of the safe house, classifieds in hand. Keiki bounced with happiness to see her. She had just enough energy to walk over to the step and sit down. She worked the dog for a while, practicing various commands.

Anchara came to the door, carrying a knotted T-shirt. "Can I throw this for dog?"

"Her name's Keiki," Lei said. "That would be great, tire her out a bit. I can't throw right now with my neck like this."

Anchara threw the T-shirt, and Keiki bolted after it. "I like your dog. I scared of her at first."

"I like her too." Eventually Keiki flopped down on the top step, tongue hanging as they petted her.

"What's going to happen to me?" Anchara folded her arms around her knees, her chin resting on them, big doe eyes worried. Lei had to remind herself the girl was twenty-three.

"Working on getting you an emergency green card. I don't think you need to stay here much longer."

"I don't have anywhere to go."

"Well. That makes two of us." Lei gave a short bark of a laugh. She shook out the rolled-up newspaper. "Let's check these out together."

"I don't have any money."

"Omura's doing some paperwork for you to get a stipend through Victim Assistance. It's going to be okay."

Lei was surprised to feel the Thai girl's arms reach over the sleeping dog to hug her. "Thanks. You do so much for me."

"You're welcome." Lei's cell bleeped, and she cleared her throat and detached herself. "Excuse me. This is Texeira," she answered.

"Lei? Hello, dear. This is Dr. Wilson."

Her therapist from the Big Island. Lei's pulse picked up with the combination of tension and anticipation the unconventional therapist evoked in her, even after a year in therapy. "Dr. Wilson, what a surprise! What's this about?"

"MPD flew me over to do some seminars and I heard you'd had an attempt on your life. Your commanding officer asked me to do your debrief, since I was in town."

"Wow, that's great!" Lei said with fake enthusiasm.

Dr. Wilson laughed, the unladylike belly laugh Lei had grown to love. "You bullshitter," she said. "I'm in a cab on my way."

"Okay," Lei said, and closed the phone. "Anchara, I'm going to need some privacy."

Chapter 40

*D*r. Wilson looked the same—ash-blond hair, petite figure in polo shirt and twill skirt, sensible Naturalizer sandals on legs that looked like they played a lot of tennis. She'd added a gold Hawaiian bracelet to her tanned arm, the only change Lei could see. The psychologist sat in the overstuffed recliner and concerned sea-blue eyes took inventory of Lei as she sat on the tweedy couch—an echo of their many sessions in Hilo.

"You look like you've been through a war."

"It was a bad case," Lei said. "We think there was a hit on me. There were several attempts—hit me with a car while I was out jogging, burned our house down, and ran me off the road in my truck."

"Oh my God. That must have been horrible."

"It's been a lot, yeah." Tears welled. She got up, began to pace, reached into her pocket and missed her black worry stone for the hundredth time. "This foam neck thing is from the last attempt. One of the suspects, Karen Walker, stole a car from her employer, and as part of her 'scorched earth' departure, ran me off the road."

"Jesus," Dr. Wilson said. "Just when it seemed like things were settling down for you and Stevens."

"About that. He wants to get married. Gave me the ring again, and you know that's what freaked me out and sent me to Kaua`i last time. I said I'd wear it on a chain until I knew what to do with it, and I had taken it off in the kitchen when the house burned down."

Dr. Wilson inclined her head.

Lei swiveled, paced back. "I've been trying not to deal with this, but Marcella Scott, my agent friend, has been trying to recruit me for the FBI. I have to make a decision soon. And now I have literally nothing but my dog and my boyfriend stopping me from going."

"So you feel like all the things that might hold you back have been severed."

"Not all. I mean, Stevens and I…We're good." She felt a blush roar up to prickle her scalp, and she rubbed her head, smiling. "We're really good. He's—amazing." She knew her grin was the sappy lovesick type. "He's done more to heal me than all the therapy in the world."

"I can see that. Nothing like the love of a good man to restore what a bad man took."

"Oh. And about that." Lei took a breath, blew it out. "I tracked Kwon, my molester."

"You told me his name. I saw in the news he was shot. Part of why I came here—I wondered if you had anything to do with that." Calm blue eyes seemed to see into her soul. Lei felt a tingling like heartburn under her sternum. That visit to Kwon could still ruin her life.

"How much of this interview is confidential?" she asked.

"All of it except suicidal or homicidal confessions."

"Well, I'm bummed you think I could do something like that—but I guess it's a fair question. The answer's no. I went over there, gave him a piece of my mind and a taste of the butt end of my pistol, but I left him alive. I'm worried someone's going to connect me with that, but so far they haven't."

"Well, they won't hear anything from me."

"It's a good thing, too. It was awful seeing Kwon." She blew out a breath. "He didn't recognize me."

"You grew up," Dr. Wilson said gently.

"I reminded him of that name he had for me. 'Damaged Goods.' He didn't react. Made me think I wasn't the only little girl he made damaged goods." She coughed around the lump in her throat. "Anyway, the bastard got his, and in the end, I'm glad someone else did it."

"That must have been hard."

"I didn't know what I was going to do until the very last second. It was scary." Lei picked up the threadbare cushion, hugged it. "I expected him to be bigger, to look evil like I remembered. He was just an ordinary little man."

Tears brimmed again, and this time Lei put her face into the pillow.

"I'm proud of you for facing him. Often the worst monsters are wolves in sheep's clothing, just little, ordinary men." Dr. Wilson handed her the box of tissues. Lei mopped her face, blew her nose.

"Or women. Like Walker. She's a sadist, gets off on others' pain—and so is the House, apparently."

"Did they escape together?"

"We don't know, but the timing is interesting." Lei got up, paced again, hugging the pillow. "So people keep trying to kill me. And get killed around me. I'm bad for Stevens; he could have died in the fire."

"Oh, don't even go there, Lei. That old 'I'm bad luck and bad news' line isn't going to fly with me. You've chosen a dangerous profession. Take up teaching or nursing or social work if you don't want people trying to kill you."

Lei sat back down. "But I can't be something I'm not. I'm a cop, first and foremost. Stevens knows that, respects it, but I think he wants the white picket fence thing, too."

"Nothing wrong with that. There are other officer couples who make that work."

"Not hard-core. Not the way I work." She got up, paced again, rubbed her hands on her jeans. "The job comes first, but—I love him."

"I've never heard you say that before."

"I've been saying it more. It gets easier."

"So what are you going to do?"

"I don't know."

"Dang." Dr. Wilson glanced at her watch. "Well, I hope you'll call me when you do. I've got a plane to catch. Anything else?"

"No. Just…Thank you. For coming, for all you did to help me get better on the Big Island. I'll keep you posted."

"You'd better." The petite psychologist hugged Lei fiercely. "Let me know what you decide. But I think you should decide soon."

Chapter 41

Lei and Anchara got out of the cab at Lei's old address. Lei sucked in a breath at the sight of a pile of blackened rubble that was all that remained of their former home.

The cabbie, a kind-faced, older Portuguese man, frowned. "Sure this is the right place?"

"Yes. We'll need a ride in about an hour," Lei said through numb lips. The cabbie pulled away as the two women stared at the wreckage. A few bits of wooden wall still stood, sculpted along the edges with charcoal as if a black monster had reached down from above and eaten the heart out of the house in a few big bites. The grass was charred, and smoke scored the side of the propane tank.

Nothing appeared salvageable.

"Good thing the toolshed had those gardening boots," Lei said. Anchara nodded. Both women wore rubber gloves and the boots. They had each chosen a pair of pants and a shirt to sacrifice, since they didn't have any old clothes, and Lei was back in the foam collar. "I know where the kitchen was. Are you sure you want to help?"

"I like to help," Anchara said. "What we looking for?"

"A ring. It's valuable, and I have to at least try to find it." Lei drew in another deep breath and stepped forward into the debris. "Follow me."

The two women crunched forward. Lei tried not to think of the fire victims she'd seen in her career, curled and clawed as sinews in their bodies retracted. That could have been her and Stevens. The fire was over now, and they were safe—but the ring was unfinished business. She owed it to Stevens to try to find it.

The ring wouldn't be here, lost in the ashes, if she'd been wearing it.

Lei stood at the steel door of the morgue and took a couple of relaxation breaths to calm herself. She'd continued on in the cab to the hospital on impulse after dropping Anchara off—her gut was telling her something. She'd stripped off the gloves and boots, but nothing could be done for the soot-streaked pair of stretch pants and T-shirt she'd ruined at the fire site.

She'd barely cleared the acrid tang of the fire out of her nostrils before coming, and getting her nose involved was a mistake— the morgue had a mouthwash-over-decomp scent that clung to the back of her throat like cobwebs. Morgues also carried memories of things she wished she'd never seen—friends, foes, and victims, all roadkill left by murder's impact. She lifted her hand and knocked.

Dr. Gregory's pale moon face appeared, and she held up her badge in case he'd forgotten her. He opened the door. Salsa music bounced off the tiled walls, and his cheery parrot-covered aloha shirt peeped out from behind a blood-spattered rubber apron.

"What can I do you for?"

"I'm here to see the Jane Doe."

"Which one?"

"There's more than one?" Lei came in, taking shallow mouth breaths as she followed him through the tables, carefully not looking at their contents. He moved with a confidence she didn't remember seeing at the crash site to the bank of refrigerated boxes, shiny as the hood of a new car.

"A few. We keep them a while, you know, before we cremate 'em. Give them a chance to be identified."

"Of course." She wondered who the other Jane Does were. Decided she couldn't worry about more than one.

He popped the handle of one of the lower doors with a sound like a Coke can opening and rolled out the shelf. A shadowed shape lay before her in a clear plastic body bag. He unzipped it, a long ripping sound, almost drowned by the samba playing in the background. Almost, but not quite.

Lei pushed the foam collar around her neck down under her chin so she could look at the girl who'd started it all.

"What happened to you?" Dr. Gregory's voice broke the spell cast by the girl's perfect features, the blue eyes Lei remembered so well closed at last, transparent lids lying over them like bruised petals. Lei touched a vivid strand of the girl's red hair.

"Car accident."

"Most dangerous thing we do each day." Dr. Gregory put on the magnifying glasses dangling around his neck to look at the body. "She was a brunette, you know."

"Yeah. Skin doesn't look like a redhead."

"Hair either, if you know what I mean. So. What did you need?"

"I'm not sure. Just saying goodbye, I guess, now that the case is wrapping up. We think we know who her killer was."

"Get your man?"

"A woman this time. And no. She seems to have gotten away." Lei felt the regret and frustration in her voice. "She's being pursued by the FBI and she's on the Interpol watch lists. Someone's going to get her."

"Too bad. Well, good thing we have the broader law enforcement community to take the investigation outside little old Maui."

"Yeah, good thing."

Lei's voice sounded hollow as she looked down at the still face. She'd had to come here, see this girl, to get the message her gut had been telling her. Something about Jane Doe—her life, her struggle, and her death, was a part of Lei's life now.

She'd made a decision about Stevens and her future.

Dr. Gregory had turned away, spraying down an adjoining table as Lei stood there, still not ready to zip up the bag.

"Any closer to an ID on her?" he asked over his shoulder.

"No. Nothing. No prints or DNA anywhere on record. None of the other women we interviewed knew her by anything but her stage name, Vixen."

"That's nothing to be buried with." Gregory gave her a kindly glance over his glasses as he rinsed gore off his instruments before dropping them into the kettle of bubbling water on the stove. "Why don't you give her a name?"

"She deserves one. She died trying to be free, and she set someone else free."

"Well, it can't be official, but I don't see the harm." Gregory handed her a ballpoint pen and a toe tag. "Put it on her other foot."

Lei had always liked the story of Amelia Earhart, a woman who defied the odds, and even though Amelia's story had ended badly, it was unforgotten. She wrote "Amelia Texeira" on the toe tag, and before she could lose her nerve, tied it around the girl's left toe. She zipped up the plastic shroud and pushed in the shelf, locking the door with a pneumatic sigh.

She turned to Dr. Gregory. "Thanks."

"Stop by and visit anytime. I get lonely in here when my assistant's not around. These guys and gals aren't known for their conversation."

"Maybe I will." Doubtful, though. She liked Dr. Gregory, but not his environs. Heading out into the sunshine and fresh air, she felt inexplicably better.

She knew what she had to do.

Chapter 42

Wind plays with my choppy, short hair. I stand against the rail near the bow; leaning over, I can see a ceaseless bow wave purling off the steel wall far below. Dark, swift shapes of spinner dolphins alternately duck and leap, surfing the wave. I feel well-being rise up from somewhere deep inside, bubbling up from my newly pedicured toes in the gold slippers Dr. Aurora Middleton favors for lunch on a cruise ship.

He's texted me on the burner phone I'd kept just so he could. Earlier this morning, I'd seen a helicopter land on the VIP deck. He could be here anytime.

I haven't been this excited since I was a kid. If ever.

"This spot taken?" That gravelly voice.

It's him. I keep my head turned away, savoring the moment, the anticipation. I know what he'll see—a shapely athletic woman in a short white denim skirt that showcases great legs, strawberry-blond shag blowing in the wind.

"Only by you." I turn, look the House in the face for the first time.

A long moment passes as we take each other's measure.

"I thought you had blue eyes," he finally says.

"I thought you…were smaller," I say.

He's a large man. Not in a good way. A shiny shaved head sits like a bowling ball on huge wrestler's shoulders; a barrel gut strains at an elegant snakeskin belt. Eyes gray and hard as bullets run over me, and I feel an unfamiliar chill.

"You aren't who you said you were."

"Who did I say I was?"

"Magda. Magda Kennedy. Tall, thin, blue eyes, black hair."

I'm beginning to be pissed. He must have been fantasizing about Magda, not me, when we phone-fucked. A ridiculous oversight on my part. But he isn't Brad Pitt, either, and my pride's stung. I'm not exactly ugly.

"I did business in her name. Stupid society bitch took the fall for me." Something dark and ugly moves behind his eyes, but it's gone before I can really see if it was there. "Besides, I'm in disguise. Aren't you?"

"I had hair before. A beard too." He drops mirrored aviators over his eyes so I can't see them anymore.

"Men. It's all so easy for you." I turn away. Disappointment curdles my stomach. Guess this isn't what either of us was imagining.

He touches me then, a bold ass grab on my left buttock. "You aren't her, but you'll do."

"And what if you won't do for me?"

He finally lets go of my ass and gives it a hard smack. I flinch. I like to be the dom. This isn't turning me on the way the phone sex did.

"Let's go to your room."

"I don't think so," I say. My voice sounds tiny, reedy and unfamiliar.

"You don't have a choice, babe." I look down. He has looped a meaty arm around me and there's a blade in it, a foldable stiletto almost entirely concealed by his hand—his palms are the size of salad plates.

I find myself walking down the lush hallway to my room, watch my hand being clumsy with the keycard. I can't figure out how to get the card in. I feel the sting and burn as the blade scratches the skin of my waist. He looms beside me like a wall.

I break out in sweat, and my mind scrabbles like a rat in a cage.

I think of something—a last resort I always keep handy. Ingredients for the drink. An overdose of roofies should do the trick. I fumble with the key and finally get the door open. I twist away from him and switch on some charm.

"Okay, I think we got off on the wrong foot, House. Let's start over. I'm Karen Walker."

"That your real name?" *He's let me move away, but now he tosses the knife back and forth, a hypnotic movement. I find my eyes following it and break them away.*

"No. It's not. But you owe me yours, too."

"Gabriel. Like the angel, if you can believe it." *His bark of laughter, I recognize.*

"Well, then. My name is Jasmine. Really. I haven't said that name out loud in seventeen years."

"Good. We're being honest now. So you fooled me. I don't like being fooled."

"I'm sorry about that. I never felt safe telling you my endgame. But I did want to meet you. I wasn't lying about that."

"I know you weren't."

He looks around the room. The bed's big and takes up most of it. I try not to look at it, gesture to the little side table and chairs.

"I have some champagne chilling for us. Why don't we have some?"

"I guess." *He wanders over to the glass slider and opens it to the tiny balcony with the ocean rippling by, dressed in sparkling sunshine.*

This is my chance. I palm the packet of GHB powder out of the bar area where I'd stashed it and dump the whole thing, surely a lethal dose, into his glass. I slip the empty baggie under the foil of the champagne bottle, unwrapping it, popping the cork.

I throw the foil wrapper into the wastebasket and pour, turning back with the bubbling glasses in my hands, the powder in the bottom of his dissolving almost instantly. Odorless, tasteless, colorless, and wonderfully effective.

"To us," I say. He nods, clinks his glass against mine and drains it.

"Fill 'er up." He holds his glass out again, and I refill it.

Bubbles rise up and tickle my nose as I sip. I feel my confidence come back—I can handle him. He's a man like any other, and I know how to handle men. I smile my best seduction. "To us. To getting away with murder, and a whole lot more."

He smiles back. It isn't reassuring—he has the smile of a shark, only his teeth are less clean—but what is reassuring is the way he knocks back the champagne and pours another, then knocks that one back too. Burps.

Charming. My smile feels frozen. But that much of the drug, mixed with alcohol—surely he'll go down soon.

"You aren't her. But you're fuckable, so let's get to it." He sets his glass on the table.

"What a way you have with words," I say. I need to stall, wait for the stuff to take effect. It's supposed to happen fast, but he's so big...

"Oh yeah?" He grabs my hair, hauls me in, works my mouth over with those shark teeth.

I pretend to enjoy it. Any minute now; anytime now, my mind screams as he shoves me onto the bed, peeling off his shirt, fumbling with his belt. I try to roll away, get to my gun in the nightstand, but he backhands me and I fall back, seeing stars.

This sucks, and it's not sexy, and it gets worse as he gets his pants down, rolls my skirt up, and shoves himself in with all the finesse of a bull. I close my eyes, wait for it to be over, but that isn't enough for him. He backhands me the other direction.

"I thought you were into this," he pants, banging me like a pile driver. "All your big talk. Show me some tricks."

I dig deep, find the rage, find the strength, and sit up, pulling him in closer with my Stairmaster legs, and bite him as hard as I can on the chest. Blood fills my mouth along with the leathery bit of his nipple, and he screams like a stuck pig, rearing back. I feel a moment of triumph and spit out the skin.

I got him good.

Only, I forgot about the blade.

It goes in so easily, I don't feel it the first time. But I feel it the second time, and the third, and the fourth, and the fifth. His hand is over my mouth, my screams muffled in smothering meat.

Oh shit oh shit oh shit. I still can't believe this is happening. Darkness squeezes in from the sides.

Suddenly I can suck in some air, though it's bubbling in my lungs as unimaginable pain swamps me from seemingly every-where.

I turn my head. Off the side of the bed, I see Gabriel stagger-ing, holding his head. His hard, gray eyes are on mine. "What did you do to me, bitch?" he growls before his eyes roll up and he hits the floor.

It fucking took long enough.

I try to reach the phone on the bedside table. I can see my hand reaching, pulling on the bedspread as if that will bring the phone closer. Blood is spreading around me, a crimson lake I sink into. My breath bubbles wetly.

I don't think I can reach the phone.

I want to cry, but there's not enough water left for tears.

I'm so cold.

Chapter 43

Lei was tossing a newly purchased ball for Keiki in the side yard, trying not to jar her neck, when her cell rang. Marcella's voice was sharp with suppressed excitement.

"They found them."

"Who?" Lei threw the ball one more time. Keiki barreled after it, late-evening sun glimmering on her shiny black coat.

"Walker and House. They're on the *Rainbow Duchess*."

"Shit, I can't believe Stevens called it!" Lei broke into a grin. "I take it you're on your way."

"Heading for the helicopter as we speak. It gets better—it looks like they killed each other."

"Holy crap! What the hell?"

"Yep. Apparently something went badly wrong in the bedroom—according to the ship's medic, who checked things out after the maid found them. He looks poisoned, and she's been stabbed."

"So much for sailing off into the sunset," Lei said. "Wow, just when it seems like they had it all and were getting away with it."

"You'd think. But there's a relationship from hell, if you ask me."

"Lucky you, get to take a helicopter out there to bring them in."

"I'd rather they weren't in body bags, but it saves us a trial."

"Well, I've got something to tell you."

Lei talked to her friend until the roar of Marcella's transport helicopter cut them off. She closed the phone and slipped it back into her pocket as Stevens pulled the Bronco into the driveway. He jumped out, and she opened the gate for him.

He grinned at her, lit with suppressed excitement. He'd never looked so good, his rugged face almost handsome, blue eyes twinkling with rich satisfaction. Her heart squeezed.

"You're never going to believe it. It looks like Walker and Millhouse offed each other."

"I just heard. Marcella called me."

"Unbelievable, isn't it?"

"Justice is what it is."

"Get over here." He encircled her wrist with his big hand, pulled her to him. Bent his head to kiss her, his other hand wandering freely, and she sighed as she leaned in to him, sinking into sensation that instantly ignited her senses.

He lifted his head eventually, eyes hazy with passion. "Anchara around?"

"No, thank God. She's downtown, meeting with a social worker for some program."

"Good."

She giggled as they ran into the house and toward the back bedroom, shedding clothes along the way.

It didn't take them long the first time, but the second time, long and slow in the shower, was when Lei let herself feel something other than hunger…and found tears sliding down her face as her cheek pressed against the cool, wet tile, and she wept with passion and sorrow.

He dried her hair with a towel after they got out, rubbing her neck gently, kneading. She closed her eyes.

"You okay?"

"You make me feel so good."

"Likewise."

"Sometimes it's just too much."

"I know."

"I have to tell you something."

"Please don't."

She opened her eyes and looked at her naked self in the mirror. The bruises had faded to yellow. She almost looked back to normal but for big eyes full of shadows. He encircled her waist with corded arms, rested his jaw on her shoulder as blue eyes met brown in the mirror.

"You're going, aren't you?" His voice was a husky whisper.

"I have to. I just have to."

"I wish you wouldn't."

"Please. This hurts." She leaned over, opened the bathroom cabinet, and took the ring off the little glass shelf. "This is yours."

He took the ring, melted and slumped, the diamonds sunken into blackened metal occluded by char. "I can't believe you went back and found this."

"It's the least I could do."

"Goddamn it." He stepped back, let go of her. Handed her a towel, wrapped one around himself. "Can't say I didn't see it coming. You weren't exactly enthused about house hunting. Does Marcella know?" he asked, walking away into the bedroom.

"I told her today. I had to see if she was serious about bringing me into the Bureau. It just seems like...something I need to do, like it's now or never. I'll come back to Hawaii. That's always been the plan." The towel hung from her limp fingers as she gazed at him. He strode over and wrapped the towel around her forcefully without looking at her, as if he couldn't stand the sight of her a second longer.

Lei felt her heart breaking—an actual pain, like being hit in the chest. She gasped with the stab of it. He turned and tossed his towel over the office chair in the corner, dressed. Brisk, hard movements as he pulled on boxers, jeans, a T-shirt so new it was still in plastic wrap. Watching him, she remembered the very first time she'd watched him dress in Hilo, a fascinating process. She watched him rip the overwrap on the T-shirt savagely with his teeth, shake the shirt out, haul it on.

The pain in her chest hadn't abated.

"It won't be right away. I have to go through the application process, interviews, background checks and such."

"If I know Marcella, she'll grease those wheels."

"We'll see. It's competitive. I might not make it."

Stevens snorted, went out. She heard him banging pans in the kitchen.

She dressed. Each item of clothing scraped over skin rendered sensitive by a thousand kisses. Her breath was short around the pain in her chest. She told herself that she could do this. This was what she had to do, what she felt called to do. It was going to be worth it.

She followed him into the kitchen.

Stevens stirred a pot of soup on the stove, his back to her, selkie-dark head bent. His shoulders were wide, wide enough for her to duck under as she put her arms around him from behind, sliding herself around, tucking her head against his collarbone, wedged in front of the stove.

"I'm so sorry. I wish it didn't have to be this way."

"I know. Me too." And he pushed her firmly aside.

Chapter 44

*L*ei sat in the seat on the plane, turned to look out the oval
window at the long, low Maui Airport building. She knew
Stevens was still there, standing against the window, and Keiki
waited in the Bronco.

Leis piled around her neck impeded her vision, and she
detached the stack, shoveled them into a plastic bag Torufu had
given her, redolent with greasy malasadas in a box at the bottom.
The sendoff at the station had been over-the-top, so many hugs,
leis, and local food items, she needed a small army to eat them.
Where she was going—Quantico, Virginia—she'd be on a strict
training program with no room for malasadas.

The plane's engines switched to the high-pitched whine that
signaled departure as it trundled to the end of the runway. She
looked back, watched the airport building until it was gone,
replaced by vivid sugar cane fields and wind-whipped turquoise
ocean. Ah, Maui.

She closed her eyes, took a breath in through her nose, out
through her mouth. Then another. It was done. For better or
worse, she'd chosen her path.

"I can't wait for you," Stevens said. "I don't know if we'll ever want the same things."

"I know. It's okay."

It wasn't okay, but she wanted it to be. She'd given him Keiki, not just to dog sit but to keep, and she might as well have handed him her heart on the end of the leash.

She had nothing else.

Her hand stole into her pocket, and she removed a little black velvet box he'd slipped in during the send-off party.

"Don't look at it until you're gone," he'd whispered in her ear.

She took the box out and set it on the plastic fold-down table. Her heart beat with heavy thuds as she opened the lid.

Inside, resting on the plain cotton batting, was a round piece of melted metal. She took it out, held it up. She could see glitters and glimmers in the gray and pitted surface, but it had been flattened and smoothed to around the size of a nickel, if a little thicker, and just the right heft to keep in her pocket.

Stevens's grandmother's ring, dug out of the fiery rubble. Melted down. Banged a few times with a hammer, sanded to a satin finish that felt good to her hand, even with the dimples and pits of diamonds still embedded. A little something rough to rub.

In case it took longer than she hoped to get back to Hawaii.

Acknowledgements

Black Jasmine takes place on my current home island, Maui. As with the other books, "real life" seeds my imagination with ideas for the story. I knew I wanted to write about human trafficking, cockfighting, and something about the arts scene on Maui—but had no idea how to tie it all together.

I had my husband drive me out to Pauwela Lighthouse because we'd recently gone through the murder of a young teenager (unsolved) and disappearance of a young woman teacher (also unsolved) out there. Tramping around on that desolate, beautiful bluff with its hidden homeless encampment and wrecked cars, I knew it was the perfect spot for Black Jasmine to begin.

Identity theft is something that has long intrigued me from a psychological standpoint—people who just shuck off the past and make up a new one, or steal one from someone else and step into it like a new pair of shoes. These folks are drawn to Hawaii as a place to start over, reinvent themselves, and with a high degree of transience here it's probably pretty easy to do. And after two books with male perpetrators, I had a lot of fun developing a plot that centered around strong female characters on all sides the chase.

Contrary to rumor, I am NOT a shoe person myself. I'm much more like Lei, with bad hair most days and a pair of slippers to cover most occasions. And if you're mad at me for the way the book ended, I have to tell you I cried too, and say. . . Didn't it *have* to end that way? A good ending feels inevitable, and bittersweet. This one had a good ending.

You'll just have to wait for *Broken Ferns*, and it'll be worth it.

As always, I thank my beta readers, writers' group and book production team—you truly give form and substance to my work. Jay Allen, detective extraordinaire—you were incredibly helpful with this one with everything from first responders on the scene of the crime, cop lingo/

dialogue authenticity, to writing me after you took a cruise about how you thought human trafficking could be done on board a ship. You helped me keep it in the ballpark, and all mistakes are mine.

Finally, I thank the Maui Police Department for your ceaseless work to keep our community safe, and in hopes that we can someday find answers to what really went on at Pauwela Lighthouse.

Much aloha,
Toby Neal

Look For These Titles In
The Lei Crime Series

Blood Orchids (book 1)

Torch Ginger (book 2)

Black Jasmine (book 3)

Broken Ferns (book 4)

Companion Series Books:

Stolen in Paradise: a Marcella Scott Romantic Suspense

Twisted in Paradise: a Dr. Wilson Novel

Middle Grade/Young Adult:

Aumakua

Sign up for email updates at

TobyNeal.net

for upcoming book announcements!

ed at www.ICGtesting.com

5/P

CPSIA information can be obtai
Printed in the USA
LVOW12s0913020814

396986LV00003B/7